# JESSE ANDREWS

AMULET BOOKS
NEW YORK

Library of Congress Cataloging-in-Publication Data
Andrews, Jesse.
The Haters / by Jesse Andrews.
pages cm
Summary: A road trip adventure about a trio of jazz-camp escapees who, against every realistic expectation, become a band.
ISBN 978-1-4197-2078-9 (hardcover) — ISBN 978-1-61312-948-7 (ebook)
[1. Bands (music)—Fiction. 2. Musicians—Fiction. 3. Friendship—Fiction. 4. Humorous stories.] I. Title.
PZ7.A56726 Hat 2016
[Fic]—dc23
2015030408

THE ART OF BOOKS SINCE 1949

115 West 18th Street
New York, NY 10011
www.abramsbooks.com

To Cory, Matt, and Victor; Sam, Ryin, Lenng, George, Yang, and Victor again; Sam and Dylan; Jared; Scam, Jake, Alec, Eric, Danny, Ari, Large, Alex, Brett, Ben, Malaika, and Spencer; Ben again and Matt; Alec again and Brett again; Alan, Matt again, and Pete; Tom, Jilly, and Gigi; Joel, Jack, and Jon; Matt again, Mike, and Dave; Matt again, Micah, Rob, Joe, Geoff, Heather, and Sedgie; Micah again, Dave, Nina, and Josh; Micah again and Dave again; and every other bandmate I've ever had.

# 1.

## WE DIDN'T KNOW JAZZ CAMP
## WOULD BE THIS MANY DUDES

Jazz camp was mostly dudes. It was just a scene of way too many dudes.

Corey and I were in Shippensburg University Memorial Auditorium for orientation, and it was dudes as far as the eye could see. Dudes were trying with all their might to be mellow and cool. Everywhere you looked, a dude was making a way too exaggerated face of agreement or friendliness. And every ten seconds it was clear that some dude had made a joke in some region of the auditorium, because all the other dudes in that region were laughing at that joke in loud, emphatic ways.

They were trying to laugh lightheartedly but it was unmistakably the crazed, anxious barking of competitive maniacs.

Corey and I found some seating way off to the side, and our hope was that we would not absorb or be absorbed by other dudes. Inevitably, however, a dude approached us. He was white. Jazz camp was mostly white dudes. This dude was clutching a gold-embossed tenor sax case, and on his head was a fedora with two different eagle feathers in it.

Corey was drumming on some practice pads and had spaced out completely, so I was the one addressed by this dude.

"You cats mind if I make it a trio?" he asked me, and it was not a huge surprise that a dude of his appearance was speaking in Jazz Voice.

This dude was attempting a big relaxed smile, but his eyes were needy and desperate and I knew we had to accept him at least for a little while.

"Sure thing, man," I said. "I'm Wes."

"Adam," said this dude named Adam, trying to lead me through the stages of a way too long handshake. "Sorry—could you lay your name on me again?"

It was even less of a huge surprise that this dude was not prepared for my name to be Wes, based on his careful appraisal of my face and skin.

"Wes," I said. "Wes, like uh, Wes Montgomery."

*"Wess,"* he repeated, pronouncing it sort of Mexican. "Very cool, very cool. And where in the wide world are you from, Wes?"

"Me and Corey are both from Pittsburgh," I said, hoping Corey would help out.

Corey stared at the dude but did not stop drumming. Corey basically has no sense of social cues, and you would think that would make his life harder, but it's the opposite.

"Pittsburgh," repeated Adam finally. "Great little jazz town. Well, I'm a reedman from Jersey. My axe of choice is the tenor horn."

"Cool," I said. "I play bass. And Corey here is obviously world-class at jazz bassoon."

For a couple of seconds, *we* were an auditorium laugh bomb. Adam threw his head back and went, "OH HA HA HA HA

HA. 'JAZZ BASSOON'?! OH MAN. WESS, YOU ARE ONE FUNNY CAT." A number of dudes looked over at us. I attempted to come up with a decent I Guess I Just Made a Good Joke Face that wouldn't make anyone want to punch it, but it turns out that's an unmakeable face.

"For real, though, we should all jam sometime," said Adam, but fortunately at that moment Bill Garabedian walked onstage with his band, and everyone started cheering and trying to freak out the most.

Bill Garabedian was the famous jazz guitarist whose jazz camp it was. He was an emaciated white dude with a shaved head and a complicated soul patch/goatee arrangement, and it was kind of clear that he had not written his Opening Address out in advance. He spoke a mellow adult variant of Jazz Voice, and his points were these:

—I'm Bill
—Thank you, thank you
—Ha ha
—Okay, settle down, for real
—Thank you, all right
—Welcome to my fifth annual jazz camp
—Ha ha, yeah! I think fifth, anyway
—What do I even say? Someone else want to get up here and talk?
—I'm serious
—Ha ha, though, all right
—You know, I'm getting too old for this, man
—Every year you kids just keep getting younger and younger

—Ha ha, though, but for real

—I'm up here looking out at all these young *faces*

—You know, I remember when I was your age and all I wanted to know was, where's jazz headed?

—What's the future of jazz, you dig? The *future* . . . of *jazz*

—Then when I was seventeen I got my first Grammy nomination

—And that's when I realized: the future of jazz is now

—Because before you know it, the future is the *present*

—Think about that. Future sneaks up on you

—And before you know it, you're old

—Old and wrinkly and the girls don't like you as much! Ha ha

—Okay, you don't have to laugh so much, Don

—They don't like you that much, either

—Anyway, what was I saying

—For real, though

—Russ, you remember what I was gonna say? No?

—We weren't just talking about it?

—Maybe that wasn't you

—Well, uh, look

—Oh, I remember now. Okay. Dig this. These next two weeks are about exploring your *musical personalities*

—We really want you guys to form combos, you know, mess around on the side and really stretch out, all right

—And here's what we did to make that possible

—This year we admitted *double the rhythm section players*

—Double the drummers, double the bassists, double the pianists, double the guitarists

—So you horn players got *double the opportunities to jam*

—Ha ha, don't mention it

—You're welcome, horn players

—And rhythm section players, don't you worry, you'll get plenty of opportunities to play, all right

—We're gonna have tryouts in a minute, divide you up by skill level

—But first, the other teachers and I need to stretch out a little bit

—Let's see Miley Smiley do *this*

And with that, Bill and the teachers launched into this super angular, up-tempo, hard-bop thing.

The goal was to demonstrate that they were all jazz geniuses with insane chops, and they completely achieved this goal. The entire song was sort of a way of making sequences of musical notes that refused to form melodies of any kind. That's incredibly hard to do, and accomplishing it is one of the final stages of becoming a hard-core jazz dude.

Our new friend Adam was almost orgasmically psyched. Literally every fifteen seconds he said something along the lines of, "Shit! Those cats can blow!" or "Bill is a real motherfucker of an axeman!!" He could not decide whether he was supposed to pronounce the *r*'s in "motherfucker." But this was the only thing limiting how amped he was.

Corey and I were not as amped. I mean, on some level, we were also admiring the ridiculous chops of these jazz assassins. But on a deeper level, we had become apprehensive about our roles at this camp. You see, we were solid at our instruments, but not exceptional. And Bill Garabedian's Jazz Giants of Tomorrow Intensive Summer Workshops had the reputation of only being for the highest-level jazz kids. Back in the winter, we had figured we had no chance of getting in. We really just applied because our music teacher made us. And when we learned we got accepted, it sort of made us more confused than amped.

Now, however, it was starting to make sense. Corey and I were two of the lower-quality drummers and bassists that the camp needed in order to inflate its rhythm section numbers. We were jazz-nerd chaff. The worst of the best. And I was familiar enough with the tactics of music educators to know that Bill Garabedian's promise of "You'll get plenty of opportunities to play" was also the promise of "You'll get even more opportunities to irritably sit around listening to other kids who are roughly as mediocre as you."

We were coming to terms with the enormity of our situation. We were stranded for two weeks in a little town three hours east of Pittsburgh, awash in a veritable sea of anxious strivey dudes, not even going to get to play half the time, and it was making us not amped at all.

Another thing that made us not amped was Bill Garabedian's band's encore, a smoothed-out fusion song entitled "The Moment." Basically, it was the soundtrack of any time a high school principal decides to have sex.

# 2.

# TRYOUTS DIDN'T
# GO GREAT

There were nine other bassists at tryouts. The bass instructor was a big tired-looking Asian American dude named Russell, and he laid it out for us:

1. You're trying out for five big bands: the Duke Ellington band, the Count Basie band, the Thad Jones–Mel Lewis band, the Woody Herman band, and the Gene Krupa band.

2. Each band will have two bassists alternating song by song.

3. They're all great bands to get into, okay?

4. So don't get all hung up about what band you're in.

5. Unless it is Gene Krupa.

6. If you get put in Gene Krupa, you may want to consider spending the next two weeks not being at this camp and instead living under a bridge.

Maybe he didn't make the last two points out loud. But I felt like I could hear him thinking them.

Obviously, I got Gene Krupa, the lowest-skill-level band. My tryout didn't even go too badly. But I think it hurt me that I was the only bassist playing bass guitar and not string bass. It probably made me seem less committed to jazz. Another thing that hurt me was that pretty much every other bassist was an unspeakable beast.

Corey got Gene Krupa, too. He was as despondent as I was. We commiserated about it over lunch.

COREY: does this mean i have to drum like gene krupa?

WES: if you even get to play which may never happen

COREY: gene krupa drums like a herb

WES: no he doesn't

COREY: he drums like the king of all herbs

WES: he doesn't drum like anything because he is super dead

COREY: that's a good point but he did drum like the biggest herb in america

"Herb" is just a generic term for someone lame. Corey is probably the last person on earth who uses it. I think he likes it because it reminds him of Herb Alpert, a smooth jazz trumpeter who both horrifies and fascinates us.

COREY: i have a new favorite song

WES: oh yeah what

COREY: the song is known as . . . "the moment"

WES: ohhhhhh yeah

COREY: i was lucky enough to hear it performed recently

WES: yeah i was there

COREY: it was a performance so buttery and smooth that i had to do harm to my dick

Dick harm is a thing that comes up with us a lot. It's kind of our go-to trope.

WES: oh hell yeah
COREY: specifically i had to go to the reception desk and unload an entire clip of staples into the side of my dick
WES: right in that side part. a classic gambit
COREY: yeah right into the side part of my dick skin

Basically, the idea is, if something is really great, we get so amped that we have no choice but to do harm to our own dicks. That is the true measure of how wonderful a thing can be.

WES: i didn't want to say anything but upon hearing that beautiful and mysterious song i also had to inflict grievous harm upon my own dick
COREY: i would like to hear about that in the maximum detail
WES: i wandered the parking lot for what must have been hours or even days until i happened upon an unlocked parked car at which point i summoned a boner so that i could slam the car door on my own boner
COREY: well that just sounds great

It is important to note that dick harm also happens when something is terrible. But usually when things are terrible, it's less you harming your dick and more your dick just trying to flee the situation at all costs. So there's all kinds of nuance to dick harm that we've been developing over the years.

COREY: that soprano sax solo in particular was so velvety and pure that i had no choice but to pluck my dick off like a ripe tomato from the vine and feed it to cats

We were forced to stop when Adam came striding up to us. He had become much more relaxed, and his jaunty walk was causing liquids to spill off of his lunch tray.

"Tryouts were crazy," he told us. "There are some talented cats in this muthafuckerr!"

"Yeah, man," I said.

"Rurnh," said Corey, who was unable to pretend to be interested in talking to this dude but knew he had to make some response noise or it would be weird.

"It kills me to be around so much talent," marveled Adam, not yet sitting down. "I was listening to some of the other reeds and I was thinking, do I even belong here?"

"Sure," I said.

"But I did okay."

"Oh, good."

"I mean better than I expected, for sure."

"That's good at least."

"I might even be in over my head!"

"Oh yeah? Probably not, though."

"I don't know, man! Ha ha. I just don't know."

Clearly this would go on indefinitely until I asked him what band he was in. "Do you mind if I ask what band are you in?"

"Count Basie. First chair."

"Oh, nice."

"Will I be spying you fools behind the skins and the bass fiddle? Or did you crack the Ellington outfit?"

"Actually, we're Gene Krupa," I said.

"Oh," he said.

He kept smiling, but some kind of almost-invisible flinch traveled across his eyes. And then he actually began slowly backing away from us.

I am not making this up. It was like he thought our jazz mediocrity were contagious or something.

"Very cool, very cool," he said, his eyes darting around. "Well . . . I gotta chow it up, on the lunch side."

"Maybe we can jam soon!" I said, hoping to make him feel guilty.

"No *doubt*," he said. His head was already aimed in a completely different direction so he ended up saying it to someone else.

COREY: why would you ever want to jam with a private-eye-hat-with-bird-feathers-wearing dude

WES: there is no risk of him jamming with us or even talking to us again now that he knows that we are gene krupa

COREY, *eating so fast that it is messing up his breathing*: ernt

WES: we will be choosing jam partners from an exponentially lamer pool of dudes

COREY: my point is that i may have to slap you around a little if you keep befriending random herbs

WES: thank you for that warning

COREY: there is a hundred percent chance of the following scenario

WES:

COREY: a second tiny private eye with bird feathers hat is delicately perched on the tip of that dude's dick

# 3.

## FINALLY A GIRL IS SIGHTED

We finished lunch early. Corey's mom called him, so he had to deal with that. I wandered into the Gene Krupa practice room twenty minutes before rehearsal was supposed to start. There were a few other kids in there, too.

One of them was unmistakably a girl.

Now, look. I'm not girl crazy. I'm not the kind of dude who's going to be a huge jackass to the other dudes in order to try to improve my chances with girls. It drives me completely insane when dudes do that.

I'm also not the type of dude to bust out a special persona to make girls like me more. Like the kind of dude who is perched on the front steps of your school with an acoustic guitar trying to convince girls that he is Jason Mraz. Or the dude who is a dick to all girls because he thinks it will make them fall hopelessly in love with him. He has grown his hair out super long and fastidiously washes it many times a day, and it hangs over his face so he is constantly pushing it out of his eyes and then looking around to see if anyone is witnessing this battle he is having with his own unspeakably beautiful hair and then rolling his eyes or quietly snarling to himself.

I think we can all agree that nothing is worse than those dudes. So I don't try to reengineer my behavior in order to get with girls. But this does not mean that I am not thinking about girls all the time. At all times, at least part of my brain is going, "Girls girls girls. Girls who are cute and girls who are nice. Girls who are sexy and funny and smart. Girls. It would be so great if a girl liked you. It would be a happiness so extreme that you probably wouldn't be able to function. So maybe it's for the best that that never seems to be what is happening, or will happen. In conclusion, girls."

So yeah. Ignore what I said earlier. Clearly I am sort of girl crazy. It's not on purpose, I can tell you that. Being girl crazy is a good way to end up looking like an idiot. But I can't really help it.

The only reason I play bass is a girl. To quote my history teacher, that's a true fact. In middle school I had a crush on a girl who liked the Nicki Minaj song "Super Bass." Her name was Lara Washington, and I spent a number of months not talking to her in a state of barely manageable fear. Then we got put in lab together, and she was singing about how a dude had that boom ba doom boom boom ba doom boom he got that super bass. So I was like, what's super bass, and she said, super bass is when a man is sexy. She told me that super bass meant everything you could want in a man.

So immediately after that I started playing bass. And for whatever reason I picked it up pretty quickly, and that felt great. It was good to be good at something. And even if I hadn't been good at it, it was really nice just to have a thing. Because I had always been jealous of the kids who had a thing. Kids who had soccer practice and ballet recitals and it wasn't just something for them to pass the time. It was their thing. Even Kerel Garfield, who did origami with all of his paper homework in this obsessive kind of uncontrolled way. That was definitely his thing and you had to respect him for it.

So music became my thing. And that felt great. And it continues to feel great. I'm good at it, and I know a lot about it, and I never tell anyone about the messed-up part, which is, I don't love it.

Well, okay. Hang on. That's not true. I do love music. But I also hate it.

That's not right either. Because "hate" is not quite the right word. What I'm really talking about is hating *on*. I'm talking about being a hater.

Haters aren't people who hate stuff. Haters just hate *on* stuff. And just because they're haters doesn't mean they don't love stuff, too. You can love something and hate on it at the same time. In fact for me it's kind of impossible not to.

This is going to get complicated, but maybe if I make a new chapter it will not be as complicated.

# 4.

## NOPE, STILL AS COMPLICATED

Look. I know we should be getting back to the girl in the practice room. But this is sort of important to know about me. Any music I love, I end up hating on, too.

I'm embarrassed to tell you who this started with. But that's the whole point. It started with a band called Kool & the Gang.

Once upon a time, I was *way* way into Kool & the Gang. I got into them through my dad, who is also super into the Gang, and above all, Kool. As an impressionable child, I was completely on board with Dad's love of Kool & the Gang, and in particular, his belief that their fourth studio album, *Wild and Peaceful* (De-Lite, 1973), was the greatest album ever made. We felt that the bass lines were unstoppable and that the horn section was crazy tight. Additionally, the party guitar stylings of Clay Smith made me want to roll around on the carpet like an animal.

But really the best part was, these dudes were having epic amounts of fun. Everyone is having so much fun that they sound like they are on the brink of a crippling panic attack. Here. Go look up a track off *Wild and Peaceful* called "Funky Stuff." Put that track on and then keep reading this. Okay. Yeah.

Do you hear how much fun these guys are having? Do you hear the dudes shouting uncontrollably from sheer happiness? And the dude just completely going to town on a slide whistle of the variety that a clown would use? Are you bopping around in your seat with a huge grin on your face? Of course that is what you are doing. Because that groove is the funnest thing ever.

Once you're done, throw on a track called "More Funky Stuff." *Yeah.* You hear that? That's a different track from the same album. But it is also *a hundred percent the same groove.* That's how good that groove is. They reused the groove in a completely unapologetic way. And until I was thirteen, I saw *nothing wrong with that.* I would have listened to, literally, a hundred songs of that groove. A thousand.

I thought Kool & the Gang was nothing less than the soundtrack to pure human happiness. Then one day I played it for my newfound buddy Corey Wahl, the drummer from school jazz band. He had recently demonstrated our friendship by yelling at a dude who knocked me down in soccer. So I attempted to reward him with some K & the G.

But somehow it did not get him fired up.

"I don't know, man," he said after about twenty bars. "It's kind of corny."

I didn't know how to respond to that.

"Ha ha!" I said, assuming he was doing a weird deadpan joke thing. "No, but for real. How funky is this."

But Corey just kind of nodded in a way that meant the opposite of what nods are supposed to mean. And we sat there wordlessly continuing to listen to it.

And for the first time, doubt about Kool began to creep into my heart.

I remember pretending, to myself, that I wasn't suddenly understanding how you could hate on Kool & the Gang. I remember thinking, in an increasingly desperate way, *This is super funky and great. I am enjoying this a lot. There goes the guy with the clown slide whistle again. It is very cool when he does that.*

"This is the band that does 'Celebration,' right?" Corey said.

"I mean, yeah," I said.

"Let's listen to that," he said.

"Another thing we could listen to is 'More Funky Stuff,'" I suggested kind of feebly, but he was already putting on "Celebration."

Look. If you love Kool & the Gang, you're fine with "Celebration." It's not the funkiest tune out there, but when you put *Kool & the Gang Greatest Hits* on shuffle, and "Celebration" comes up, it's not hard for you to get into it. It's an upbeat track with satisfyingly clean production. Also it automatically suggests that whatever you're doing, e.g., chemistry homework, is a celebration. And sometimes that is exactly what you need to get through five pages of chemistry homework.

But we sat there listening to it, and Corey had this intense, absorbed, critical look on his face, and for the first time, I found myself hating "Celebration."

"It's just pretty cheeseball," said Corey.

"Yeah, but I mean," I said. But I didn't have anything to finish that sentence with.

"But what?"

We listened to Kool tell us to bring our good times, and our laughter, too.

"I mean uh . . . I don't know. I mean yeah obviously but uhhhh."

". . ."

"Mmmmmmm. Well . . . *cheeseball*, I mean, sure, but that's, uh."

We listened to Clay Smith strum his party-guitar octave sixteenth notes in his relentless and increasingly unbearable way.

"That's what?"

"Well but yeah though, but I do know what you mean and, obviously, yeah."

"I kind of feel like I'm in a furniture-store commercial," said Corey.

As we continued listening to the hits of Kool & the Gang, I realized that I could never love Kool & the Gang ever again. "Celebration" *did* make you feel like you were in a furniture-store commercial. "Funky Stuff" *was* kind of corny. And in retrospect, the existence of "More Funky Stuff" was *not* awesome. It was instead ridiculous and embarrassing. Because why couldn't they come up with a different groove? They really thought, we can just do a second song of exactly the same groove? That's for real what they thought?! What was wrong with them?

Every subsequent song was another nail in the coffin. "Jungle Boogie" was trying too hard. "Ladies Night" was trying *way* too hard. "Get Down On It" was the song you would hear if Hell was experiencing high call volume. "Cherish" was the song you would hear when you finally got through.

You're probably thinking I hated Corey for humiliating me like this. But I didn't feel humiliated. I felt grateful. I felt like he had saved me from what could have been a lifetime of listening to corny, cheeseball music.

We quickly became close friends. And pretty much all we've done from then on has been listen to stuff. We just sit around Corey's basement eating his parents' bright-orange cheese surplus and going on epic deep dives with Rdio and Spotify and Grooveshark and YouTube and searching for the Unpoisonable Well. The well that can't be poisoned. The music that you can love forever with all your heart, because it's impossible to hate on.

Obviously by jazz camp, we were still looking for it. Because everything we listened to, every band and artist and album, we always found ways to like it, but we always found ways to hate on it.

**The Beatles:** You can't really be a fan of them so much as a historian or paleontologist

**James Brown:** His life's work is basically the soundtrack to an infomercial for cocaine

**LCD Soundsystem:** Their life's work is basically the soundtrack to an infomercial for the random pills in the outstretched sweaty palm of a rich kid in a hoodie

**Pharrell:** His songs are fun except after a while they're actually not that fun because he's kind of too cool to express true unguarded joy or any other deeply felt emotion or actually any emotion at all because he's probably a robot

**Kanye:** Kanye's artistic output is like if a corporation's only product was commercials for itself, so I guess GEICO

**Can:** Enough with the bird noises

**Bon Iver:** Way too emotionally high stakes for casual listening in the sense that it makes every single part of your life feel like the part of a TV show where you are in a hospital saying goodbye for the very last time

**Vampire Weekend:** Any given lyric might require you to have memorized *Ulysses* or the entire Bible or something

**My Bloody Valentine:** Can only be correctly enjoyed while lying semiconscious on a filthy mattress in an abandoned apartment

**Django Reinhardt:** Can only be correctly enjoyed while riding around the Alps in a tiny car with a poodle and a baguette

**Odd Future:** You can only listen to dudes ironically rapping about killing and raping everyone for so long before you realize that, despite all the irony and playfulness and everything, when you get right down to it you're still just sitting around a basement listening to a bunch of dudes telling you about killing and raping everyone

Okay. I'll stop. I love all those guys. But that just makes me an expert at hating on them.

That's me and Corey. We're expert well poisoners. And forget about trying to *make* unpoisonable well music.

I mean, Corey had a drum set and an amp down there in his basement, but we barely ever played stuff. Anything we did was just the less-good version of something else that already had some kind of fatal flaw. Periodically we'd try to do some Afrobeat or some shoegaze or some proggy fusiony thing, but sixteen bars in,

I knew it wasn't good enough to put into the world. And so did Corey. Our basement sessions were always over pretty much before they started.

And we played jazz at school, obviously, but in my head that didn't count. Jazz was music we were comfortable liking because there was no danger of us loving it and then eventually being betrayed by it. It was safe somehow. It was basically a game on your phone that you would periodically whip out and try to beat your high score. It was fun and challenging but not really something that you would think to show other people.

Also, it's not like that high score was super high, because I wasn't amazing at jazz or, frankly, anything.

I mean, no one was going to write a Wikipedia article about me anytime soon.

# Wesley Namaste Doolittle

From Wikipedia, the free encyclopedia

**Wesley Namaste Doolittle** (born September 15, 1999) is an American person.

## Early life [edit]

> ⚠ This section of a biography of a living person does not include any references or sources. Please help by adding reliable sources.

Doolittle is adopted.[citation needed] His birth parents are Venezuelan. Hopefully he is still in the early part of his life.[?]

## Career [edit]

> ⚠ This section of a biography of a living person does not include any references or sources. Please help by, um . . . okay. Yeah. Look. We know there is nothing written about this person's life anywhere. Because he is completely unremarkable. Don't worry. An editor will be deleting this page soon. In the meantime, we apologize for its entire existence and would like to offer you a full refund for your Wikipedia expense of $0. Yeah. This whole thing costs $0. So maybe just chill out.

Doolittle has no career to speak of. And when he finally is forced to get one, it is really not clear what he is going to do. Odds are it will probably[according to whom?] be something horrible like corporate lawyer or guy who demonstrates kitchen products on the Home Shopping Network.

## References [edit]

There is no reason for you to be reading this section and probably we should just get back to the girl in the practice room.

# 5.

## YES CAN WE PLEASE GET
## BACK TO THE GIRL NOW

Okay. So, in the practice room, there was a girl. She seemed to be deep into a very demanding guitar solo. However, I couldn't hear if she was any good or not. The guitar was not plugged in. It was a brand-new-looking Les Paul that momentarily gave me a guitar boner.

Was she beautiful? I would have to say probably yes. To me, anyway, she was very beautiful. But I sort of have a low Is This Girl Beautiful Threshold. She was also definitely kind of strange looking.

Maybe the best word for what she was is look-at-able. You could look at this girl for an incredibly long time. I mean, obviously, you couldn't, because she would probably get pissed. But if it *were* an option, like in some magical dream scenario where she wouldn't get bored either and was happy to just sit there being wordlessly looked at, you could look at her basically indefinitely. Maybe she'd be on her phone.

Here's what she looked like: Her hair was a normal length but bleached kind of creamy papery white and her skin was pretty dark and moley. She had small, black, somehow very sharp eyes and this intense comet-shaped eyebrow situation that made her look sort of concerned and skeptical at all times and a nose that was feminine and womanly but a little bit also made you think of a Labrador retriever. I know none of this is helpful at all. She had a scrunched sort of puffy mouth and round cheeks that I think you would call "apple cheeks" and a chin shaped like a hammock with a giant bowling ball in it. Maybe a less heavy ball. A giant soccer ball.

So in other words it was the shape of basically every chin.

Okay. I am going to stop trying to describe how this girl looks. She was a highly look-at-able guitar-playing girl, and obviously I started crushing on her immediately, because that's just how crushes work. Great.

As I began setting up nearby, she stopped playing and glanced at me. I racked my brains for something charming to do. But somehow what I went with was frowning and scrunching my eyebrows and nodding for no reason. It was a pretty alienating display that I chose to follow up by announcing, "Shredfest."

"What," she said. Her voice was low and sounded like it didn't get used a lot.

"Shredfest," I repeated. "A festival of shredding."

"Huh."

"Shredding on the guitar."

"Ohhh."

"You were shredding pretty hard. Then I called it Shredfest. And . . . that brings us just about up to date."

"What?"

"Up to date on what has happened so far."

"Yeah."

"Good," I said, and frown-nodded a *second time,* and then I made a big show of turning to my bass and tuning it, and she went back to shredding, and I spent the next five minutes not suddenly sprinting out of the room and into traffic.

# 6.

## THE MEDIOCRE GENE KRUPA
## BAND PLAYS A BLUES IN F

One by one, the other rhythm section members appeared. They were mostly pretty chill and reasonable. The exception was the guitarist who wasn't the girl. His name was Tim, and he was a scumbag.

The primary indicator of him being a scumbag was that he did not acknowledge the presence of anyone except the girl, who turned out to be named Ash.

He began by positioning himself directly in front of her. Then he adopted a casual stance. "Well, hello there," he said to her. "I'm Tim."

"Hi," she said, kind of distractedly. She did not stop playing. So he put his head right up next to her guitar. He kept his head there for a while and listened and scrunched his eyes shut with this doofy I-am-appreciating-your-guitar-skills face.

"Oh my goodness," he said. "We've got a lady Robert Johnson in the house."

Unfortunately, this made her look up at him as if maybe he wasn't a huge scumbag.

"You like Robert Johnson?" she asked.

"I wouldn't say I like Robert Johnson."

"Why not."

"Because I *love* Robert Johnson."

"Oh. Okay, good."

"They say he sold his soul to the devil. I say, it was *worth it.*"

"I'm Ash."

"Ash. My goodness gracious. That's quite a name."

"No. It's dumb. It's just less dumb than 'Ashley.'"

"Ash, it honors me to share with you this humble chair," he said, giving off the vibe of a forty-year-old man who has been divorced at least three times.

I was sitting there silently listening in and becoming inflamed with inappropriate territorial rage, like a rival elk or something. Meanwhile, by now literally every horn player was trying to play the loudest possible thing, which is the standard pre-rehearsal procedure of all jazz horn players.

All of this was brought to a halt when Bill Garabedian's drummer, Don, entered the room and started yelling. Don had black curly hair, a mild underbite, and a neck that was a little bit wider than his head. The pit stains of his white T-shirt made him an intimidating presence. They seemed to say, *You will probably never be able to sweat this much out of your armpits. Because you will never truly be a man.*

"Turn it down," he yelled. "Hey. Turn it down *at least* 90 percent. Okay? I couldn't hear myself talk *out in the hallway.* All right. Y'all tuned up? Need to tune? Tune up if you need. But do it quiet. We gotta get started. All right. Welcome to Gene Krupa. I'm Don. Some days you'll have me, some days you'll have a couple other teachers. If you have a calendar, it's probably on there. We all got charts? Share if you need to. Okay. Now, I don't have a ton of *teaching experience.* So

I'm up here figuring it out, just like you. So give me some slack, all right? You guys gonna be cool? Great. But don't forget you're supposed to have fun."

He paused for a moment to stare at us with a kind of dull, blank horror. Then he continued.

"Let's stretch out with a blues in F. First rhythm section, give me, uh, Corey, Wes, Jeremy, and uh . . . Tim. Everybody gets twelve bars. No more than twelve, because there's a lot of you. Jeremy, start me off. Five, six, uh, uh."

And so we embarked on a fifteen-minute journey through the blues, hopeful that each of us would have something new and cool to tell each other in the language of jazz.

Unfortunately, our hopes were completely in vain.

It was pretty rough. There was just kind of a stressed-out fraudulent vibe that was sort of the dark side of all that strivey-dude energy from the auditorium. The trumpets were all switching back and forth between grumpy squawking and trying to hit the highest and loudest possible note. The trombones were botching goofball quotations like "Flight of the Bumblebee" and then signaling surrender with sheepish atonal elephant noises. And each of the saxophone solos was basically the equivalent of the small talk that you are forced to make with the friend of your mom who cuts your hair.

As for me, I hate soloing. It just never feels like something the bass is designed to do. Basically every bass solo that I have ever taken is the soundtrack to an overweight cartoon bear putting on women's clothing and then trying to dance.

Corey didn't have it, either. He got through about eight bars of pleasant, forgettable snare patterns and then froze up and spent the turnaround just sitting there in total silence. Don frowned and nodded thoughtfully at this. But it was sort of the face you would make if a super little kid told you there is no God.

After Corey we got the first good solo of the day, a spare and haunting jazz haiku from Tim. He definitely played the fewest notes of anyone. That is a time-honored approach by jazz kids who are technically proficient but also have great soulfulness.

So that pretty much sucked, too. The most sensitive, brilliant musical mind in the room seemed to belong to an unignorable scumbag. But that should not have been surprising. That's just how the music world works a lot of the time.

Halfway through this long and monotonous blues, Don had the other rhythm section take over, and as soon as they did, the whole room perked up, because they sounded way better than us.

Part of me was bummed out about that. But the other part also enjoyed listening to them. Or at least three out of four of them. The stubby, pale drummer was a lot flashier than Corey, the ponytailed, huge-handed bassist had a richer, jazzier sound on his upright bass than I did on my Fender, and the swim-team-captain-looking pianist basically just tried to impersonate Bill Evans, i.e., probably the greatest jazz pianist of all time. The soloists were way more energized by this group. Even Don started relaxing and muttering, "There it is" and "Yup."

A third part of me was stressed out and upset that their weak link was Ash.

Her sound was the first problem. It was not a jazz sound in any way. Jazz guitar typically has a pretty soft attack and a clean sustain.

But Ash had this raw, chunky distorted sound with a big crunchy attack that really fought what was going on in the rest of the rhythm section. Another problem she had was a clear lack of knowledge of jazz chords. Mostly she was trying to comp with these garage-rock power chords that make no sense in the context of jazz.

It was sort of like a ballet recital where most of the kids were doing competent, reasonable ballet, in frilly skirts and leotards and stuff, but then off to one side this girl Ash was wearing a football uniform and doing the Worm.

This went on for a few solos. During the baritone sax solo, Tim tried stepping in.

"Hey, Ash," he said. "Lady, I dig what you're doing. Why don't I try to give you a cleaner sound."

She did not respond or make eye contact with him. But her cheeks turned bright red.

So Tim started messing with her knobs. And he did succeed in giving her a cleaner, jazzier sound. But power chords with a jazz sound are kind of the wimpiest, most pathetic possible thing. So now she was wearing a frilly skirt and leotard like everyone else but still writhing around on the floor doing the Worm.

I should have said something. But I didn't. So instead Corey was the one who said something.

"Hey," he said. "Don't mess with her knobs."

Tim ignored Corey completely.

Corey stared at Tim the way large dogs on porches do sometimes.

"HEY," repeated Corey. "She doesn't want you fucking with her amp."

Unlike Corey, I have an overpowering fear of confrontation. But I still got in there. To back Corey up but also to back Ash up but mostly because, fuck Tim.

"Yeah," I said. "Hey, man."

Tim, sensing that I was the wimpier one, chose to address me.

"I think she just forgot to switch it over," Tim told me.

"Uhhhh," I said, shrugging meaninglessly. I followed that up with, "Well, I don't know."

Corey, impatient with my being a huge confrontation-averse puss, yelled, "Dude. No. She wants it the way it was. It sounds like ass now."

"*No talking*," yelled Don. "Come on. Have some respect."

We all shut up. Meanwhile, the whole time Ash was staring rigidly forward and pretending like none of this was happening. But she definitely started playing quieter, and less. Which was probably an improvement, because the rest of the rhythm section sounded great. But now there was this sort of combative anxious atmosphere in the room because someone had gotten yelled at.

At the very end it was Ash's turn to solo. She soloed in E.

If you don't know music, just know that if the band is playing in F but you're playing in E, it's going to sound simultaneously very whimsical and very horrible. It's basically a horror movie starring the Muppets.

The bassist and pianist didn't know what to do. The pianist started doing these minimalist stabs that were not really key-specific, and the bassist stayed in F but looked terrified.

It was a huge enough train wreck that Don tried to intervene.

"F," he called out. "Ashley. It's a blues in F."

But she just shut her eyes and bore down on her solo, which also was not really a jazz solo, or even a solo at all. It was really just a bunch of gritty Delta blues comping, over which ideally a grizzled old man would be singing about how some woman had ruined his entire existence and now he lived in the river and had no shoes.

Don clearly felt obligated to continue trying to help.

"Now B-flat," he said. "Sweetie, you're on B-flat now. The four of F."

But she didn't acknowledge him in any way, unless it was via the quiet wordless grumbling she had begun to do, while continuing to crank out Delta blues with her eyes closed.

"Back to F," he said. He started looking at the rest of us and shrugging and shaking his head, like he was apologizing to us for what she was doing, and I fantasized about slapping him around, or just if a giant hawk showed up and started eating him.

At the turnaround, he lost his patience. "Okay," he said. "Band. Stop. I gotta stop you guys. Ashley? Hey. Ashley. Honey, I need you to stop."

The band stopped. Ash continued for a bar or two, then also stopped. She refused to make eye contact with Don or say anything.

"Hey," he said, kind of quietly and soothingly. "What just happened? What was that?"

Excruciating silence.

"You knew we were in F. I heard you comping in F. So why would you solo in E?"

Even more gut-twisting silence.

"Sweetie, it's not a rhetorical question. I'm not trying to embarrass you. I actually just want to know why you soloed in E."

"Because she wanted to solo in E," Corey kind of yelled.

"Yeah," I said.

"I am not talking to you," Don said to Corey.

"Why didn't the *band* switch?" Corey wanted to know. "Shouldn't the band follow the soloist?"

"Wrong, and I will talk to you in a second. Right now, I'm talking to Ashley."

"I gotta go," said Ash abruptly, and she stood and started packing up her stuff.

But it didn't seem like she was doing it out of embarrassment. It sort of seemed like her attitude was, she had finished what she had come to practice to do, i.e., take two-thirds of an alienating solo in the wrong key, and now that she had accomplished that, it was time to leave.

Some of the horn players started muttering to one another.

Don pretended to try to stop her from leaving. "Oh," he said. "Now, hold on. You don't have to leave. Hey."

"Band should've switched," said Corey.

"Yeah," I said again.

"*Wrong,*" said Don again. "Honey, you sure you want to leave?"

She looked at him with a completely blank look on her face, except for her perpetual-skepticism-expressing eyebrows. She nodded and butted the door open with her shoulder.

"Okay," said Don. "Go hit the practice room. Brush up on the basics. And hey."

But the door had closed before he could say whatever piece of encouragement he was about to say.

"Band should've switched," said Corey again.

"You want to leave, too?" asked Don.

Corey looked at Don, then me, then Don again.

"Yeah," said Corey. "We both want to leave."

Oof, I thought.

"We gotta go do stuff, unfortunately," I explained.

"No," said Corey. "We don't have to go do *anything*. The only reason we're leaving is that this is *bullshit*."

This did not really give me too many rhetorical options, so I tried to salvage the situation with, "All right all right."

"I'll be outside," said Corey to me. And then he left.

It would have been nice to make a quick dramatic exit. But first I had to pack up my stuff. So I did that, trying for brisk defiance but probably accomplishing something more like panicky haste. The various groups of horn players were mumbling to one another and Don was gazing at me with mostly just pity.

"Kid, you don't have to leave just because your friend told you to," he said.

This was an ideal time for a biting retort, except that it wasn't. Because deep down I knew we were being melodramatic and ridiculous, and the real reason we were leaving was that we just didn't want to be there.

And also obviously a little bit because there was a girl.

# 7.

## THE THREE OF US BOND OVER DICK HARM AND THEN PLAY ACTUAL MUSIC

We caught up with Ash outside the music hall on her way to the practice spaces across the quad. She still looked blank and unruffled.

"Why did you guys leave?" she asked. "I thought you were both pretty good."

"What that guy did was bullshit," said Corey.

"That whole scene was just kind of tough," I said.

She nodded a little uncertainly.

"Basically, this entire camp makes us want to harm our own dicks," announced Corey.

It's always a risk to introduce people to our go-to trope of dick harm. People tend to find it confusing and frightening. But it turned out Ash was receptive to it.

"Yeah?" she said. "This camp makes me want to harm *other people's* dicks."

"*Fuck* yeah," said Corey.

"Bear in mind," I said, "to have any kind of impact, you'd have to harm at least twenty or so dicks. Because this camp has serious issues with dick surplus."

She laughed this kind of rusty, squeaky chuckle and my heart got hot.

"So are you guys super into jazz," she wanted to know.

"I mean," I said.

"Some jazz," said Corey.

"Jazz among other kinds of music, I would say," I said.

It was clear to us both that we were not going to win her over by making a point of how much we loved jazz. "Here's the thing," she said. "I do like jazz some of the time. But I don't think any of the jazz I like was played by someone who went to jazz camp."

"One billion percent yes," said Corey.

"Who do you like," I said.

"Miles Davis," she said.

"Miles Davis is a beast," Corey said.

"Huge huge beast, obviously," I said.

"If you sent Miles Davis to jazz camp," said Corey, "he would have responded by becoming a professional terrorist."

She laughed a little at this, too.

"I mean, he probably would have just left," I said.

"To *suicide bomb an airport*," said Corey.

"Or play a show somewhere," I said.

"Somewhere like the smoldering ruins of an airport that he just bombed the shit out of."

"Sure. Or, the Village Vanguard, where he played many noteworthy shows."

"Or, the Village *Deadguard, where he played many noteworthy dead.*"

"Hey," said Ash, to get us to stop. "Do you guys want to play some stuff?"

"Sure," we both said.

"Not jazz, though," she said, but that kind of went without saying.

Like I said, our previous attempts to play music other than jazz had all failed. So I was a little nervous going into this one.

And I was right to be nervous. Because we started playing and immediately sounded horrible.

For whatever reason—probably a combination of anxiety and just panicky self-sabotage—as soon as he got behind the kit, Corey immediately launched into a very busy fusiony beat, like from a lesser Headhunters or Weather Report song. It was the kind of beat that was unfollowable, because it kept changing every single measure. The bass pattern changed, the snare pattern changed, and there was basically nothing to latch on to.

And I knew it wasn't going to be a ton of fun to play to or listen to. But out of pure reflex, I launched into my own complementary Jaco-Pastorius-but-dumber-and-worse bass line that had a million notes and made it sort of unclear what the key was or what the melody could possibly be.

So Corey and I hammered away at this complicated, difficult, rootless groove for a while. Now and then Ash did a little aimless noodling on her guitar. Mostly, though, she didn't play anything. She just looked at her fretboard like she was waiting for a video to load.

After about a minute, which felt a lot longer, she held up a fist. We stopped playing.

"No," she told us. "That's not gonna work."

We both nodded.

"Can you guys just dumb it down," she said.

So we tried again. It was what we were playing before, but dumbed down. But when you take the braininess out of what we were doing, there's nothing really left. So, unsurprisingly, it sounded even worse.

This time Ash didn't even noodle. She just watched us, with her skeptical eyebrows and scrunched mouth.

After nine bars she stopped us again.

Corey's jaw was jutting out the way it does when his parents are preventing him from leaving his house.

"I don't mean dumb that beat down," she told us. "I mean dumb yourselves down. Just shut off your jazz brain. Give me something really, really simple."

We nodded.

"In E," she said to me. "Not whatever key that was. E, okay?"

I nodded.

"Just make some room," she said to us. "Try to give me a lot of room."

And she started snapping off a very slow tempo.

Corey and I looked at each other.

I played the dumbest, simplest thing I could think of, which was just ringing out a low E.

Corey held his sticks up in the air. He let his hands go theatrically limp, above his head. His sticks dangled uselessly from his fingers. He lifted his right knee. And he started thumping his bass drum on Ash's slow beat.

On one, I let E ring out again, and then muted it on three.

That was the beat. It was just me playing long half-note E's, and Corey thumping quarter notes on the bass drum. That was it. It was incredibly simple and dumb.

And yet, somehow it didn't sound bad.

We kept doing it. And I can't tell you why. But pretty soon it started to sound good.

Actually, it was sounding kind of great.

It was so dumb that it was hypnotic. It was eerie and intense. And Ash was really comfortable letting it grow on all of us. She just stood there, not smiling but nodding a little, while we kept cranking out this beat like we were both possessed or snake-charmed or something.

Then without warning she pushed her volume up and rang out an E, too. It was huge and jagged-sounding and she let it sit in the air for two bars.

Someone screamed, "OH."

Then we started playing.


I'm not going to give you the details. I'm not going to do them justice. But we played for three and a half hours, and we sounded incredible.

I don't know if you'd call it rock, or blues, or punk, or what. It felt a lot simpler and earthier than those. There was some mid-career Miles Davis in there, some Ramones, John Lee Hooker, AC/DC. Some James Brown and some Talking Heads. Parts were a little bit like Sleater-Kinney, and there were a few moments that sounded like Cat Power. But none of these are really going to give you the right impression at all.

What it was, honestly, was just about locking in. We were just all completely fused together. We got quiet together, and loud, and quiet again, and rhythmically it was like we weren't capable of playing outside one another's beat. And somehow the whole time I knew exactly what to do, like I could hear every note the moment before I played it, and honestly the whole time a part of me was terrified that there was a limit to whatever was happening, and it was going to suddenly run out, but it didn't.

After about an hour of just playing, without any song or plan, Ash started giving us little bare-bones sketches of songs she had written. The lyrics were pretty hard to make out but seemed to be a little bit gonzo '90s fringe lyrics like Ween or King Missile and a little bit not-super-rhymey conversational lyrics like Courtney Barnett. The titles were, too, but more intense.

**God Has No Thoughts**
**Suburb of the Abyss**
**Everyone at Wendy's Was Dead or a Robot**
**Trees Are Eating My Dad Right Now Pt. 1**
**Love Plague**
**This Sex Sucks**
**Shark Contest**
**I Am Such a Mess from Werewolf PMS**
**They Told Me You Are What You Eat So I Ate Roger Federer**
and my favorite,
**If You Love Your Dog So Much, Why Don't You Fuck Him**

Ash plugged a microphone into her guitar amp and did all

the singing, and her singing voice was sort of like she took her speaking voice and gave it fresh batteries. It was a voice that cut. It was the voice of someone who gave zero fucks and rode around on a bear. It was the kind of voice where you didn't care if you could tell what she was saying, because you knew what she meant.

The bass and guitar were all thick and distorted and buzzy because we turned our amps up higher than they were supposed to go. Corey ended up mostly thumping things out on his bass drum and toms and used his cymbals only when he absolutely had to. So the effect was this chunky thumpy sound that kind of made you think of the most badass possible rabbit. I know that sounds idiotic. I don't care. That's how it sounded. It was like the war music for an elite army unit of giant, bear-riding, eyepatch-wearing rabbits who were riding off to a battle that was actually just a huge party.

Ash took audio of the whole thing by hanging her phone from the ceiling with a shoelace. We played for three and a half hours, and between every song Corey and I were afraid to do any talking. The entire time it was incredible. Then we went out into the hall and tried not to freak out too much.

At that point, I would say Ash felt like one of us.

WES, *punching a wall*: yeah

COREY, *punching himself*: yeah

ASH: fuck yeah guys

COREY: heeeeerrrrrrrrRRRRNNNNNNNNNN

WES: i know this is gross but it feels like we all just had sex with each other for three hours

COREY: i can never play jazz again

ASH: fuck jazz

WES: to continue to play high school–type jazz would be a catastrophic mistake for us

COREY: the very thought of having to play another two weeks of jazz with the many herbs of this camp is making my dick retreat into my body like the head of a turtle

[*a hyped-up silence during which corey punches himself again*]

ASH: so actually that was the first time i've ever gotten to play those songs like with a band and everything

COREY: no

WES: what?!

ASH: i've just never had anyone to play with

COREY: fuck you! that's not even possible!!

WES: you're telling us Trees Are Eating My Dad Right Now, for example, you've never gotten to hear that song played by a band before

ASH: no. i mean i tried to play it with one of my sisters on piano once, but that doesn't count

COREY: that probably sounded like ass

ASH: it did sound like total ass

WES: that song could work with guitar and piano if your sister had a certain kind of approach but it sounds like she did not

ASH: she plays like you gave billy joel mittens and a concussion

WES: daaaaaaaamn

COREY: real talk

[*a silence in which everyone is thinking something different*]

[*the silence intensifies*]

[*he has been suppressing them pretty hard but wes's hyper-developed hater reflexes finally kick in*]

WES: so just,

COREY:

ASH:

WES: i mean, uh

COREY, *with growing irritation*:

ASH:

WES: i mean that was as good as we thought it was, right?

COREY: oh goddamn it wes

WES: what

COREY: wes. why would you *even say that*

WES, *babbling like a maniac*: it's just that i just want to be prepared in case we listen back to it and it turns out we were being dumb or naive or whatever because i mean it was definitely good but what if it wasn't *as good*

COREY: you have to stop talking immediately

WES: okay

COREY: if you keep talking i am going to commit an atrocity against you

WES: okay but let's just listen to it and make sure

COREY: no

WES: what

COREY: no. we can't listen to it in fear

WES: oh

COREY: we can only listen to it when you're no longer at risk of hating on it

This was a tough thing to hear. Because I was, deep down, preparing to hate on it. But I figured Corey was, too. He's even more of a hater than me.

We were at kind of an impasse, and fortunately Ash was there to break it.

ASH: let's listen to it after dinner
WES: okay great
COREY: what's for dinner though

# 8.

## COREY LITERALLY EATS HIS TONGUE AND ASH LEARNS THE TRUE MEANING OF GARFUNKEL

Dinner at Bill Garabedian's Jazz Giants of Tomorrow Intensive Summer Workshops was an array of steamed meats and vegetables that looked and tasted like we were getting them secondhand. There was also a pasta bar way off in an abandoned corner somewhere. Corey filled an entire bowl with sauce and drank it as if it were soup.

At first we were mostly silent, ignoring our gross food and gazing around the room in secret triumph at these other jazz kids in their various jazz-camp-hierarchy postures: the alpha kids sitting in too wide of a stance; the beta kids hunched over, intensely making Important Points; the gamma kids slumping around all demoralized.

We were feeling completely superior to these kids who were too chickenshit to throw a tantrum and walk out on jazz camp band practice for basically no reason.

ASH: oh my god this food sucks dick

WES: i feel like someone pre-licked all of these zucchinis

[*ash chuckles again and wes feels a happiness so extreme that he momentarily cannot function*]

COREY: the soup's okay but there's too many tomatoes

WES: corey, that's spaghetti sauce

COREY: no it's a soup

WES: you got it from the pasta bar

COREY: i think it's the soup and pasta bar

WES: well

WES: hmm

ASH: you guys want to get second dinner?

[*a silence in which it is clear that corey and wes had not even considered the possibility of second dinner*]

COREY: oh hell yes

WES: like pizza?

ASH: i was thinking sushi

Second dinner was at a sushi place that Ash drove us to and then paid for, and it taught us a number of things about Ash. For one, she had a car. The car was a huge, black, new-smelling SUV that felt more like a rental than anyone's day-to-day car. It certainly didn't feel like the one my parents had. There weren't inexplicable hair and crumbs ground into the seats, or ancient mud-encrusted stacks of papers and binders sloshing around everyone's feet. There were no stray objects of any kind, and every surface felt cool and pebbly, like the skin of a lizard, but from space.

Another thing we learned was that Ash had an entire strategy for ordering sushi:

1. buy the sushi chefs a beer
2. tell them the magic word

The magic word is *omakase.* It is Japanese for "Just make whatever." And if you utter this word after buying the sushi chefs a beer, these sushi chefs are going to make you some epic stuff. I would not be able to tell you what any of it was, except that the production values of this sushi were top-notch. A lot of it didn't even look like food. It was fish art. There was a little fish volcano. There was a seaweed pond with little fish stepping stones and ripples coming out from each one. And then they gave us each a sea urchin.

Sea urchin is called *uni,* and it looks like a human tongue, except orange and with bigger, more diseased-looking taste buds. Ash slurped hers up immediately. I put mine in my mouth without thinking about it too hard and managed to enjoy it. It tasted kind of like the sea, kind of like a burger. But Corey just stared at his with unconcealable horror.

The sushi chefs thought this was hilarious.

"Ha ha ha!" the main one yelled. "You should eat it!!"

Clearly, Corey and I had stepped into someone else's life. It did not resemble our lives anymore. It was someone with an infinitely more baller lifestyle. But Ash was kind of guarded about how it had come to be.

WES: so how come you know so much about sushi?
ASH: i don't know that much. i've had it a few times
COREY: what's up with your crazy nice car
ASH: it's my mom's
COREY: how come you have it though
ASH: i dunno, she wasn't using it

COREY: tell your mom she's crazy because that car is baller

WES: so ash where are you from and everything

ASH: new york what about you guys

WES: uh, pittsburgh

COREY: and your parents they're also from new york?

ASH, *shrugging*: they're from a couple places what about yours

It didn't take us long to figure out that she was kind of uncomfortable talking about herself and was going to deflect every question back onto us. So pretty soon we were just rapidly volunteering things about ourselves.

COREY: my dad's jewish and my mom is irish catholic

WES: our high school is called benson and it's like medium size with a couple thousand kids

COREY: my older sister becca made us get two different cats

WES: it's an inner-city public school, so budget-wise kind of hurting

COREY: one of the cats is named fish-fish and he literally has feline AIDS

WES: the gym department is so strapped for cash that one of their units is called "the block run" and in it the gym teacher just forces everyone to run around the block

COREY: wes is adopted

WES:

ASH:

COREY: he doesn't like to talk about it but it is kind of obvious from his name and then how he looks

WES: there are other possible explanations for that, but okay

COREY: sorry, maybe i shouldn't have said

WES: i guess it was gonna come out sooner or later

ASH, *deciding to ignore the adoption thing*: so you guys have played a lot of music together, huh

[*corey and wes both nod a little and then stop*]

COREY: i mean not that much outside of jazz band

WES: we more just listen to music

COREY: sometimes we play the game garfunkel

ASH: i don't know garfunkel

COREY: yeah because we invented it

Okay. We need to copyright Garfunkel. Because it's the greatest game on earth. It's incredibly simple and elegant. Literally all it is is, someone puts on a song, and the other person or people have to guess who it is. Not the song, but the person or band. That's the entire game. If you're playing it right, it's all deep cuts and artists people think they know but actually don't. But there's no wrong way to play it really.

You get five points if you get it on your first guess, three if you get it on your second or third, otherwise one if you get it by the end of the song. And if you don't, the other person gets a point, EXCEPT you can prolong the point by asking for a second song by the same artist/band/rapper/etc., in which case, you still get one point if you guess it, but if you don't get it, the other player gets three. First person to fifteen wins, or you can just keep score for your entire lives, which Corey and I have been doing. Right now he is up 2,063 to 1,849. He went on an epic but controversial run last summer with Modernist classical composers that I'm still recovering from.

If you choose someone who it turns out the other players have never heard of, then the point is a wash. So obviously there's an honor system component, because if you're guessing, you can always be a dick and just lie and say, oohh, sorry, I've never heard of Mobb Deep, or Carly Simon, or Brahms.

But probably the strongest thing about me and Corey's friendship is that neither of us has ever even accused the other of violating the honor system.

ASH: do you guys ever play with anyone else

WES: we've tried to

COREY: you can really only play with people who are at your level or it gets frustrating

[*ash gulps a scallop and points to corey's phone*]

ASH: try me

Bear in mind, we've been playing Garfunkel for years. Also we invented it. So our game is ridiculous.

And Ash's early lobs, Run–D.M.C. and the Jesus and Mary Chain, were pathetic and quickly destroyed by each of us.

But soon it became clear that she was a hundred percent at our level.

She threw on a Gary Numan arrangement of Erik Satie. Then she followed it up with a track that sounded like luau music but turned out to be the Strokes. She hit us with a Jonas Brothers ballad that stumped the hell out of us because who knew the Jonas

Brothers had ballads. And on the guessing front she was holding her own, too. She was able to get Stewart Copeland's solo work. She got the Baha Men on her first try. She had never heard of Hank Mobley, which admittedly was a little strange for someone attending a jazz camp, but we accepted that without argument and moved on.

We were in there for two hours just cranking tunes on her phone and munching high-grade artistic sushi and yelling bands and musicians at one another. And honestly, I know I told you how great it was jamming out earlier. But I think in terms of just overall happiness and contentment, playing Garfunkel with Ash and Corey in that sushi restaurant was probably the pinnacle of my entire life.

I just felt like maybe for those two hours I actually was being a person I could feel good about, or living a life that I could be happy about, or whatever. I don't know. I know it's stupid.

Corey got so psyched after Ash nailed the Baha Men that he immediately picked up the *uni* with his bare hands and swallowed it whole.

"TONGUE OF THE SEA," he yelled.

"OH YEAH," responded both of the sushi chefs.

Then Corey leapt to his feet and sprinted into the bathroom to throw up, and I panicked and ran after him because I thought he was having a fatal allergic reaction, but it turns out he just literally thought it was a tongue.

# 9.

## RETURN TO THE JAZZ GULAG

So if this was a VH1 *Behind the Music* episode, now would be the part where the narration would get all ominous, and it would go something like:

> "On the evening of Monday, June 13th, Ash, Corey, and Wes were riding high. They had just made the best music of their lives and then eaten a sophisticated and challenging sushi meal. But little did they know . . . that up ahead . . . the road was *going to get super bumpy.* Because they were about to be arrested and thrown into jazz prison."

Okay. That's not technically true, because jazz prison does not exist. But if there was one, we probably would have been sent to it.

Russell, the bass teacher, stormed up to us in the dorm parking lot as we were getting out of the car.

"This is not good, you guys," he told us. "This is really not good."

It turned out we weren't allowed to leave campus unsupervised. But then why was it so easy? This was not a question he was interested in answering.

"I want us to be cool," he said, louder than I think he meant to. "But look. I gotta write you up for this. I'm sorry. I don't want to be a cop about this whole thing. I'm a musician, like you. But I got no choice. I hope you understand."

I nodded sheepishly. Corey nodded sullenly. But Ash just looked him up and down.

"No," announced Ash. "I don't understand."

The way she said it brought some kind of new crazy electricity into the air.

"You don't," Russell repeated.

"I don't understand."

"You do not understand."

"Nope."

"You don't get why I can't let *minors* off the campus, out of camp jurisdiction, just running around."

"I'm not a minor. I'm nineteen."

"Oh. Okay. So, you're saying, first of all, nineteen is an adult. And second—"

"Yup. Legally, an adult."

"I don't mean legally, I mean, come on. Nineteen? Sorry. Not an adult. Second—let me finish—*second,* you're telling me if something happens to one of these guys here, you're trying to tell me, you're liable. If, say, *he* gets hit by a car, or you know, *he* freaks out and, you know, runs away to join the circus, you're liable."

"Does that happen? Do you guys have a chronic problem of kids leaving jazz camp to join the circus?"

"Don't be smart with me. My point is, *we're* liable, and, look. Do you think this is easy? You think having to police you guys, being responsible for you guys . . . you think that's easy for us?"

"I don't think *any* of this is easy for you. Because I don't think any of you want to be here."

Russell just stared at her. And suddenly he grinned, in this defeated, tired way.

"Okay. At this point, I think you need to come with me and talk to Bill."

"Whatever you think."

"Your issues with the workshops, you need to take that up with him."

"Whatever you need to do."

"Come with me," he said, and turned to go.

"We're coming, too," I heard myself say.

Russell turned back and stared at me, like, why are you doing this. And I stared back at him.

I was trying to make a Defiant Face, because that was obviously the face that the circumstances were calling for. But also, because I wanted to communicate to Russell that I understood that he had a tough job and wasn't trying to be a dick, I was also trying to make an Apologetic Face.

Russell continued staring at my increasingly unsustainable face.

"Are you okay?" asked Russell.

"Don't worry about me," I said, grimly committed to making two completely incompatible faces at the same time.

"You're making kind of a strange face."

"No. I'm not."

"There isn't something in your eye or something?"

"Don't come," said Ash. "I don't want you guys to come."

"You sure," I said.

"Yeah," she said, and gave me a little smile.

"Sounds good," said Corey uncertainly.

"Let's go see Bill," she said to Russell.

And they left. And Corey and I went into the dorm, alone.


The common room was full of dudes. But no one was interested in talking to us except Tim, the scumbag guitarist.

"You cats caused quite a stir," he said to us in a voice that was trying to be at least half an octave deeper than it actually was. "Especially the *lady*."

Corey actually just sped up and walked out of the room.

"Join me for a square?" Tim said to me, twirling a cigarette pack and almost dropping it.

And before I knew what was happening, I found myself out behind the dorm's fire exit for fifteen minutes, watching Tim chain-smoke Parliaments and listening to him tell me How It Is. He was talking in Stage Four Jazz Voice about Ash in particular and ladies in general and how he always found himself falling for crazy ladies, ladies with *fire*, where sometimes the fire burns slow and sometimes it burns hot, and the only thing they like better than bossing you is when you step up and boss *them.*

"They *jones* on you mannin' up, down, and sideways, my froond," he told me. "And it's the *only* game in town that'll get 'em to quit bossin' you every which."

Then he took a long drag, chuckled, and looked me in the eye.

He was probably trying to get his eyes to twinkle. But the effect was sort of just squinty and intense. It was the face of when someone is trying to fart, except there's a razor's edge between farting and pooping.

I had restricted myself to politely murmured agreement up to that point. But "froond" was just a bridge too far.

"Froond?" I repeated. I didn't even know how to begin raising objections to it. I found myself just repeating it over and over. "Froond? . . . froond. *Froond.*"

"Froond, like 'friend,'" said Tim.

"Yeah. But, uh. But, Tim. Who says 'froond.'"

"Speakers of the lingo known as Ger-manical, my froond."

"Okay. Well, German. Not Germanical. Second, *in* German, according to every German class I've ever taken, it's *froynd.*"

"F-R-U-E-N-D? Believe that spellifies *froond.*"

"Well, that doesn't, but also, it's E-U. Not U-E. Pronounced *froynd.*"

"Depends on the, uh, dialecticaciosi-*cality.*"

"The dialect. No. No dialect has 'froond.'"

"Agree to disagree."

"Tim. It's always *froynd.* Everywhere. Also, you're wrong

about women. Women hate being bossed around. That's the whole reason feminism exists. And in general, man, you gotta not talk like that."

Tim kept smiling, but his face did something between a blink and a flinch.

"Talk like what," he said.

"Talk, like, this whole made-up thing, where every sentence you're trying to remind people that you play jazz and aren't just some other suburban white kid with orthodontist parents."

Now his face had gone a kind of ugly blank. But I had to keep going.

"You gotta not try to talk black. Because let's be honest, that's what you're trying to do. You're trying to do blackvoice. So stop. You're not even doing it right. I mean, you just tried to throw 'froond' in there."

We gazed at each other.

Then he said: "Well, this is how I talk with the brothers back in South Philly. And they've never had a problem with it. But if *you* have a problem, man . . ." He nodded slowly. "Then I got to thank you," he said. "For speaking your truth."

"Oh," I said, immediately feeling exhausted and stressed out.

"As a person of color, when you speak your truth to me, it helps *me* to grow."

"Okay."

"And understand who *I* should be when I'm around *you*."

"Hmmm," I said, needing to end this conversation at all costs.

"Because man. When you think about it, language is such a powerful thing."

"It really is. It really is powerful. Hey. I gotta go. But . . . good talk."

"Come on, man. Rap with me five minutes. I'm digging this back and forth. *Language*."

"No, yeah, but, I have to take a call, but, great talk."

"All right, but come find me after, all right?"

"Yup. Sure thing."

"Because this is the *realness* right here."

A conversation with Tim was never going to be good. But it would have been way less painful if he had gotten mad at me and said, fuck you, don't tell me how to talk. Because that was what *should* have happened. I had been a dick to him. But he was white, and I was visibly not, and so it became this whole other thing that happens with white people that a lot of the time I just don't have the energy for.

I was so out of sorts that I went inside to the rec room and let myself just stand there for another ten minutes while another white dude talked at me. This time it was Steve, the ponytailed bassist, and it was a little more chill. He was giving me a scouting report of himself as a ping-pong player.

"My weaknesses are all psychological," Steve told me. "By that I mean, if I had to play myself, I'd lose every time."

Corey and I got the text around midnight.

meet me in parking lot 2am. dont get caught. bring cloths

We knew who it was. But we didn't know what she meant with the cloths. And when we asked for clarification, she didn't write us back.

I figured "cloths" had to mean bring a change of clothes. Corey thought it was bring washcloths. So we brought both.

She smiled when she saw us, and it wasn't a smile I had seen her do before.

COREY: so what's going on

WES: yeah what did bill say

[*ash shrugs*]

WES: did you get kicked out?

[*some kind of nothing flickers through ash's eyes*]

ASH: yeah

WES: damn

COREY: fuck that guy!

ASH: sshhhh, shut up, don't make noise

COREY: i'm just pissed!

WES: corey, shut up

ASH: it's fine. i basically gave him no choice. he had to kick me out or else look like a huge pussy. but listen

[*ash ushers us closer, and whispers*]

ASH: here's the deal: i'm not going home. i'm going on tour.

COREY:

WES:

ASH: i'm going to drive south and find some places to play. and i think you guys should come with me.

She said this, and I realized that she actually wasn't really one of us at all. She was completely different from us.

"I think we could be a great band," she whispered to us. "But not if we stay here. Summer camp is not where bands get good."

By "different" I mean she actually was an adult, despite what Russell said. And we weren't. That really was the entire difference right there.

"Out on the road is where bands get good. That's where they figure out who they are. They need to play tough crowds and figure shit out the hard way. And I think if we do that, we have a shot at being great."

You become an adult when you decide you don't need anyone's permission to do things. That was Ash. That was definitely not us.

"But we'd have to go tonight. We'd have to go right now and swipe into the practice spaces and load your stuff into my car and be out of here ASAP."

I mean, Corey and I couldn't even give ourselves permission not to play jazz. It took Ash to come along and do that. I was thinking all of these things and my mouth was puffy with spit and my heart was hot and shaky.

"Do you guys want to do this?" Ash asked us.

Corey was nodding. *What is wrong with him*, I thought. Then I realized I was nodding, too.

There was no one in the practice spaces. Load-out went quickly. Corey and I were so keyed up that we couldn't stop accidentally smashing into walls and doorframes with our drums and amps, and then shout-whispering *FUCK*. But no one heard us, or if they did, they didn't care.

We left a note where Corey's drums had been in practice space G:

GOING ON TOUR
BACK BY END OF CAMP
A/C/W

Then Ash put her phone next to the note.

"Put your phones here," she told us.

"What," Corey said.

"I've been thinking about it," she said. "And I think we need to leave our phones behind."

I frowned thoughtfully and pretended to consider this insane and terrible suggestion.

"What," I said.

"We can get tracked with our phones," she said. "After a couple of days, if people really want to find us, they can figure out where we are, and come get us, and then the tour's over."

Corey was nodding.

"But also, if we don't have phones, it's more old-school. It's just us. It just feels right to do it the way bands used to have to do it."

"Makes sense," said Corey. And he put his phone on the floor next to Ash's.

Ash looked at me.

"Uhhhh," I said.

Ash waited for me to say something.

"No, yeah, but it's just, maybe we should have one phone—"

"Nope," said Ash.

"—that we can sometimes use just for maps or something, because we're gonna get super lost without our phones, I think—"

"No phone," said Ash.

"—which, okay, if you're sure, but we won't be able to call anyone, or contact places to set up shows for ourselves, or anything. Or listen to music. Or play Garfunkel. Or do a whole lot of kind of basic things that we might need to do."

"I'm not too worried," said Ash.

"Okay, but it is gonna make things harder for us, like maybe a lot harder," I said, but I realized as I was saying it that that was the whole point.

"That's the whole point," said Ash.

No one stopped us. No one even seemed awake. It was sort of terrifying how easy it all was.

"What's up with the washcloths," said Ash as we pulled out of the parking lot.

# THE HATERS
## SUMMER OF HATE
## WORLD TOUR 2016

JUNE 14th • 5:30 P.M. • KNOXVILLE, TENNESSEE

PERFECT TASTE

## 10.

## AIR HORSE

By 3 A.M. we were across the Pennsylvania-Maryland border. I was still having trouble getting comfortable with the phone situation.

"So, just to go over the plan," I said. "The plan is, basically, drive at random into the South."

Ash nodded, not looking over at me.

"And show up at places without calling first."

"They'll let us play somewhere," she said.

We all sat with this for a while.

"Corey's parents are going to have a massive panic attack when they find out he's missing and doesn't have his phone," I said.

"They'll be fine," yelled Corey from the backseat, sounding pissed. I felt bad for bringing it up. But it was true that this was going to cause them a possibly life-threatening panic attack.

"I don't know about 'fine,'" I said.

"They just need to chill out," he said.

"What's wrong with Corey's parents," murmured Ash, not looking away from the road.

She drove between seventy-two and eighty-seven miles

per hour and had no philosophical issues with passing on the right.

"They're kind of clingy," said Corey finally.

"They don't want to give up control over your life," suggested Ash.

"Sure. I mean, yeah."

"Great. So what you have to do is take it from them."

"No, yeah, I know."

"That's what this is. You're taking control of your life. For what sounds like the first time ever."

"Yeah yeah yeah, no, I know, and that's why I'm on board with no phones."

"They're never going to just give you control. They've been running your life since the beginning, and it makes them feel big."

"Yeah yeah yeah yeah yeah," muttered Corey, trying to get it to stop. "Yeah yeah yeah."

"Ash, is that what your parents are like," I said.

"My parents stopped giving a fuck about what I did a long time ago," she said.

"*Nice*," I said.

We were all quiet.

"Are they dead," said Corey.

"No," said Ash.

Then on instinct, I reached for a phone that was not there. It would be the first of literally thousands of times that this would happen.

Ash noticed and kind of grinned.

By 4 A.M. we were in Virginia and discussing band names. Ash wanted us just to be the Ash Ramos Three.

"That might be a little boring," I said.

"It's not boring," said Ash. "It's classic."

"Yeah," I said, "it's sort of classic but the problem is, it's not memorable. It's just your name, plus how many people are in the band. A band name needs something mysterious about it that makes you think, huh. What even is that."

"Agree," called out Corey from the backseat.

"I guess we could just bill ourselves as Ash Ramos," said Ash.

"No no no. We need a band name. And we need a name where, if you've never heard of the band, the name makes you go, holy crap, I need to find out who this band is immediately."

"So give me a name like that."

I knew this challenge was coming, and I was ready for it. But I pretended not to be, so it would have more impact.

"Oh man. Uh . . . let's see. Just off the top of my head, I mean . . . oh! Well, what about this. Air Horse."

"Nope."

I was dumbfounded at how quickly she dismissed Air Horse.

"Wait," I tried to reason with her. "Come on. Sit with it for a second. Air Horse. That's actually really good."

"Air Horse is not good."

"Corey? Air Horse?"

But Corey was clearly influenced by the crazy swiftness with which Ash decided to hate on Air Horse.

"I guess I like the 'Air' part," said Corey doubtfully. "But the 'Horse' part is making me wonder: Is each song going to be about a horse? I don't like horse songs."

"Okay," I said. "Horse songs aren't a thing."

"It's like how the name Band of Horses makes me imagine that all the members are horses and the lead singer's voice is the voice of a horse, and you know. Ugh. I hate thinking about that. It fucking sucks."

"Okay. That's idiotic. Ash, you seriously don't want to go see a band called Air Horse?"

"Nope," said Ash. "Look. I already know what that band is. That band is two pasty bearded men in skinny jeans. They both play vintage synthesizers and sing in falsetto. Their songbook is basically just eighties-type ballads about how no one will fuck them because they're too sensitive."

Immediately, it was impossible to think of Air Horse in any other terms.

"Nawww," I said feebly. "Come on."

"Yeah," said Ash. "'Air Horse'? Yeah. Close your eyes. It's clearly two hipstery dudes. One of them has a curly Jew 'fro like the guy who paints happy trees on public television. The other is a fat pale redhead. His stomach is bulging out from under the bottom of a very small pink T-shirt with a Pegasus on it. That's Air Horse. And you'd never go see them."

We were quiet.

"Air *Wolf*," I tried.

"YES," shouted Corey.

"Air Wolf is the exact same band except maybe there's also an even fatter guy playing tenor sax," said Ash.

"DAMN IT," shouted Corey.

"That's best case," mused Ash. "Actually, Air Wolf is probably just a third-rate metal band who found each other on Craigslist."

"Air Wolf's probably like eight bands already, so let's look them up," said Corey.

"Corey, you don't have your phone."

There was a brief silence from the backseat.

"That's right," said Corey, trying to sound amped. "And I am *amped* about not having my phone."

"Give me a name that describes a band that I would actually want to go see," Ash told us, "and we can go with that name. But I don't think you guys have one."

The gauntlet had been thrown down. We were racking our brains for a name that Ash couldn't destroy.

We were up against an even bigger hater than ourselves, and I think it's safe to say that both of our hearts were sick with fear.

"I got one," said Corey.

"I'm listening," said Ash.

"Ash and the Shitheads."

"Nope."

"Yeah. I know it's not good. But I can't figure out why."

"Here's one reason why it's not good. Swear words in the name tend to mean no one in the band has any idea how to actually play their instrument. Everyone met at like a summer art program and decided they were going to suddenly form a band, despite never having played an instrument before, and now they're Ash and the Shitheads. They sit around smoking

Camel Lights and trying to convince each other that it's cool that they sound terrible."

I could actually hear Corey trying to think.

Eventually he said, "What if you pronounced it, Shuh-theeds? Is that still not good? Ash and the Shuh-theeds."

"That's probably worse."

"Yeah. I know."

"Ash and the . . . Burnouts," I said.

"Jesus," said Ash. "No."

"Fine, but it's at least better than Ash and the Shuh-theeds."

"No. No, it definitely is not. Ash and the Burnouts is the worst one so far."

"It's not the worst *so far.*"

"It's even worse than Air Horse. Because the best-case scenario for Ash and the Burnouts is, they play Earth, Wind & Fire covers at corporate events. That's best case."

"I agree but why," said Corey.

"You guys have to stop with Name and the Somethings," said Ash, "Because that's never good. That formula is just played out and it's never coming back. But when you add a pun in there, I mean, come on. *Ash?* And the *Burnouts?* They don't even pretend to have self-respect. They're a cover band, and they've opened every performance they've done with 'Celebration' by Kool & the Gang."

"Wes loves that song," announced Corey.

"No I don't."

"You did in eighth grade though."

"Corey. Shut the hell up."

"The song's not the problem," Ash said. "Ash and the Burnouts playing that song is the problem."

We kept lobbing band names at her, but it wasn't because we actually thought any of those names would work. It was just amazing to see a hater of her caliber in action. It was like watching a great athlete ferociously dunking on people.

**Ensign:** "That's a prog-rock band with too many members. They all take turns singing and none of them is any good. The drummer has one of those huge, three-story rigs where it's kind of like he's in a hamster ball. Halfway into their first song, they're playing something in seventeen, or some other horrible time signature, and everyone has left the dance floor and is never coming back."

**Thundergarment:** "All right. That name is sort of likable, but in a coked-up way that is actually completely *un*likable. This is a punk-pop band that is the less-good version of one of those angsty bands where one of the members is famous for being something other than a musician, like an actor or a soccer player or whatever, and then *that* band is the way-less-good version of, I guess, Fall Out Boy or Imagine Dragons or whatever cokey emo thing. So basically Thundergarment is fifth-rate Blink-182."

**The Jacobins:** "Acoustic guitars . . . way too precise rhyme structures . . . uh, contrived love metaphors using like astrophysics . . . and two lead singers who are married to each other. They met at their day job at Google, which they still have. This band has a pathological fear of kicking even a little bit of ass, and NPR brings them into their studio every four days."

**The Magical Singing Boner:** "Ugh."

**What The . . . ?!:** "Okay. I do like this name, but we can never use it, because it can only belong to a band that sucks. Because the unnecessarily elaborate punctuation means this is a band pretending to be way more experimental and interesting than it actually is. At heart, this is a disco band that's ashamed of itself. So it's got like harpsichords and tablas and, I don't know, a bass clarinet. But that is all a smoke screen for entry-level disco. Or like prog disco. It wouldn't be a bad name except that it dooms you to being terrible forever."

**Ramos Wahl & Doolittle:** "Stoner organ trio, dropped out of Juilliard, now they open for Phish, none of their songs has words or is shorter than ten minutes, and a decade from now they'll have given up music completely and instead be a pickle company."

**The Magical Singing Dick Surplus:** "Great. Ash Ramos Three it is."

By 5 A.M. the sun was starting to come up and Corey was asleep. Ash and I left him in the car at a rest stop and committed what would be the first of many irresponsible food purchases. We bought a twenty-four-pack of Coke, a twenty-four-pack of Mountain Dew, and family-size bags of every varietal of Airheads,

Skittles, Doritos, and Dale's, an off-brand potato chip whose flavors were just REGULAR, ONION, CELERY, and BEEF. I made an effort to get stuff without nuts in it, because Corey is fatally allergic to certain kinds of nut, and I was pretty sure Corey had left his EpiPen in Shippensburg.

The CELERY chips were my favorite. The BEEF chips had a taste that I would categorize as like a locker room, but for dogs.

Back at the car, I stacked everything on top of Corey's sleeping body, hoping he would wake up and freak out. But he just opened his eyes, nodded at us in a strangely authoritative way, and closed them again.

I offered to drive and Ash accepted.

"Are you guys gay," she said when we were a few miles down the road.

"What?" I said. "Are *we* gay? No. Of course not."

"Fuck you 'of course not,'" she said. "I get to ask if you're gay. You act like you're married. And you talk about your dicks a lot."

"What do you mean, act like we're married."

"You do a lot of married-couple-type bickering. It's like you guys are sick of each other but can't escape."

It felt wrong to say that he's like my brother, or basically we're each other's dog. Or to say, in ninth grade a kid slide-tackled me pretty hard during pickup soccer and I started crying and Corey decided to go bananas and get way up in that kid's face for messing with the jazz band rhythm section, making crazy eyes and bellowing that that kid was about to have a *big* motherfucking problem, and it probably should have been weird between us afterward, like I was a woman who got mugged in an alley and he was Batman, but somehow instead it cemented our doggy brotherly bond.

The best I could do was, "Real gay dudes don't talk about harming their dicks."

She shrugged. I glanced over at her. She looked back at me. We made kind of a lot of eye contact. I didn't know what to do.

"You're in two lanes," she said, and I was, so I dealt with that in hopefully a calm and commanding way, causing Corey to make an irritable groaning noise.

It's impossible to talk about how a girl is hot without sounding gross or embarrassing, but here's how she was hot. She was just very, very confident. I mean, she was also pretty and vaguely athletic and stuff, but the main thing was she had this way of carrying herself with her chin tilted up and her shoulders kind of back in this way that was like, yeah, I have kind of small probably great-looking boobs and in general am just really hot, and if you don't agree, then definitely go fuck yourself. Somehow all of that was conveyed by how she carried herself. It was hot. Okay. I'll shut up.

"What about you? Are you gay?" I said, in a transparent attempt to turn the tables.

"I used to think I was gay," she said. "Now I think I'm not."

"Why," I said.

"Why which."

"Uh, why both."

"I thought maybe I was gay because I didn't want to hook

up with boys. But after a while I realized I didn't want to hook up with girls, either."

"Mmmm," I said. I was both disappointed and extremely interested in hearing more. But I didn't want to tip my hand. So I was attempting to say "Mmmm" in a way that would convey the idea of, "Cool. Thanks for telling me this. By the way, this is no big deal. Girls tell me about their evolving sexuality all the time."

"You've always liked girls, huh," she said, and turned to me, and in my peripheral vision I could tell she was looking at me in this careful, studying way, and I tried to make a face of relaxed uninterestedness, but it was probably more the face of someone in a coma.

"Yeah," I said.

"Have you hooked up with a bunch of girls?"

"I wouldn't say a bunch."

"How many would you say."

"Uhhhhhh."

I probably spent a few too many seconds pretending to count how many fake hookups.

"Zero," she said.

"No. Hang on. I'm counting."

"It's fine if it's zero," she said. "We're in a band. We have to be open with each other or this isn't going to work."

"It's just embarrassing saying zero," I kind of blurted. I hated the sound of my voice. I sounded like a little kid.

"Hey," she said. I looked over at her. She had a look on her face that I couldn't really classify. "Zero's not bad. Zero means someone gets to be your first. That's a good thing to have. Once you've lost it, you'll want it back."

"I definitely won't," I told her.

"You're in two lanes again," she said, and I was.

"What if you drove not like a herb," mumbled Corey from the backseat.

By 6 A.M. the sun was above the horizon. The Virginia landscape looked more or less identical to the Pennsylvania landscape except maybe the trees were fluffier. Every five minutes I found myself reaching for my phone, and it wasn't there, and I felt a little bit like my mind was disintegrating.

"How come Corey's parents are going to freak out but not yours," Ash said.

"Wes has the greatest parents of all time," Corey announced. "They probably won't even notice he's gone."

"Nnnnnnnope," I said. I was trying to sound amped about it.

# 11.

## MY PARENTS VERSUS COREY'S PARENTS

Here's the difference between my parents and Corey's parents. Corey has never once successfully left his own house without at least a twenty-minute interrogation by one or both of his parents. I have been present for a lot of these interrogations. They don't vary a lot in substance or tone. I can reproduce the beginning of one here basically verbatim from memory.

[COREY'S MOM, *appearing from nowhere as Corey opens the front door en route to trying to leave his house*]

[COREY'S DAD, *yelling from other room*]

—Whoa, whoa, whoa. Where are you headed off to?

—Close the door!

—Slow it down. Slow-w-w-w it down. Tell me *where* you're going.

—Corey! Close the front door! Cold air is entering the house.

—I *see* that you're going somewhere with Wesley. Hello, Wesley. It's very nice to see you.

—Okay. You're going to be at the Oh Yeah Ice Cream store for *how long*?

—An hour and a half? It takes that long to eat ice cream?

—Corey, don't slam the door.

—You *did* slam it, but it's fine.

—An hour and a half is how long it takes to eat ice cream? Isn't it kind of cold for ice cream anyway?

—Fine. Fine, fine. Don't get mad. Listen. Make sure they *wash absolutely everything* before serving you. Okay? Everything. Are you coming home after?

—Then what are you doing?

—I can *feel* the cold air coming into the house, *up here.*

—*Close the door.* CLOSE. THE DOOR.

[*Corey's dad appears at top of stairs*]

—COREY. CLOSE THE DOOR.

—Not "slam the door." "Close the door." I asked you to close it a number of times. Hello, Wes. How are you.

—Wes, it's funny—last month's gas bill came out to *precisely the same dollar amount* as Corey's entire college savings. What do you think of that?

—I know! It *is* a coincidence. It is *quite the coincidence indeed.*

[*Corey's dad pauses to stare at Corey in exaggerated alarm*]

—Are you going to at least call me and tell me *when* you know?

—If I don't hear from you in an hour, I'm going to call. So pick up. I don't care. Pick up or I'm going to come find you. Do you have your EpiPen?

—Is your phone charged all the way?

—That'll run out. Here's a charger. Use one of the outlets. I am sure they'll let you use one if you ask. Now let's just go over your homework situati— hey. Don't get mad at *me*.

—My God, Corey. Are you planning to go out in public like that?

—Your T-shirt is decrepit. In fact, to the naked eye, you appear to be wearing the Shroud of Turin.

—And your jacket looks like a Sex Pistol died in it.

—Wait here. Let's see if we can find you some clothes that weren't foraged from a landfill. By raccoons.

—Diseased, sightless raccoons.

So you can't really blame Corey if sometimes he gets kind of surly and dickish with authority figures and people trying to make him do stuff. He has basically spent his entire life under constant assault.

My home life is a little different. If you're Corey, Corey's parents constantly want to hang out with you in this state of half love, half panic. So they're a lot like dogs. Mine are more like cats. If you're me, my parents are happy to have you around, but they also seem perfectly happy to have you not around. Plus, like cats, they themselves are mysteriously not around a lot of the time. I mean, I guess it's not that mysterious. They're at work.

My mom and dad are first- and second-grade teachers at Mellon Elementary, a public school in South Oakland. And together they do this very effective two-year bilingual thing that wins awards every year and gets the school a ton of federal grant money and clearly has major impacts on kids' lives.

But it means they have to be at the school kind of a lot, like from 7 A.M. until 8 or 9 P.M. during the week, and then on the weekends they're sort of exhausted and checked out. So we're not all that tight-knit of a family unit. Family Dinner is not a thing that happens in our household, for example. I mean, even on an individual level none of us eats in an organized enough way that you would call it Dinner. Or Lunch. Instead you would probably have to call it Constant State of Distracted Grazing, and it is in effect at all times throughout the day and happens to foods that require the absolute bare minimum of preparation, e.g., uncooked vegetables dipped into a two-gallon vat of hummus that Dad gets every Saturday from a restaurant supply store. It's also been at least a year since either of them checked a single piece of my homework.

But look. I realize this might sound sad or self-pitying. That's not how I'm trying to sound. I love my parents, I know they love me, I know how awesome and rare it is that I get to be so independent, I try pretty hard not to let them down, and it makes me happy that they do really important work really well.

I guess my point is just that when Corey's parents smother him with intense caringness every time he tries to leave his house, it doesn't always seem so horrible.

# 12.

## ASH BRIBES A RECEPTIONIST

Obviously Ash was someone who was used to having money. She had her own new-seeming car, played a very expensive Les Paul, paid for group sushi dinners, and gave no shits about which gas station candy had a two-for-one deal. And we had pretended not to notice. But this became impossible when she booked a $519 room at the Knoxville Clinton Hotel and then bribed a receptionist named Wayne.

Wayne had asked us for ID to show that we were all twenty-one.

"My brothers don't have theirs on them," said Ash, handing Wayne her driver's license and two fifties.

Wayne glanced at each of us in turn.

"We're adopted," she said. "Will this work?"

"That will work," said Wayne in a high voice.

"Ash, we should probably talk about band finances," I said, once we were alone in our enormous Jacuzzi-equipped room.

She gazed at me without a facial expression.

"I mean, this is all starting to run into a lot of money. Gas, hotel rooms, food."

She blinked.

"And uh—Corey and I don't really—"

"Everything's on my dad," interrupted Ash. "The whole tour. All the expenses. If anything gets busted, he'll replace it. So just don't worry about it."

Corey was examining the unnecessarily spacious bathroom in what seemed to be a state of shock.

"Does he know we're doing this?" I said.

"Nope," she said. "But he won't care."

"So are you nineteen or twenty-one," called Corey from the bathroom.

"Why wouldn't he care, though?" I said.

"What are some rules of thumb for bribing people without getting arrested," Corey said, coming back out of the bathroom and sniffing a bar of soap.

She sighed.

"I hate talking to people about my shit," she told us. But she ended up telling us a lot.

Her dad was a billionaire. So her family wasn't the kind of rich where they were super comfortable and everyone went to private school and took summer vacations to Europe. That's millionaire or multimillionaire rich. This was billionaire rich, a.k.a. the kind of rich where everything that happened to everyone in the family was completely insane and usually terrible.

Frankly, it all would have sounded made up, except you could tell from how she was talking about it that it wasn't. Because she clearly wished that it was.

Her dad was João Ramos, a Brazilian mining-fortune billionaire who mostly lived in New York, and her mom was his second wife, a French model named Clotilde. How did they meet? He saw a picture of her in a Calvin Klein underwear ad and decided to have her flown to his house on a jet. Because that is just one of the things you can do when you're a billionaire and you don't give a shit.

Apparently, he did this kind of a lot. If he thought a model in an ad was really beautiful, he would just straight-up order her delivered to his house like a pizza. I mean, the pretense was, he was friends with the model's agent, and the agent would suddenly get the idea that maybe his client and his good friend the Brazilian billionaire should go on a date. But in reality it was just João ordering women like pizzas from the basically infinite menu of all magazine ads everywhere.

João and Clotilde went on some dates and got married in less than a year, when he was forty-three and she was nineteen. A year and a half later, Ash was born, and João and Clotilde were already in the process of getting divorced, because João was having affairs not just with more underwear models but also with an honest-to-God princess, specifically of Monaco, the world's most rich-person-intensive country.

At this point Corey attempted to tell Ash that her dad was actually kind of a beast. But she was not receptive to this idea.

Anyway, after having Ash, her mom spent a bunch of years trying to get back into modeling. So Ash was raised north of New York City at her dad's house, along with her two older half sisters, Natalie and Jessica. Mostly the parenting was done by a combination of West Indian nannies, private tutors, and a

Russian tennis instructor named Evgeniy. And mostly her life was about tennis.

João was obsessed with the idea of his daughters crushing at tennis. He took them to the US Open every year, where they would all spend hours hanging out in a luxury box with whoever João's girlfriend was and then at the end of the day get hastily introduced to sweaty, exhausted tennis superstars who clearly just wanted to be alone. And he forced all three daughters to train with Evgeniy from the age of six.

Evgeniy was responsible for many of the deeply terrible child-of-a-billionaire things that Ash experienced. Because Evgeniy was a sadist. For example, he did not value happiness or spiritual growth. What he valued was winning.

His worldview was: winners are just people who want to win more than anyone else on earth. So if you want to win, you must become pathologically obsessed with winning. You must come to find it viscerally revolting to lose to anyone, ever. The desire to win and the fear of losing are the same thing, and they must become the most powerful part of your soul, eclipsing all other wants and fears. Also, no sugar.

"He literally made an unflavored nutritious slurry that we had to eat at every meal for almost a year," said Ash.

"Jesus," I said.

"What's a slurry," said Corey.

"A slurry is a semiliquid mixture," I said. "Like something with the consistency of mud."

"Yup," said Ash.

"Holy shit," said Corey.

Evgeniy liked to talk about the time Joseph Stalin ordered a scientist to breed apes and humans together to create a new kind of super warrior, "insensitive to pain and indifferent to the quality of the food that they eat." Stalin's breeding project apparently was a failure. But Evgeniy still felt that it taught the world a valuable lesson about the benefits of being indifferent to the quality of the food that you eat.

João put an end to the slurry after he found out about it. But this turned out to be only because he believed eating flavorless gray food would make his daughters less beautiful. And being beautiful was his number-two priority for all three girls behind crushing at tennis, a priority that took the form of constant access to Japanese skin-care products and occasional fatherly suggestions of plastic surgery for Natalie, who eventually got a nose job that collapsed two years later after getting hit by a serve from a ball machine.

Anyway, the slurry episode led to the hiring of a family chef/nutritionist, a mysterious, ageless, soft-spoken Scottish man named Onnie, who had trained under the chef Thomas Keller at the French Laundry and also once briefly filled in as the lead guitarist of Slayer.

At this point Corey proposed that maybe this dad didn't do everything for the best reasons, but you did have to admit that he was somewhat of a beast if he was hiring the guitarist of goddamn Slayer. But Ash did not feel that she had to admit any such thing about her fuckface of a dad.

So the three Ramos girls grew up playing an absolute dickload of tennis, becoming remorseless winning machines, and not having a ton of friends. Natalie, the oldest, with the still-a-little-bit-fucked-up nose, had been an undistinguished junior tennis player but managed to grind out a respectable pro career as an all-court player who had no glaring weaknesses but no overpowering strengths, either. At twenty-nine she was now ranked forty-first in the world, which was probably as high as she was going to get. Jessica had been a top-ten junior player with a 95-mph serve and actual sports people on ESPN saying she could become the Next Big Thing when at age seventeen she tore the rotator cuff in her right shoulder. Then at age eighteen she tore it again. Then, despite no longer having a huge serve, she made a moderately successful comeback as a gritty, tireless, annoying, hyper-defensive counterpuncher until she tore the ACL in her left knee at age twenty-three. Now she was twenty-six, unable to serve or run at a very high level, but still doggedly pursuing a comeback that only she and Evgeniy believed was possible and not, in actuality, depressing and doomed.

Ash was ten years younger than Natalie and seven years younger than Jessica, and apparently she was the best prospect of the three. She was fast, played smart, and had a monster serve like Jessica's, except smoother and less likely to blow out her shoulder. Most importantly, she was great at hating to lose. Her signature move after a loss was squatting on the baseline like a frog, gripping fistfuls of her own hair, and letting out bloodcurdling screams as long as ten seconds in length. If the loss was really bad, she would then slash up her racket with a pocketknife that she carried around. She had a reputation on the junior circuit as an absolute psychopath. So in other words, she was the pride and joy of Evgeniy's entire life.

Then at fifteen she had her appendix taken out. She was in bed for two weeks. Evgeniy, on the road with Natalie, had assigned her to watch a twelve-hour History Channel miniseries about horrible protracted wars. It was called *Attrition.* So she was lying there, watching *Attrition,* and Onnie came in with her dinner on a tray, and the narrator was saying stuff like, "Of the fourteen thousand men to set foot on that island, *only three survived,*" in way too intense and grave of a voice. It was the over-the-top dramatic voice of just some guy in a sound studio somewhere. Some gleefully dire, comfortable guy wearing comfortable clothes who you could just tell had never experienced any kind of real violence or danger at all, so there was nothing that qualified him as the guy who got to be the voice that told you about all these tens of thousands of deaths, each of which happened to someone and was awful. So somehow that plus Onnie walking in gave Ash the suspicion that her life so far had been pointless.

I think my life so far has been pointless, she told Onnie.

He told her that was far from the truth.

Can you put on something to watch that isn't this, she asked him.

Onnie nodded, fished around on the Internet for a moment or two, and ended up putting on a John Lee Hooker concert. Why? Who knows. He never said. He must have just thought Ash would like John Lee Hooker. So they sat there and watched the whole thing. And then he left and she watched it again. And then she found some other John Lee

Hooker videos. And for the next two weeks all she really did was lie there and watch and listen to Delta blues guys: John Lee Hooker, Robert Johnson, Howlin' Wolf, Charley Patton, Ishmon Bracey.

Once she was on her feet, she told her dad and Evgeniy and her mom that she was done with tennis and was going to play guitar instead.

Evgeniy did not take it well. In a yelling match on the court behind João's house, he told Ash she was being irresponsible. She told him she hated tennis. He told her that she hated tennis because she loved it so much. She told him that didn't make sense and anyway it was her life. He told her she was being a coward. She told him actually it was taking a lot of courage to leave the game especially if he was going to be such a dick about it. He told her she was throwing away thousands of hours of not just her time but his and had she thought about that for even one moment no of course not. She told him it wasn't her fault he chose a fucked-up line of work where you spend all your time thinking about how to develop the muscles of a girl's body and also trying to give them basically the mindset of a Nazi conquistador rapist sociopath. He told her millions literally *millions* of girls would be ecstatic to have the instruction and expertise and care and everything else that had been invested in her and now she was just tossing it all in the garbage like the spoiled impulsive brat that he had always secretly suspected her to be. She told him the thing that excited her most about music was that she would never again have to pretend to listen to his dumbshit lessons from nature about how the spider lies in wait for hours but the wasp is never still or whatever the pointless creepy fucking thing and also she would never again have to smell his gross breath. He told her he was too much of a gentleman to tell her what he really thought of her, and then he told her she was a cunt.

But João took it worse. He frowned and nodded and got kind of cold and formal and told her if that's what she wanted to do, then that's what she wanted to do, and there was nothing he could do about it, because she was her own person, and he respected that, and perhaps it was best if she moved in with her mother. So Ash moved in with Clotilde on the Upper West Side and started going to a high school and more or less never saw her dad again. He paid off her credit cards every month and made a point of dancing with her at his next wedding but that was about it.

Meanwhile, Clotilde was sort of supportive, but not really a mom. She was preoccupied with her fashion label and going out most nights and having rich boyfriends and abruptly being in Rome or Buenos Aires without telling anyone.

So Ash was alone. For a while she had Onnie, who gave her secret guitar lessons for two years, but then he left to start a restaurant in New Orleans, and then she had no one at all.

She spent all her time outside of school shredding guitar alone in Clotilde's apartment and writing songs and listening to music constantly and sometimes going to shows and thinking about the band she would start but not having anyone to start it with.

Also she briefly was the underage girlfriend of a member of Animal Collective. She refused to say who because he could get in big trouble.

So that brought us pretty much up to date.

"So how old are you," I asked.

"Nineteen," she said. "I got my ID from the equipment manager of the New York Knicks."

I sort of wanted to hear more about that, but mostly didn't.

"Did you graduate?"

"Yeah. In June."

"Are you going to college?"

"Taking a year off."

"To play music or what?"

"I physically can't talk about myself anymore," she said, and we left the room and the hotel and spent the afternoon staggering red-eyed and jittery around Knoxville looking for a place to play that night, like jazz-camp-escaped zombies.

## 13.

## THE ASH RAMOS THREE BOOKS THE PERFECT TASTE

It took us five hours to find a place that we could book. It was an all-you-can-eat Chinese buffet restaurant called Perfect Taste in a strip mall on Route 70, and it had no stage or sound system. So there were some clear early signs that it wasn't going to be the smoothest possible beginning to the tour. Also a lack of sleep paired with a diet of Coke and Airheads had made us all temporarily psychotic.

How did we find Perfect Taste? Basically, a huge amount of getting rejected by actual music venues, followed by an even huger amount of random driving around.

The rejections were uniformly swift and impervious to whatever script we used:

1. Hi. We're a band called the Ash Ramos Three. Can we play here tonight? Oh. Okay. Well, uh . . . okay. Thanks. Actually, why are we thanking you.

2. Hi. We're a band called the Ash Ramos Three. Can we play here tonight? Oh. Then can we talk to the guy who does the booking? Oh. Well, what hours is he in here? Wow. That's a cushy job. Honestly, it sounds like you don't even need him. You should

just do the booking yourself! Just book us and maybe your boss will give you a raise and a new title. And then you've truly begun your ascent up the corporate ladder. Dress for the job you want, not the job you have. No, we don't want a table. We're obviously not here for a table. We're here to play a life-changing show that you can use to catapult your career into places you've never even thought possible. Well, fine. Bye. Enjoy never having a good job. Sorry, we didn't mean that, we're just stressed out because Corey ate the entire bag of Dale's BEEF potato chips and now he won't stop burping.

**3.** Hi. We're the Ash Ramos Three and our manager told us he had a gig booked here, but it turns out he was lying about that and a bunch of other stuff, so we fired him, and now we're seeing if we— yeah, it's just us. We fired him. Yeah, we're all twenty-one. Blues, punk, like a blues punk roots power trio, but really a lot of critics say we transcend genre. Unfortunately we have nothing you can listen to because our manager stole all our CDs for no reason other than he's vindictive. Well, also Ash stabbed him in the dick. The foreskin. He's fine. We're pretty sure he's a rapist. Can we just play here tonight? We don't have anywhere to play. We can play after the other bands are done. We'll seriously go on whenever. Okay. Sure. Bye. If you see a guy with a bloody dick, then you'll know. Although, you guys are probably already best friends.

**4.** Hi. We're Meatflower, and we're here for soundcheck. Meatflower who you booked for tonight like it says out front. Our slot's at ten after Fangs of the Mutant. Ugggh. Look. Yeah. I can't believe they keep doing this. Those guys from earlier *weren't* *the Meatflower that booked this gig.* WE'RE Meatflower. Those fucking guys are just a bunch of assholes who call themselves Meatflower so they can steal our shows! We went to high school with them, Corey stole one of their girlfriends, and now we're mortal enemies and they've been fucking with us the entire tour. But we're the real Meatflower! Don't let them back in here. Okay, fine. We'll wait here until they come back. Sure. We'll just wait right here. Okay. Hey. Look. We're not Meatflower. But fuck Meatflower. We're definitely better than them. Just let us play instead. Okay. Chill out for just one second. We haven't even done anything.

5. Hi. If we pay you one thousand dollars, can we play here tonight instead of Coach Nasty Cat? A thousand bucks in cash. Hmmm. Okay. Well, look. It was worth a shot. Where would it even say in the legal code that this is illegal. Oh.

Eventually we found ourselves just driving around, not really saying a lot, and on Route 70, without asking us, Ash pulled into the parking lot of the strip mall that Perfect Taste was in.

"Fuck it," she said.

The cashier of Perfect Taste was also the owner, a woman named Lucy with enormous permed hair, and she seemed delighted and amused that a band wanted to play at her restaurant.

"What kind of music?" Lucy wanted to know.

"We're a blues roots punk power trio," said Corey.

"Oh!" she said. "That's a lot of things!"

"Yeah," Corey agreed.

There was kind of a standoff where she smiled intensely at each of us.

"I like the blues," she announced eventually. She had one of those smiles that made you feel great about yourself. "We get most people around five-thirty, six P.M. You can play then. Play blues music."

It was already four. We had a band meeting out in the parking lot.

"That buffet looked rock-solid to *me*," I said, trying to be positive.

"I probably shouldn't eat any of it because I don't have my EpiPen," said Corey.

"Fierce," I said.

"Ash," said Corey. "Is this really a place where bands could play."

"We just booked it, so yeah," said Ash.

"We might be playing for zero people, though," said Corey.

"She told us we were gonna play when they get the most people," said Ash.

"I do worry a little that the acoustics are a giant bucket of dick," said Corey.

"Shut the fuck up and listen," said Ash, suddenly losing all patience. "Good. I *want* to play here. I *want* to play for strangers in basically a Chinese prison cafeteria. Because that's how you become a great band. Okay? This is exactly the shit I'm talking about. We have to play at *tough places to play*. If we can play a great show here, we can play a great show anywhere. So I'm fucking excited about this shit."

Corey did a Robert De Niro–type face scrunch. He was pissed

off because on the one hand he hated being told what to do, but on the other hand he did not want to be the one who was anti-greatness.

"All right all right," I said, attempting to build consensus. "All right all right all right."

"Let's fucking do it then," said Corey.

"We're gonna play a great fucking show," said Ash.

"Let's play the *fuck* out of the Perfect Goddamned Taste."

"We're gonna rock the shit out of it."

"We're gonna rock it so hard they have to shut it down. For safety reasons."

"We are going to fuck this place with our guitar dicks," I said, and then immediately made eye contact with a nearby man who was bringing his two young children out of a FedEx.

Anyway, as it turned out, we did not play the fuck out of a great show. Instead, we found ourselves playing a show that was epically terrible.

First, the only place to set up with electric outlets was a little rectangle of space crammed in next to the buffet itself. So we had to wedge Corey in next to the combination egg rolls and spare ribs tray and then set up directly in front of him. We couldn't see him, and he couldn't hear us, and also we were in the way of anyone who wanted egg rolls or spare ribs, which literally everyone at a Chinese buffet wants.

Second, the audience came and went but was never more than twelve people, all of which were old or families. So they did not constitute the ideal audience for loud warlike songs about eating Roger Federer and fucking your dog. The acoustics were bad enough that it was impossible to tell what Ash was saying, but her intent was still clear.

Every single person in the restaurant chose to sit as far away from us as possible, and either tried to behave as though we were not there or just sat there munching and glaring at us like resentful cows.

Third, as a band, we sucked.

We sucked in every way. Ash's guitar was out of tune. My bass sounded like you were hearing it through a mattress, except still loud and in fact way too loud. Corey's bass drum kept sliding away from him. I forgot entire parts of songs. Corey forgot even more entire parts of songs and kept panicking and switching to super fast disco, first as a joke but then increasingly as a kind of nihilistic statement about the bleak absurdity of what we were doing. Ash apparently got bored of singing actual notes and switched to a combination of retching and shrieking. We were physically incapable of all ending a song at the same time. In fact, we couldn't do *anything* at the same time. We were an animal with three different kinds of leg. We were the soundtrack to a mental illness.

We probably should have stopped after our first song. We definitely should have stopped after a completely improvised fifteen-minute blues during which two different children started crying. And we even more should have stopped when an angry old dude came over during "Sex Plague" and yelled at us over and over, for two entire choruses and a verse, "This isn't music!! THIS ISN'T MUSIC!!!"

So it was a traumatizing forty-five minutes. For the audience, sure, but I think even more for us. When it was over, no one applauded and multiple people loudly thanked God.

"I just came here for my moo shu," yelled the old dude, aiming his head around in search of people who agreed with him. "I didn't come here for *that*. I came for the moo shu and that's *it*."

The only person who thought we were any good was Lucy, and actually in retrospect she was almost definitely just fucking with us.

"You kids have real talent!" she came over to tell us as we were packing up. "Real emotion! Ha ha ha ha ha ha!"

But she also gave us a three-for-two deal at the buffet. So we hung around for twenty minutes, eating noodles and General Gao's chicken and saying little. Ash was stony-faced. Corey kept sighing miserably.

At least it felt like Ash was one of us again.

ASH: wes

WES: what

ASH: stop saying that

COREY: for real

WES: stop saying what

ASH: "all right all right"

COREY: yeah you're muttering it like an insane person

WES: oh

ASH: you've said it like a billion times

WES: i wasn't even aware that i was saying anything

ASH: well you were so stop

COREY: why the fuck were you saying it so much

WES: i guess it's a reflex

COREY: why would you have that as a reflex though

WES: it's just like a thing to say to make peace or build consensus

COREY:

ASH:

WES: like in times of difficulty

COREY: i am going to kill myself

We loaded up Ash's car and managed to drive back to the hotel without getting lost or having a horrific accident.

It would make sense if we were all consumed with terrible shame upon entering our over-the-top lavish hotel room, with its hot tub and very rich-feeling carpet and enormous bed and panoramic views. Shame about how little we had done to earn this. But what I felt, at least, was relief. Who even knows why. It was somehow a big relief to get to hang out in this incredible room with a hot tub. I walked over and stared at the hot tub for a while.

"Fuck it," I said, I think out loud, and without asking permission or guidance or anything, I turned on the hot tub, and it started roiling and foaming, and I stripped to my boxers while trying not to be weird about it. And after a while the water was hot, and I got in there and sat there for a while.

Obviously, on some level I was hoping that Ash was going to get in there, too. Maybe on most levels. If that meant Corey was getting in, fine. He would also be in there. I mean, getting in the hot tub wasn't like a *move*. I didn't think it was going to lead to me hooking up or anything. I just thought at least it was a chance to be in a hot tub in my underwear with a girl in her underwear, and that would be something.

But within a few minutes it was a moot point because I had passed out.

# THE HATERS
## SUMMER OF HATE
## WORLD TOUR 2016

JUNE 15th • 10:00 P.M. • FARGO, ALABAMA

CHARLIZE AND ED'S BACKYARD

# 14.

# A TURBULENT MORNING
# AT THE KNOXVILLE CLINTON

I woke up on the floor. My mouth tasted like a landfill and my neck felt like horses had been standing on it. Also, the fly of my boxers was open, because there was a full-on Code Red sleep boner awkwardly lunging out of there.

It was definitely my boner. So immediately I was wide awake and consumed with panic.

Fortunately, no one was awake to stare in disgust at the lurchy jailbreak of my sleep boner. Corey was asleep, fully clothed, on top of half of the bed. Ash was under the covers of the other half. So I ran into the bathroom, contorted myself over the toilet so that I could pee into it and not onto the wall or ceiling, laboriously peed, still had the boner, masturbated in a brisk businesslike manner into the sink with the hotel conditioner, rinsed out the sink, took a shower, and then put on clothes.

Everyone was still asleep. And I still did not have a phone. So I turned on the TV and flipped around until I found David Attenborough's *Blue Planet* and watched the segment about tubeworms for probably the seventy-fifth time in my life.

Corey was next to wake up. He went straight for the bathroom.

Pretty quickly he came back out again.

COREY: wes

WES: what

COREY: what's in the sink

WES: i don't know

COREY:

WES: what

COREY: well i don't know either but it looks a lot like jizz

WES:

ASH: nnnggh

COREY: wes, true or false: that's your jizz in our sink

WES: *corey stop talking so loud*

COREY: wes you gotta at least clean up the sink after you've jizzed in it

WES: *shut up i thought i did clean it*

ASH: both of you shut up about wes jizzing in the sink

It turns out that rinsing isn't always enough to get jizz all the way out of a sink. Anyway, I hastily cleaned up the rest of it, but the damage was done, and things were awkward at breakfast in the hotel buffet afterward.

But I figured it wasn't just awkward because I had masturbated into the hotel sink. I felt like the awkwardness had just as much to do with the disgrace we had all brought upon ourselves the day before at Perfect Taste.

How had it happened? Could it really just have been the

circumstances? The lack of stage or sound system? The super inappropriate audience?

My suspicion was that those factors were not it. They served only to conceal the deeper truth. And that truth was, perhaps we were awful.

You can talk about circumstance all you want. It was still *us* up there. It was us whose performance had constituted an atrocity against music and possibly humanity itself. Circumstance or not, we had proven ourselves capable of limitless monstrosity.

And not even the good kind of monstrosity. Not "monstrosity" in the sense of eating Roger Federer. "Monstrosity" in the sense of being so lame that it makes everyone question the very project of human life. Monstrous not like the sudden eruption of a completely ass-kicking volcano, and instead monstrous like a desert, which will also kill you, but mostly by being so monotonous and irritating that you finally decide to lie down and be eaten by a vulture. That was the kind of band that maybe we were.

And that's what I figured we were all sitting there silently thinking. Then when Ash got up to look for coffee, it became clear that I was at least part wrong.

COREY: um
WES: what
COREY: so uh
COREY:
WES: corey what
COREY: so just so you know ash and i hooked up last night

My first reaction was, I found myself doing Corey's signature Robert De Niro Face Scrunch. I did it for kind of a really long time.

I was overcome with something. But it wasn't anger. I think it was more just the question, *How*. It was just a huge existential bafflement at how someone like Ash could ever want to hook up with someone like Corey.

COREY: so yeah

WES: all right all right

COREY: yup

WES: you guys just hooked up while i was lying there in the tub?

COREY: first we moved you out of the tub and onto the floor because we were worried you would fall in and drown

WES: hmm

COREY: you were in like a coma or something

WES: and then you guys, uh

COREY: yeah

WES: well uh

COREY:

WES: well . . . good job?

COREY:

WES:

COREY: are you mad

What I was thinking was, Look. I know I'm no prize. I'm somewhat walleyed. I have dumb floppy hair and no visible muscles of any kind. In general I look like I'm twelve and probably will for the next two decades. The list goes on and on. But *Corey*?

Corey has one of those heads where the back of it extends an unnaturally long distance, like a dinosaur's. His breath always smells like a corpse. Speaking of corpses, his hands and feet are frequently cold and purple, from terrible circulation, which I guess you shouldn't hold against him, but I'm just saying. Also, if I look like I'm twelve, he basically *is* twelve, like psychologically.

WES, *lying*: no i'm not mad
COREY: okay
WES:
COREY: well thanks
WES: thanks for what
COREY: thanks for being cool about this
WES: sure
COREY:
WES:
COREY: i have to say you do seem a little bit mad

It was just, we had a ninety-ninth-percentile girl on our hands, in pretty much every respect, the smartest, sexiest, most interesting girl we were definitely ever going to meet, *and* it turned out she had a totally bizarre and crazily permissive taste in dudes and was willing to hook up with a completely subpar dude, a dude flailing around in the forties or thirties, in terms of percentile of dude, which meant *I maybe had a chance* with a girl like Ash. But because Corey had blundered in there first, now there was definitely no chance at all and an opportunity like this was never going to happen again. So actually I was suicidal with rage.

WES: yeah i'm a little bit mad

COREY: yeah i could tell

WES: i mean i'm mad because it's gonna make things weird for the band now if you keep hooking up, because this band is now gonna feel like it's a married couple on tour with this third random dude, i.e., me

COREY:

WES: but it'll also be weird if you *stop* hooking up, because then you guys will probably start fighting or getting mad at each other

COREY: oh

WES: so yeah it feels like something that'll fuck up the band no matter what and i'm a little mad about that

COREY: i figured you were mad because you wanted to hook up with her

It was like this. Have you ever suddenly realized that someone older than you, whom you've always assumed is smart, because they're in a position of authority, actually isn't very smart? Like you're getting nachos at a Pirates game with your Uncle Bill and he tries to pay with exact change and he keeps getting it wrong? Even after the cashier has explained it to him? Until finally the huge dude behind you guys has to physically take the right change out of Uncle Bill's hand? And you're standing there feeling embarrassed for Uncle Bill but even more for yourself and you just want to get out of there?

Okay. Now imagine having that feeling about the entire universe. Like God and everything. That is what I felt like when

I found out that Ash had decided to hook up with my idiot best friend. There was a God who was in charge, and He was just way dumber than you had ever even suspected.

COREY: i mean i'm just saying

WES: fucking drop it

COREY: okay

WES: jesus

COREY: i knew you weren't gonna be cool about this

WES: *i'm* not being cool?!

COREY: yeah you're freaking out

WES: you're the one insisting on talking about it right now like a big freckly tampon

COREY: i'm just being honest with you

WES: i'm also being honest when i tell you that you're being a gummy wad of used horse condoms at this time so please shut up

COREY: i knew you'd be mad

WES: yeah i'm fucking mad because you did some typical selfish impulsive destructive bullshit because you're the dinosaur-headed goat foreskin that you are somehow always incapable of not being, so just shut the hell up

The small part of me that was able to have some perspective and not just selfishly feel horrible about Corey and Ash was feeling horrible about what I was saying to Corey. Because this was different from the ambient low-level bickering that we often do. That stuff is just riffing and no one's out to make anyone feel bad. This was clearly something else. This was not playful dogs-romping-around behavior. This was shitty spiteful human behavior, but I couldn't help it.

COREY: just tell me this and i will shut up

WES: tell you what, ass

COREY: would you have hooked up with her?

WES: what?

COREY: just would you have hooked up with her if she was like, wes, let's hook up

WES:

COREY: that's all i'm asking

WES: the answer is no

COREY: what? bullshit

WES: the answer is no so choke to death on sasquatch's dick

That was the point at which Ash returned. So we shut up about it and resumed our awkward wordless consumption of low-quality sausage.

We tried doing Internet in the hotel's business center, a dank, windowless, fluorescent-lit closet of ancient computers that kept asking us to update their versions of Windows. But when we tried updating one computer, it had a panic attack. So we ignored the other ones' software update pleas, which was difficult, because they kept popping up every thirty seconds or so in front of everything you were trying to do, and also because you did feel pretty bad for these poor dinosaur computers.

ASH, *reading email*: fuck

WES: what

ASH: we can't use my car anymore

WES, *alarmed*: what?!

COREY: hey i'm getting the software update message again

ASH: yeah we're all getting it so just ignore it

WES: ash what's wrong with your car?

ASH: my mom emailed me. she's pissed off because the jazz camp people keep bothering her. she says the police are looking for my license plate and are going to pull us off the road

WES: fuck

ASH: so we should stop using my car

COREY: how do you get this message to go away

WES: click "cancel"

COREY: it won't let me

ASH: uncheck the little box and click "cancel"

COREY: it says don't uncheck the box

WES: uncheck it anyway

COREY: ok

WES: christ

COREY: in my defense i didn't know you could do that

WES: so what are we going to do?

ASH: we need another car

WES: oh

ASH: with its own plates

WES: how much does a new car cost?

ASH: we don't want a new car. we want a used one that already has a plate

COREY: the box came back

WES: corey jesus christ

ASH: get rid of the box every time, don't update the software, and hurry up because we need to get moving

WES: how much cash do we have?

ASH: i'll take some out today. it shouldn't cost more than a couple thousand to get a car that works

WES: whoa

COREY: uh wes

WES: what

COREY, *typing*: uhhhhhh

WES: corey what

COREY: wes do you remember any of my passwords

WES: oh my god of course not

COREY: i don't remember them either but i know they're all super complicated

ASH: wes what have you heard from your parents

I had heard nothing. They hadn't emailed me, or Facebooked me, or chatted me, or left me any voice messages. They had made no effort to get in touch with me at all.

Honestly, it was just embarrassing. If they had sent me something about how angry they were, or worried, or disappointed, or whatever, that would have made me feel pretty terrible. But this made me feel worse. I was sitting there thinking, *Come on, guys. Even Ash's delinquent mom is making you look bad right now.*

WES: they seem very upset and worried

ASH: what did they say specifically

WES:

ASH:

WES: well i'm assuming they're upset and worried

ASH: oh

WES: they haven't contacted me in any way

ASH: huh

WES: but uhhhh

ASH: that sucks. fuck them

WES: no they're pretty busy. it's not a big deal

ASH: no fuck them

WES: i mean i guess a little but they don't usuall

ASH: your parents need to get it the fuck together

WES: well

ASH:

WES: i guess yeah

COREY: uh guys

ASH: what

COREY: i think i just tried to update the software

WES: you *think* you tried to update the software

COREY: well i did try to update it

WES: corey why the fuck would you do such a thing

ASH: we've been saying this whole time not to

COREY: just to get it to shut up but now it's all fucked

WES: how are you even still alive

ASH: let's get the fuck out of here

We did, but there was a part of me that did not want to leave that room. For one thing, it had Internet. I was really starting to feel like I was going insane without my phone. I was reaching my hand into my pocket like every thirty seconds and then realizing yet again that there was no phone in there, and every single time that realization was unbearable. I was dead to the world minus two people, and it felt like all around me terrible things were probably happening, and I didn't even get to know about them.

Basically going through your life with no phone is like driving a car from inside a chicken suit.

But for another thing, I sort of just didn't want to be on the run anymore, with my nitwit best friend and the girl who was choosing to hook up with him and not me. I really just wanted to sit on the floor of the business center like a four-year-old until someone came to pick me up.

Honestly, the only thing that kept me from doing that was that I still had this stupid desire to be in a band and play shows. I was beginning to realize that this desire was eventually going to destroy the rest of my life.

COREY: what's good about my password system is that it's essentially unhackable

ASH: unless you no longer have your phone

COREY: well

ASH:

COREY: well yeah

## 15.

## HOW TO TRADE YOUR REALLY NICE BUT POLICE-SUSPICION-AROUSING CAR FOR AN INFINITELY LESS NICE AND COME TO THINK OF IT PROBABLY ALSO POLICE-SUSPICION-AROUSING CAR IN THREE EASY STEPS

**Step One. Get a bunch of money from Citibank**

Specifically, five thousand dollars. If you're not a minor, you can just walk in there and do this. The bank people might put up some resistance, like, sweetie, what do you need the money for, do your parents know about this, etc., but this resistance is easily overcome, especially if the kind but patronizing Citibank manager is made aware that you are part of a family that could remove a bazillion dollars from Citibank tomorrow in response to what feels like unfair, ageist, possibly sexist treatment, an awareness that will make the Citibank manager drop the kindness but also the patronizingness and get all thin-lipped and wounded as the teller silently fills your envelope with five thousand goddamned dollars while you try not to do a fist-pump so triumphant that it blows out your shoulder and then you have to play guitar left-handed.

*Note: Step One requires that you already have five thousand dollars and are part of a family with a bazillion dollars.*

**Step Two. Cruise around neighborhoods where cars seem to be for sale a lot and eventually buy one from a person named "Relph"**

In Knoxville, it's not super hard to stumble onto a neighborhood where every block or two there's a car with one of those black-and-orange FOR SALE signs taped to the side window. So get in there and start cruising around. Because you don't have a phone, you're going to have to knock on some doors, which will excite some dogs and confuse some old people and irritate some strung-out jobless weirdos, and when you do finally find someone who actually does have a car to sell, you will discover that the car is not running right now, and then the next one is running but it only gets six miles per gallon because there is a puncture wound in the gas tank from a knife that will be displayed to you in a frighteningly casual way, and the one after that runs fine except there are no brakes or windshield, and after a while it is going to seem totally hopeless but that is about when you will find a suitable transaction partner. He will be a genial courtly older gentleman named Relph who corrects you with a wheezy giggle when you try to pronounce it "Ralph." "Nope," he says. "*RELPH.*" Okay. Relph's car makes it all the way around the block, so you agree to buy it for $2,300 cash, no questions asked. It is a boxy little 1998 Honda Accord the color of your dad's teeth, it smells like menthol cigarettes and a barbecue that happened at least five years ago, and the backseat is patterned with entire stain continents from wine or blood. It is an atlas of stains, and Atlas of Stains will strike one of you, very briefly, as a decent band name, until you say it out loud and only then do you realize your mistake, but it's too late because already one of your bandmates is shooting it down by comparing it unfavorably with a number of sweaty earnest sexually frustrated Christ-core type bands while you mutter I know I know I know I know I know and maybe try to climb into the trunk to escape except it's already got the amps in it.

**Step Three. Deposit the nice car in long-term parking at Knoxville's McGhee Tyson Airport**

After transferring all of the equipment to the Honda Accord, which already has the Check Engine light on and is making a quiet but piercing hungry-dog whine at all speeds below 20 mph, you can split up and one of you can drive the brand-new SUV into the Knoxville airport's long-term parking section and park in a random indoor spot and walk away without once looking back, feeling pretty badass, like Vin Diesel walking away from something exploding, except there is no explosion and you actually do look back and the big black SUV is just kind of still there in the parking spot looking enormous and blank like someone else's dog that has already forgotten everything about you.

You walk over to Departures and stand there waiting for your bandmates to show up in the Accord, imagining the beat-up yellowish car pulling up to the curb, trying to make yourself okay with the idea that they will be furiously making out or, who knows, casually fingering each other, or even just holding hands, which would actually be worst of all, but then when they do show up they're not even sitting next to each other. Ash is in the backseat wedged in next to some drums with her guitar on her lap, just wordlessly shredding away, and Corey glances at you from behind the wheel and the look on his freckly bucktoothed face says to you, something is happening here, and he has no idea what that is.

# 16.

## WE DRIVE INTO ALABAMA AND ALMOST
## GET MURDERED IMMEDIATELY

The band tour vehicle experience became dramatically different after Knoxville.

| BAND TOUR VEHICLE EXPERIENCE CHECKLIST | BEFORE KNOXVILLE | AFTER KNOXVILLE |
|---|---|---|
| air-conditioning | yes | no |
| is engine probably going to make it | yes | no |
| does radio sound good | radio sounds great | radio sounds like if corey and i tried to make a radio out of the world's oldest amplifier and some bees |
| smells | almost puzzlingly few | a new inexplicable one every thirty-five minutes, e.g., latex, marijuana, burnt hair, oranges |
| does passenger-side seat seem to have been upholstered with scorpions | no | yes |

So we were all sweaty, and punchy, and kind of afraid. And yet, as the Accord rattled and whined down the highway in the muggy midafternoon heat, the air roaring through the open windows, with no phone, I found myself in a good mood. Who even knows why. It's just a good feeling to be in a band even if everything's going to shit.

The windows had to be down so that we did not all immediately die, and it was hard to hear anything over the noise, but after an hour Ash started yelling at us from the backseat anyway.

ASH: I'M CALLING A BAND MEETING

WES: SOUNDS GOOD LET'S DO IT

COREY: WHAT

WES: ASH SAID SHE WANTS TO HAVE A BAND MEETING

COREY: OH

COREY: AREN'T WE ALWAYS KIND OF HAVING A BAND MEETING

ASH: WHAT

WES: COREY SAYS AREN'T WE ALWAYS KIND OF HAVING A BAND MEETING

ASH: WHAT IS THAT SUPPOSED TO MEAN

COREY: WHAT

WES: SHE WANTS TO KNOW WHAT DO YOU MEAN

COREY: WE'RE JUST ALWAYS TOGETHER AND TALKING AND STUFF SO ISN'T THAT ONE NONSTOP BAND MEETING THAT'S HAPPENING ALL THE TIME

ASH: I CAN'T HEAR WHAT HE'S SAYING

WES: CAN WE DRIVE SLOWER OR CLOSE THE WINDOWS BECAUSE THIS IS GETTING ANNOYING

Corey didn't want to get off the highway. So instead we closed the windows. Immediately everyone's Sweat Levels shot up about 20,000 percent.

COREY: what i'm saying is right now our entire life is a band meeting so when you're like let's call a band meeting, how is that diff

ASH: item one: band philosophy

WES:

COREY:

ASH: i think it's going to help us if everything we do comes from a central unifying philosophy

COREY: you mean like buddhism

ASH: no

COREY:

ASH: i mean what would that mean? that we're all suddenly buddhists?

COREY: wes's parents are buddhists so maybe we c

WES: OW FUCK

COREY: JESUS WHAT

WES: THIS SEAT STABBED THE SHIT OUT OF ME

COREY: oh

WES: it literally feels like this seat is full of angry scorpions

ASH: i mean more just like a philosophy about the music itself, like something really simple like an attitude or a mantra or something

COREY: you mean like "work hard play hard"

ASH: well definitely not that

COREY:

ASH: "work hard play hard" is the philosophy of being a relatively high-functioning alcoholic

COREY: i mean i'm not saying, uhh, but i guess yeah that is what that essentially means

I was starting to realize that one reason I was feeling good was, Ash was not behaving like Corey was the love of her life. She was behaving like he was a lab partner who was spilling acid all over her stuff.

Meanwhile, we were stuck behind a semi that had more than thirty bumper stickers on it:

**Driver Carries No Cash (He's Married)**

**This Truck Is Responsible for "Global Warming"**

**Made with Wrenches, Not Chopsticks** 🇺🇸

WES: what about "if it sounds good, it is good"

ASH: if it sounds good, it is good

COREY: nope that's terrible

ASH: no actually that's not bad. did you just come up with it?

WES: uh yup

COREY: what? no he didn't. duke ellington said that

WES: mmmm corey i don't think duke ellington said it

COREY: wes it's like the most famous duke ellington quote of all time

WES, *falsetto*: mmmmmmmmmmmmmmmmmmmmmmmmm

COREY:

WES: mmmmmmmmmmmmmmyou're thinking of "it don't mean a thing if it ain't got that swing"

ASH, *rustily*: heh

COREY: okay if the rest of the band meeting is just gonna be wes being a herb i propose we adjourn

We were still stuck in the right lane behind the heavily bumper-stickered 18-wheeler. In the left lane, a Jeep with tinted windows was blocking us from getting over.

COREY: ugh come on

ASH: i like "if it sounds good, it is good"

WES: sure just an idea

ASH: but it sort of means don't make anything that's going to be an acquired taste

WES: hmmm

COREY, *gesturing*: come on! let me over

ASH: like anything difficult that doesn't sound good right away that you have to give a chance, this philosophy is like don't make that thing. instead make the shiny easy-to-like thing

WES: right

ASH: i'm not sold either way but I'm glad we're thinking about this shit

COREY, *rhythmically honking the horn*: *stu*pid *tin*ted *win*dow *moth*er *fuck*er

WES: i had a teacher who used to say "the best artist is the best thief"

ASH: mmmmm

WES: like you take ideas from everywhere and you do cool like unexpected things with them and aaaeeeeeeeeehhhhhh.

COREY: UM

WES: this is not good

ASH: huh

COREY: WHAT IS HAPPENING

What was happening was, suddenly there was a laser show in our car. It was big, and it was everywhere. It consisted of all these green sci-fi-type characters and glyphs and designs rapidly blinking and rotating on the steering wheel and the dashboard and our laps and bodies and everything. The vibe of it was, basically, Evil Alien Spaceship Control Panel, like from Halo or something.

It didn't take long to figure out that the laser show was being projected from the Jeep next to us. We could see the projection in miniature on the Jeep's tinted passenger-side window. But we could not see anything else. So, for example, we could not see if they had a bunch of guns. But you would have to assume that maybe they did.

The Jeep's creepy opaque windows, combined with the fact that they were not letting us over, and just aggressively keeping pace with us and trapping us behind a semi, caused two of us to lose our shit.

COREY: NO NO NO. NO NO NO NO NO

WES: COREY STOP FREAKING OUT

COREY: *YOU'RE* FREAKING OUT

ASH: guys

WES: I GET TO FREAK OUT BUT YOU DON'T BECAUSE YOU CAN'T SHOW THEM ANY FEAR

COREY: ASH IF YOU STICK SOME MONEY OUT OF THE WINDOW MAYBE THEY'LL TAKE IT AND LEAVE US ALONE

We probably wouldn't have been as freaked out if it were possible to look into the Jeep. But it wasn't. It was just this big, black, faceless object, gliding alongside us, broadcasting this nerve-racking thing onto us like a tractor beam.

ASH: guys they're just fucking with us

WES: yeah but fucking with us is not good

COREY: no no no i would say it is not good at all

WES: should we pull over maybe

COREY: yup. yup yup yup

And so Corey hit the brakes, swerved into the shoulder, and we came to a loud, rattly, shuddery halt.

But the Jeep also pulled over. It glided into the shoulder in front of us and came to a stop, too, about a hundred feet away.

Its brake lights winked out.

We sat in silence and stared at it.

It also just sat there in silence.

We were somewhere in Alabama at that point.

Corey was the first to speak.

COREY: so

ASH:

WES:

COREY: now what

WES: maybe if we suddenly pull away and really floor it

COREY: no

WES: we can outrun them long enough to get to an exit and lose them maybe

COREY: we're not outrunning anyone. we can barely do sixty-five

WES: well maybe if we jump the median

COREY: nope

WES: and go the other way maybe they're not crazy enough to follow us

COREY: this car is not jumping any medians. it would beach itself like a whale

WES: also they probably *are* that crazy

COREY: yeah they're fucking psychos. look at them sitting there

WES: maybe if we just wait here for long enough they'll leave?

COREY: wes what if they try ramming us

WES: fuck

COREY: or start shooting or something

WES: fuck fuck fuck

COREY: i think we should try to drive into the forest

WES: yeah maybe

ASH: guys.

As soon as she spoke, it was clear again that we were us, and she was her, and those were two separate things.

"They don't have guns," she said. "They don't have shit. They're just fucking with us."

She waited a moment and then said, "So let's fuck with them." She said it in the tone of voice you might use to order the ice cream that you always get at the ice cream place you always go to.

She opened the door.

"Ash, wait," I said, but she ignored me completely.

"Pop the trunk," she told Corey.

He didn't do anything.

"Do it," she said, and he did, and she got out and walked around back and we heard her rummaging around in the trunk.

No shots were fired from the Jeep. No one got out of the Jeep. The Jeep continued to do nothing at all, and I found myself thinking, what if there is no one *in* the Jeep.

"Fucking come on," we heard Ash whisper, audibly rooting around under the amps.

No. That was crazy and stupid. There were definitely people in the Jeep. And they were definitely hostile. And they had definitely decided that they were not done with us.

Maybe they were on meth. Or acid. Or in a cult. Probably all of those. Because why else would you behave in this psychotic and terrible way.

We heard Ash give a kind of grunt of satisfaction. The trunk slammed. She walked around to my side. She rapped on the window. I rolled it down. She was holding a lug wrench.

"Wes," she said.

I stared at her.

"Come on," she said.

I didn't move.

"Corey stays in case he has to move the car. But you have to come with me."

I nodded. But I still didn't move.

"Corey, leave the engine running," she said, and she started walking, and I managed to shut up my own thoughts long enough to open the door and jump out of the car and start walking.


It wasn't quite as hot out on the shoulder. But the air was still thick and sticky on your skin. The Jeep somehow looked farther away. The ground was generously littered with food wrappers and plastic bags and empty cigarette packs and soda cans and broken beer bottles.

"Pick up one of those broken beer bottles," said Ash.

I nodded and tried to walk over to the closest beer bottle like this was a thing I did all the time. I picked it up. It was a Budweiser and it was wet to the touch.

"No," said Ash. "Like *broken* broken. Like that one."

She nodded to another Budweiser bottle that was missing the bottom part, and I picked it up by the neck, and squeezed it, and we started walking toward the Jeep.

Pretty soon it became clear to me that the part I was squeezing was also broken, and there was a jagged edge cutting into the fat part of my hand. But it was too late to say anything or do anything about it.

It was a long walk toward that Jeep. It was like you could feel the sun breathing on you. Ash spun the lug wrench a couple of times in her hand like a tennis racquet.

"What is this bottle for exactly," I said.

"Slashing their tires," she said.

"Oh," I said.

"I mean for self-defense, too," she said.

There was not a part of my body that wasn't slick with sweat. But the wetness on the inside of my hand felt stickier somehow. *That is just blood*, my brain tried to reassure me. *There is nothing to worry about. That is just the blood that is leaking out of a wound in your hand.*

We were about halfway to the Jeep at that point. It was clean and undented. It had no bumper stickers anywhere. The license plate was 5KAK924. It continued to be impossible to tell who was in the Jeep.

Then its brake lights turned on.

We heard the engine start, and we saw it begin to roll away from us. I yelled something involuntarily. We broke into a run. The Jeep picked up speed. I was screaming. Trucks were whooshing past us. A ridiculous number of them like the same one on loop. Somewhere behind us Corey was honking the horn. I was sprinting and roaring my lungs out. I was outrunning Ash and almost keeping pace with the Jeep, and I could feel a little train of blood crawling up my arm, and I squeezed the bottle a little harder and felt nothing at all and took a couple of skip steps and hurled the bottle as hard as I could. The bottle was in the air for not a long time and it was clear that it wasn't going to make it all the way. It landed in the grass next to the shoulder about ten feet short of the Jeep with a distant little *thump*. The Jeep bucked and hit a higher gear and slid out onto the highway, and I thought, *it doesn't matter, I'll just keep running, and sooner or later I'll catch it, and then they're fucked.*

Back in the Accord, my hand was bleeding a lot, so we tied one of the washcloths around it and decided to get off the highway and look for a town with a CVS. Also somewhere to play a show. We were feeling like we were more equipped than ever to play a dominant and masterful show. We knew this made us idiots. But we didn't care.

WES: OW FUCK

COREY: what is there still glass in your hand or something

WES: NO IT'S THIS STUPID SCORPION UP-HOLSTERY

Actually though there was still a bunch of glass in my hand.

## 17.

## YEAH THERE WERE SHARDS
## OF GLASS IN THERE STILL

In a lot of ways, Ash was the least girl-like girl that either of us had ever met. She had memorized multiple Angus Young solos and was completely indifferent to the cleanliness status of her own hair. It was impossible to imagine her, for example, Instagramming herself in a bathroom.

But the blood coming out of my hand brought out a relatively girl-like side of Ash.

"Fuck," she said. "I feel like this is my fault." She was holding my hand and arm and kind of running her finger over the wound.

"It's all good," I said. *I would literally cut myself with dirty highway glass every day if it led to this,* I somehow prevented myself from saying.

"There's definitely some glass in there still," she said, pulling the cut apart a little bit.

"Uuuuunnnnnnnnnnn," I said.

"Does that hurt?"

"Nnn."

"Sorry."

"No. Do it again. Because that shit does not hurt at all."

"YUP," barked Corey like a dog.

It was near sunset when we finally found a CVS. It was in Fargo, Alabama, and it was pretty busy. Fargo seemed to be mostly black. Definitely everyone in the CVS was black. So we got some attention when we walked in there. Although it may have been less about us being the only nonblack people in the CVS and more about the bloody washcloth tied around my hand. We had cleaned up my arm a little outside a gas station with bottled water, but I still looked like an extra from *The Hunger Games*.

Also we smelled terrible. So that was probably getting us some attention, too. We collectively smelled like Jennifer Lawrence's armpit.

We rounded up some medical supplies kind of at random—gauze, rubbing alcohol, silicone scar sheets, a three-pound bag of Mike and Ikes—and were waiting in line when the guy in front of us turned and said, "Buying all that for your hand?"

He was a tall, fortyish, stripey-polo-shirted guy with a brisk conversational manner.

"Uhhhh," I said.

"Do you need medical attention on that hand," he asked, this time less conversationally and more like a high school vice principal who is dealing with that one kid that he has to deal with all the time.

"Oh," I said. "This hand? No. I don't think so. But thanks."

The guy just raised his eyebrows, like, are you sure.

"He needs medical attention on his *dick*," suggested Corey.

A silence fell over all of us.

The guy stared at Corey with a total lack of facial expression.

Corey responded by inspecting various parts of the floor, fidgeting, and softly humming a goat noise.

This went on for a longer time than you would think possible.

"You know, he probably does need his hand looked at," said Ash eventually.

The guy nodded, still staring at Corey. "Charlize," he called. "Boy needs your help." Then he went to the cashier and bought cigarettes and we never saw him again.

Charlize turned out to be a woman getting a prescription filled at the pharmacist's counter. She was tiny and sixtyish looking, and she had her hair in a purple flower-patterned Russian-peasant-type babushka. Up close we saw that her arms were criss-crossed with what looked like decades-old burn marks.

She made no secret of being not amped at having to deal with us.

"You can't just go to urgent care?" she muttered, unwrapping the washcloth.

"We're in kind of a rush," said Ash.

"Also they're closed," said Corey.

"Corey," said Ash.

Charlize just shook her head impatiently. "Hand me that alcohol, please, and go fetch some cloth pads," she told Ash, and fished a tweezers out of her purse, and sterilized it, and pretty soon she was just straight-up performing surgery on my hand in the middle of CVS with a bunch of increasingly enthusiastic spectators.

"Where are you children from," she muttered to us.

"New York," said Ash. "Pittsburgh," I said at the same time.

"Around here," said Corey.

"Corey," said Ash again.

I was too busy focusing on not thrashing around and sobbing uncontrollably to investigate Charlize's medical credentials. But Ash asked her if she was a doctor.

"Nurse," she said. "Retired."

"Why'd you retire so young," said Corey.

She raised her eyebrows but didn't look up at him. "How young do you think I am," she said.

You could hear Corey trying to think again.

"Thirty . . ." he said, "four."

She clearly was incapable of coming up with a verbal response that expressed how dumb she thought this was. So instead she shook her head and made a little coughing noise of derision.

"Three. Thirty-three."

"Not twenty-three?" she said, with no smile at all.

Then she pulled out the last and biggest chunk of glass, something loosened up in my hand, and what felt like a pint of my own blood just sort of plopped out of there onto the linoleum, and almost everyone else started shrieking and panicking and a couple of spectators actually passed out, and in general it was just chaos.

Not too long afterward, we were out on the street and my right hand was wrapped up super tight, and Ash and Corey were peering around into the distance trying to figure out whether we wanted to stay in town or not.

"This seems like the direction hotels and bars and stuff would be in," said Ash.

"I don't think we're gonna find anything, though," said Corey.

"Well, let's at least look," said Ash.

"We're gonna waste like an hour, though, just driving around and not finding anything."

"How could that possibly be more of a waste than getting back on the highway."

"The highway's got signs for Motel 6 and stuff."

"Yeah, but then we'd end up staying at Motel 6."

"Yeah. That would be tight."

I saw Charlize about half a block away, lighting a cigarette and kind of eyeing us.

"No," said Ash. "That would not be tight. That would suck a bag of dicks."

"Motel 6 is badass. It's not even named after a word. It's named after a *number*, because they give no shits."

"Six *is* a word, and Motel 6 is where you go if you've been evicted from your home and you need a place to do the meth that you just stole from the corpse of a prostitute."

"You don't know anything about Motel 6. You just embarrassed yourself with how little you know about Motel 6."

"Where are you children trying to go," called Charlize.

Somehow no one could figure out how to answer as she walked back over to us.

"Are your parents traveling with you?" she said.

"We're a band," I said. "So we're pretty much on tour right now."

"We *are* on tour," clarified Corey.

"No teachers?" she pressed. "No adults?"

"I'm twenty-one," Ash told her.

Charlize gazed at Ash for a very long time.

"And they're nineteen," Ash added.

Charlize nodded, slowly.

"Where's your next show, if I may ask," she asked us.

"We're figuring it out," said Corey.

"We don't really have one," I said.

"*Right*," exhaled Charlize, like a teacher who had finally gotten us to explain what a cosine was. "Right. That was my sense. I am about to make an offer to you. Are you ready? You're listening? The offer is of a place to sleep, and some food to eat. Now. This offer is one time only. No hard feelings if you turn it down. But. The offer will not be renewed. So consider it carefully, take a moment to confer amongst yourselves, and—"

"Yeah, we would like that a lot, please," I said, and fortunately neither Ash nor Corey tried to fuck it up.

Corey and I squeezed into the back so Charlize could have shotgun and give directions to her house a few blocks away.

"How old are y'all, seriously," Charlize wanted to know.

"Seriously, I'm twenty-one," said Ash.

"If you're twenty-one, I'm Michelle Obama," announced Charlize.

There was a meditative silence in the car.

"And I am not Michelle Obama," clarified Charlize. "Because the man I married is not the President of the US of A. He is more like the President of the US of PYF."

She gazed out the window.

"United States of Picking Your Feet," she said eventually, kind of to herself, and somehow that was how we knew she didn't hate us.

"My dad picks his feet," said Corey.

The President of the United States of Picking Your Feet was not amped about the three random kids who were going to sleep in his house.

"Charlie," he announced. "These young people have *got to go.*"

We were in the living room with him. He was sitting in an armchair with a cup of tea and a book called *The Mauritius Command* with pirates on the cover. His name turned out to be Ed, and I would describe his fashion sense as "frumpcore." It was socks and flip-flops, pants that looked like they were meant to be worn in a lab over your actual pants, and an old mucus-colored polo shirt that somehow had a hole right over the belly button. It was a look so committed to late-middle-age frumpiness that you had to respect it.

"They have nowhere else to stay and you can just deal with it for one night," Charlize called down from upstairs, where she was making some beds.

"NNNNNNOPE," shouted Ed, staring squarely at me.

"Yyyyyyyes sir," called Charlize.

"I will NOT be responsible for the children of strangers."

"That's funny, because my crystal ball says you most certainly will."

"I am deeply opposed to this foolishness."

"We really appreciate this," offered Corey, but Ed just stared at him wordlessly for ten seconds. Then he repeated, "*Opposed.*"

"Oh, go oppose yourself," we heard Charlize say.

"I am *strenuously* opposed to this latest misbegotten misadventure."

"Ed, it sounds like the second-floor toilet's still acting up."

Ed exhaled a few times through his nose.

"Charlie," he called upstairs, in a more rational tone of voice. "Suppose the police come by. Suppose they make the discovery of three children in our home—*white* children—without the knowledge or express permission of any type of legal guardian. Now tell me realistically what you think might happen next."

"The police are not gonna come by, and by the way only one of 'em's white."

He did an eye roll so hard that it was kind of amazing that he didn't dislocate his eyeball.

His next move was to peer intensely at each of us in turn, clearly with the purpose of getting one of us to break. Unsurprisingly, that person turned out to be Corey.

"His parents are also white," volunteered Corey, pointing at me.

Ed turned his CIA-interrogator-type stare back to me.

"I'm adopted," I said, feeling ridiculous. "From Venezuela."

Ed nodded gravely, as if this information could possibly have been of any use to him.

"I grew up outside New York," added Ash irrelevantly, at which point Ed cut us all off by throwing his arms wide and saying, in a slow and reasonable voice, "*Now look.* You three can appreciate my predicament. Am I being asked to harbor runaways?"

It is safe to say that none of us had any idea what the fuck to do. We all just stood there nodding at him thoughtfully. We were trying to nod in a way that said, *We appreciate your predicament,* but not in a way that said, *Yes, we are runaways that you are being asked to harbor.*

"In the eyes of the law, will I be culpable of harboring fugitive minors? In the eyes of the law."

We continued nodding in our halfhearted, confusing way. Ed seemed to just be addressing me. *He thinks I am the leader,* I tried not to realize.

"Tell me," he boomed. "Am I complicit in some funhouse-mirror perversion of the Underground Railroad?"

I had to stop nodding in order to contemplate what this meant. Corey just nodded even more vigorously. And Ash started shaking her head. So we looked like total idiots taken as a group.

But somehow that response was the one that satisfied him. Because he grinned and went, "HA."

And then, mysteriously, he just let it drop. He cleared his throat, sipped some tea, picked up *The Mauritius Command,* and went back to reading it as though we weren't there.

We shuffled upstairs to three made beds in three different

rooms. Charlize was lying facedown on the floor in my room when I went in there. She got up briskly as if that was a totally normal thing to do.

"Just resting," she told me, patting me on the arm and walking out.

Charlize told us we could play a little backyard set after dinner, and neighborhood folks would come see us and have some beers and stuff. It seemed like Ed wouldn't possibly agree to let this happen, but nonetheless, we rehearsed out there for a couple of hours while the sun set, and no one stopped us.

This was clutch, because no one could remember any part of any song. Also I needed to get used to playing with the heel of my right hand all wrapped up. But the main thing was we were still just getting started on figuring out how to play with one another.

I mean, I was really just beginning to learn who Ash was as a guitarist. Like the specific things she liked to do and when she liked to do them. But also, I was starting to understand her overall musical personality, which seemed kind of sloppy and haphazard until you really started listening to it and you realized that actually she was in total control.

She was never right on the beat. She liked to come in a split second late, or early, and was always putting either too many notes into a phrase or too few. She'd shadow the bass part for a few bars, like an intro or a verse, but with all kinds of hiccups and ghost notes that made it actually a different part completely. Or she'd set you up with some very orderly squared-away blues comping and then, without warning, stamp a big weird note over it in a way that kind of made your skin jump. But it was all super intentional.

Her whole thing was about giving you whatever it was you didn't expect, and so for me and Corey it became about giving her the maximum amount of space to do that, and getting as tight and gridded-out as we possibly could, and for a couple of hours that's what we did, and we couldn't be totally sure but by the end we were starting to feel like we really were onto something.

Charlize and Ed's four sons came for dinner. Two of them brought their wives and kids. We were spared the indignity of eating at the kids' table in the living room. Instead we got squeezed in among the adults despite there being not really enough room for all of us.

Dinner itself was some kind of poached fish, plus a million delicious sides. In an effort to get at these miraculous sides, I kept accidentally elbowing the guy next to me, who turned out to be Ed Jr., a.k.a. Little Ed. Eventually he mumbled, "Just tell me what you want I'll get it, okay." He did this without turning his head or making eye contact.

That was all he said until Charlize started telling the story of how she met us.

"Well, my heart sank when I saw Walter in that CVS because you know Walter, he's like a hypochondriac but for everybody in the room, and sure enough he sees this young man with his hand wrapped up, and he hollers, Charlize! Hey! Charlize! *I need you to look at this!* And soon as I say, look at what, he just goes, whoopee!!

and—and *books* it out of there, knocking people over, leaving a Walter-shaped hole in the wall. But it isn't that false of an alarm because this young man Wesley does need some attention, and Wesley, I don't want to embarrass you, but you looked a little like a hobo standing there, sorry but you did, you had a dirty little bloodstained washcloth around your hand like you were going for your Hobo Patch in Boy Scouts—heh—Quincy, don't make me laugh—and there's all kinds of dirt and grime and shattered glass in his hand just begging to get infected. So I cleaned it out and then I sent these three on their way—"

"The evidence would suggest you did no such thing," said Ed.

"Ma, what were you doing in CVS," said Little Ed, in his mumbly scratchy voice.

"Ed, I *did* send them on their way, but then outside I catch up to them arguing and bickering about motels, not a parent or a teacher in sight, which, let me ask you three, is that normal for you young people? I'm not judging, I'm just curious, is that a normal circumstance?"

"I will answer that question," said Ed cheerfully. "NO. No, it is not. There are three runaways sitting at our dinner table."

"Pop," said Quincy.

"You three would've told me if you were runaways, I hope," Charlize asked us.

My skin got very hot and itchy and I squirmed involuntarily. Corey stared at his food unhappily like it was forcing him to watch an episode of the news. And Ash was completely expressionless, which somehow made her seem the guiltiest of all three of us.

"Their silence is deafening," said Ed, munching some fish.

"Ed, let them speak."

"You," said Ed to me. "Do you have express parental consent to be in this house."

Fortunately, I had a full mouth. And I knew that having a full mouth was going to buy me a little time. So I tried to chew the food as conspicuously as possible. But I was not able to use the time that this bought me to have any kind of productive brain activity.

Everyone continued to wait for me to say something. I knit my eyebrows and puffed out my cheeks a little bit, hoping to convey the idea of, *There is a whole bunch of food in here. So I probably will not be able to talk for a while.*

Unfortunately, puffing out my cheeks caused a small amount of stuffing to lurch out of my mouth and into my lap.

A wife giggled. So did Ash. But pretty much everyone else reacted with total despair. One son put his head in his hands and whispered, "*Dang.*"

The impasse, incredibly, was broken by Little Ed, who wanted to talk about something completely different.

"Pa, you gonna ask Ma what she was picking up at CVS," said Little Ed.

Ed turned to Little Ed.

"What reason would I have to ask her that," he said, genuinely confused.

"Ma. Are you gonna tell him."

She pursed her lips and said, "Couple of things."

"You gonna tell him or do I have to."

In a very short period of time the vibe at the table became completely different.

"Advil," said Charlize. "And, uh, toothpaste."

Little Ed just stared mournfully at his plate.

"Well, don't go making a big deal out of it," snapped Charlize. "I've been having a few dizzy spells. So the doctor prescribed me something. Now drop it."

"Told me it was seizures," mumbled Little Ed.

"*Drop it*," ordered Charlize, but everyone at the table was talking to her at this point. Everyone except Ed, who was just staring at her with this frozen terrible face that I didn't want to be looking at, but was.

It was about that point that I knew we probably shouldn't be there. But there was no clear way to leave.

"Ma—you've been having seizures again?"

"They've been barely even noticeable, and in fact—"

"Oh my goodness, Mrs. Harris. Oh my *goodness*—"

"You can't be—Ma, listen—you can't be keeping this from us. If you been having them at all—"

"All y'all, just calm down, because I am *fine*—"

All three of us were desperately racking our brains for graceful exits we could make so that this sensitive family moment could happen without three weird nonfamily spectators. Or maybe Corey and Ash weren't racking their brains. But I definitely was. "We all have to go to the bathroom"? Nope. "We just remembered that actually we do have a hotel booked somewhere except don't ask us the town or the name of the hotel and, on that note, bye"? Also nope.

"Mrs. Harris, you can't be cooking alone if you're gonna have seizures!"

"Ma, yeah, say you got some water boiling on the stove—"

"This is exactly why I didn't want to tell y'all because I *knew* y'all would start overreacting and trying to keep me out of my kitchen and—calm down, *please*—"

"Charlie," croaked Ed, shaking his head, and something in the way he said it made me react kind of in spite of myself, and I felt myself get up, and I heard myself say, "We're definitely intruding here, so please excuse us," and I got up and walked out to the backyard before anyone could stop me, and Ash and Corey must have followed immediately because pretty soon it was the three of us out there.

Each of us was making our own That Was Intense Face. Corey's was his go-to all-purpose face, i.e., the De Niro. Ash was kind of gritting her teeth and sneering with one side of her lip. Mine was the one where you push your mouth up and your eyebrows down and basically push all the parts of your face toward the center.

We could still hear them having their intense family moment through the windows. Ed was begging Charlize to tell him everything and not leave a single thing out. Charlize was taking it out on Little Ed for making a fuss about it. The two wives were making a bunch of offers of things they could do to help. The sons who weren't Little Ed were also kind of taking it out on Little Ed for not telling them sooner.

"Well, one thing's for sure," said Corey.

We waited for him to tell us what that thing was.

"We would not be dealing with this shit if we were at a Motel 6," Corey said.

"Jesus, Corey," said Ash.

"What."

"'This shit'? We wouldn't be dealing with 'this shit'?"

"Yeah. We wouldn't be intruding on other people's shit. Why the fuck can't I say that."

"They're the ones dealing with serious shit. Not us."

"Yeah, good point, except I'm already making that point, so fuck you, because my whole thing is, we're making it worse by being here, and on top of that at least I'm trying to engage people instead of being silent and weird."

"Oh right. By talking about how Wes's dick needs medical attention. And telling Charlize she looks like a thirty-three-year-old."

"That is called flirting, and when a young dude flirts with an older woman, that is always her favorite shit, ever, a million percent of the time."

"Yeah. You really know a lot about what older women like."

"Everyone in that house thinks you're a fucking sociopath, and they're probably right."

"BOTH OF YOU QUIT DICKING ON EACH OTHER," I said.

They stared at me.

I was thinking, maybe Ed was right. Maybe I actually *was* the leader of this band.

"I know you guys hooked up last night. And now it's weird for whatever reason. But at least try to be cool about it. Because we're a fucking band. And that's the most important thing. So we got to make this shit work."

Ash nodded kind of sullenly. Corey just stared at me. There

was no way either one could actually be the leader of any kind of group, I was realizing. They were too inside their own heads.

"You guys both agree that family is in there dealing with some way heavier shit," I said. "So what is there to even argue about? Can we not just all agree that we don't get to be fuckups right now? And we need to have our shit together?"

Corey hiked up his eyebrows and turned to the ground so he could stare at it.

"Look, man," I said to him. "We know what we're capable of. We know we can make some great music. So what that means is, we can give this family a really cool gift tonight, at a time when they could really use it, if we just focus up and let go of all this negative shit and *be a band.*"

Corey exhaled hard through his nose. Then he said, "Awwww yeah."

But he gave it the melody of someone walking through a front door and saying, "Anybody home?" So it was like, "Awwwww yeah??"

It was a weird good thing. And it was weird and good enough that Ash chuckled at it.

A small part of me was jealous. But mostly I was amped.

"Let's fucking do this," said Ash. "Let's do it now."

## 18.

## WE WERE THIS CLOSE TO DOING A MAROON FIVE COVER THAT WE HADN'T EVEN PRACTICED

We set up, tuned, and started playing. For the first couple of songs we had no audience. But as we started up on our third song, the door opened and Little Ed came out.

He nodded at us, lit a cigarette, and sat on the steps.

The song we were playing was "If You Love Your Dog So Much, Why Don't You Fuck Him."

He said nothing. He just watched us and took long, exhausted drags on his cigarette.

Pretty soon, more family members opened the door and joined him and watched us play.

We were locked in. We were sounding pretty good.

But I was feeling increasingly anxious about the song we were playing.

The chorus was:

*If you love your dog so much*
*Why don't you fuck him*
*I bet he would love it*
*At least you should suck his dick*

It is going to be pretty hard to describe the facial expressions of the family members that were the audience to this song.

I guess I would say, imagine you've just learned something possibly really terrible about your mom's health, except she doesn't want you to think it's that terrible, so maybe you're arguing with her and maybe you're just bottling it all up. Okay. So that's super heavy, emotion-wise. It's really hard. All right. Now imagine, you go outside, and there are three kids out there trying to cheer you up by playing a song. But that song is about fucking a dog.

The facial expression that this would cause to happen on your face is probably one of the ones that we saw that evening.

The kids tried to come out and listen, too, but the moms physically forced them to go back into the house.

"*Oh* no," they yelled. "*Nuh* uh. This is not for your ears."

We kept playing the song, and the family kept sitting there listening to it. Fortunately, the verse was completely unintelligible. But the chorus was not. It was unmistakably a recommendation that you have sex with your dog, or at least suck his dick.

Eventually, we finished. There was a small amount of ragged applause. Most of it came from a few guys out on the street who had gathered up against the fence.

"Thank you," announced Corey. "We are, What The . . . ?!"

Unsurprisingly, this announcement did not make the audience any less alienated or confused by us.

"That's our name," clarified Corey. "What The . . . ?!"

Again, nothing was clarified. Ash squeezed her eyes shut.

Next on our setlist was "Trees Are Eating My Dad Right Now Pt.1." But I stopped Corey before he could count us off.

"This song about a dead parent is not a good song to play at this time," I said.

"What do you think we should play," Ash asked.

I was realizing another thing: Even if we were playing it really well, our music had serious limitations, as far as being something you would want to play for people. And one of those limitations was, if people needed to be comforted or put at ease, our music was not going to accomplish that. It was kind of like asking the craziest possible dog to be one of those hospital comfort dogs. He's not going to sit there all docile so a frail kid with a shaved head can gently stroke his ears. No. What he's going to do is bark insanely, smush his nose into that kid's junk, and then gallop out the door in a total panic. That was the dog we were being.

"'Sex Sucks,'" suggested Corey.

"'Roger Federer,'" countered Ash.

"The one about how God is just a mindless robot without a conscience," said Corey.

"Consciousness."

"That's what I said."

"No. It's not."

"Hey band," called out one of Ed and Charlize's sons, a guy named Quincy.

We looked up.

"Do y'all know 'Free Bird,'" he asked.

Next to him, Little Ed was shaking his head. But it was from giggling.

The giggle kind of spread through the group. And suddenly some of the tension sort of melted away.

Other suggestions started coming in and they were all joke suggestions.

"'Party in the USA.'"

"'Moves Like Jagger.'"

"'You Don't Know You're Beautiful.' Because you got some One Direction fans in the crowd tonight."

Each suggestion was setting off a bigger collective giggle than the last. Ash and Corey were both looking at me. I was the leader of the band. I was frantically brainstorming stuff.

Or at least I was trying to. Because I also had the a-guy-whistling-plus-party-guitar intro to "Moves Like Jagger" ricocheting around in there, and it was kind of obliterating every other thought that I had.

I started to say to Ash and Corey, "How well do you guys actually think you know 'Moves Like Jagger,'" when I heard one of the fence dudes call, "Ed, you think maybe *we* could do a couple songs?"

We looked at the fence dude. Then we looked at Ed.

Ed's eyes were kind of red and painful looking. But he smiled and said, "Ask the kids."

We let them. I mean, of course we did. They weren't pros or anything, but I guess they played together at church, and they did some gospel and some blues and a lot of just messing around and wandering from groove to groove, and sometimes a dude would get up and rap a little bit over it, and all of it sounded good. I mean, they weren't breaking any new ground or shredding your face off. But it was music that made you relax, and music you could dance to, and pretty soon that's what people were doing in Ed and Charlize's yard, and Ash and Corey and I sat to one side and just watched it and took mental notes and stuff.

Corey managed to drink four different beers in about an hour. Then he got up, immediately sat back down, got back up, and walked very rapidly into the house, and that was the last we saw of him.

I wasn't drinking. Ash was, but slowly. We didn't really say anything to each other. We just watched the church band play while mosquitoes ravaged our flesh.

At some point the church bassist got called back home by his wife.

"Fugitive!" Ed called out, standing by the band. "Where is our fugitive bass player."

I walked up there.

"Do you know 'Mustang Sally,'" he asked me, and winked, and walked over to the back porch to pull Charlize out into the yard.

The drummer was fun to play with. He had a huge backbeat and a way of staring at you with his mouth open like he was seeing through your head all the way to space, or God. The guitarist was fine, too. His singing was a little showy and vibrato-heavy. But his playing was super precise and easy to follow.

The best part was obviously watching Ed and Charlize boogie up and down the backyard with Ed mouthing along to the song and dipping Charlize and twirling her around and Charlize's face completely transformed with this tight O-shaped smile and these hitched-up eyebrows that were sort of like, *who is this man who is dancing with me, I've never met him before in my life, I've got my guard up but I think maybe I'm in love.*

I looked over at Ash a couple of times and her face was in the shadows, but it looked like she might have been smiling, too.

It turned out Corey passed out in the second-floor bathroom, woke up, threw up, and immediately went to his room and passed out on his bed, which was where we found him. We wiped the excess barf off of his mouth, and then I went into my room, and Ash followed me in there and sat next to me on my bed.

I had no idea what was going to happen next.

"Hey," she said.

"Hey," I said.

Outside someone not very good had taken over on bass and the band had acquired a trumpet and a harmonica.

"Sorry for hooking up with Corey," she said.

"I thought you didn't want to hook up with boys," I said.

She shrugged, kind of staring me down.

"It reminded me why I don't," she said.

"Oh yeah?"

"Yeah. It wasn't a good hookup."

The harmonica playing was completely for shit. The trumpet sounded okay but sleepy.

"What do you mean."

"I mean, literally all it was was, he went down on me for like half an hour."

"Oh."

"But he wasn't good at it."

"Oh."

"And by the time I got him to stop, he was so on edge that he lost his hard-on and couldn't get it back. So we just called it quits and went to sleep."

"Okay," I said.

I felt horrible for Corey. But I also felt pretty good that their hookup was such a disaster. It put Corey back on my level somehow. I mean, I wasn't happy about it. I guess I was just kind of relieved.

The room was Quincy's old room. There were trophies and pictures of him everywhere. There was a painting he did of himself playing football.

"All boys need to know this. Never go down on a girl unless you actually like to go down on girls. If you're just doing it because you feel like you have to, and you have no idea what you're doing, it's just not gonna work out."

"Right, right."

"Your approach can't be, I'm going to jam my tongue in here until you come. If that's your attitude, you need to step back and figure some shit out."

The painting Quincy did of his team was one of those paintings where everybody's head and body are facing in completely different directions, and every eye is just a black circle in a brown circle in a white football-shaped circle.

"But why'd you hook up with him in the first place?" I said.

Ash shrugged again. She looked at me.

"Sometimes I get lonely," she said.

That sentence kind of changed everything and I became a different person for a while. I leaned in and kissed her. I pulled back and she looked at me. And then she leaned in and kissed me and I kissed her back and that's what we did for I don't know how long.

I mean, I became a different person in the sense of what I *wanted* to do was press my mouth into her mouth as hard as I possibly could and smash my body into her body and just in general completely spaz out and flail around because my heart was beating out of control and every muscle in my body was on the verge of seizing up completely, but I didn't do that. I basically just kissed her as slowly as possible. Because I knew it could end at any time, but if I slowed it down, then it would last as long as I could make it.

So I was kissing her and she was kissing me and her hands were up my shirt and on my skin, but it was kind of clear that it didn't mean This Is the Part Before We Have Sex. It just meant Sometimes I Get Lonely. But that was okay with me. Actually, I was realizing it was probably the thing I was telling her, too.

Her lips were kind of cool on my lips. They felt softer and smaller than I thought they'd feel and they had that hot-summer kind of spit-smell taste. My hands were on her waist and her back and her shoulders and touching her skin felt like licking ice cream.

"Okay," she said, meaning stop, obviously sooner than I wanted.

But she didn't leave my room. Instead we sat cross-legged on the bed, facing each other. It was at least midnight. Outside an old-sounding woman had started yelling at the party from her window.

"Wi-i-i-i-ind it down," I heard her yell. "It is *too late for all that.*"

"In general I think everyone lies to themselves about why they do whatever they do," Ash told me.

"Like what," I said.

"I mean, people say, I love you, but what they really mean is, I'm lonely."

"Oh. Yeah."

"Either it's I'm lonely, or it's I want to fuck."

"Yeah."

"It's pretty much always just one of those two things."

"Yeah."

"For me it's always just, I get lonely, but I've found that people take it the wrong way."

"Right."

"What about you," she said.

"Me?"

"Yeah."

Outside the trumpeter was trying to teach the harmonica player the horn part to "Sweet Life" by Frank Ocean. Although actually it's by Pharrell.

"It's just loneliness for me, too."

"Yeah?"

"But for me it's because I *can't* fuck."

"You can't?"

"Yeah. Because my dick and I got divorced."

"Oh."

Her reaction was kind of hard to read. But I decided to keep going for it.

"Yeah. Four years ago, we agreed to get one of those amicable divorces. It was just that classic thing of irreconcilable differences. Between the rest of my body and my dick."

"Is that right."

"Yeah. It sounds sad, but it's not really that sad. It's just that all-too-familiar story, you know, of, you get older, and you become different. You and your dick at some point just realize that you're two different people than who you were. I turned thirteen, we had a talk, we realized we both wanted out, and honestly, it was just a huge relief more than anything."

Ash smiled a little bit. But impatiently. But for some reason I couldn't stop.

"But it still hurt when, not even a year later, I found out my dick had completely moved on and found someone else. And that someone else turned out to be, get ready for this, a *dog*."

Ash snorted, and then immediately shook her head like she was trying to take it back.

"Yeah. That was super rough. A year later I see this big Bernese Mountain Dog shambling around, and it's got a human dick, and—"

"Okay," said Ash, cutting me off. "Now you have to tell me something real."

# 19.

## SOMETHING REAL

By now you're probably like, what is up with Wes and dogs. Because he talks about dogs a lot. In fact, dogs seem to be kind of his go-to thing. So what's up with that.

What's up with that is, I used to have a dog. I was eight. His name was Dad Junior. I got him when I was playing alone in the churchyard around the corner from my house. I was trying to beat my record for how many times you can bounce a superball against the upper part of a wall using only your head, which at that time was a thing I did sort of a lot. I called it "dolphin bouncing." This is the kind of thing that at some point in middle school you become super embarrassed about and stop doing, except that it does not stop being one of the funnest things ever, and in high school you're sort of like, actually, why did I ever stop doing that.

Anyway, I was eight, and I was dolphin bouncing in the churchyard, alone, when a car pulled up nearby and a bald, stressed-out, middle-aged man got out, and he asked me if I wanted a dog, and I said yes, and he coaxed this huge, shaggy, oafish dog out of the car and told me he was a great dog, shots up to date and housetrained and everything, but they just couldn't take care of him, they thought they could, but they couldn't, so if you want him, here, and he gave me the leash, and before I even knew what was happening I was just sitting there hugging this enormous dog around the neck and watching a car pull out of the churchyard lot and disappear around the corner.

My heart was racing. Nothing this incredible had ever happened to me before.

I knew that I had finally found my loyal best friend for life. There was no name on his collar, so on the way home I named him Wes Junior. But I ended up changing it to Dad Junior in a frenzied attempt to win over my dad. Because my dad really, really did not want Wes Junior to be our dog. I mean, my mom didn't, either. But it would have been stupid to call the dog Mom Junior. Because this dog was a dude.

In retrospect the obvious name was Both Parents Junior.

Anyway, yeah. Neither Mom nor Dad was in my camp when it came to Wes Junior. Clearly, the whole thing kind of shook them to their core.

[DAD, *mid-mail-sorting, standing motionless with horror in the hallway*]

[MOM, *from the kitchen*]

—Uhhhhhh.

—What exactly is going on here, bud.

—Hey, boo? Ramona? I need you in here.

—Sure thing booper!

—Okay. Wes, kiddo, we can't just take someone else's dog. So let's get him back to his owner.

—I'm sure he didn't *give you* the dog.

—Wes. Let's not play games. This is a living thing we're talking about here.

—You want me to believe he just drove away? You're telling me, *a man just handed you a huge, slobbering dog and then drove away.*

[*Dad leans out of the front door and addresses the entire street*]

—Hello? Whose dog is this? Is this someone's dog? Anyone?

—Did anyone happen to see the *unhinged maniac* who drove up to my kid and gave him a dog? Jeff, do you know anything about this?

—I'm just having a little booper snack. Does booper want a snack, too?

—Ben? Can I get you a little old snack?

—Li'l snack never hurt poor old booper?

[*Mom emerges from the kitchen, eating ice cream directly from the container*]

—Li'l boopy snack-snack? For a littlOH MY GOD.

—Oh, I really don't like this. I don't like this at all.

—This animal has a very negative energy. I am really not comfortable with this energy in my home.

—Wessie, look at its eyes. It has demented, *violent* eyes. No, it does, sweetie.

—Apparently some lunatic is driving around giving away giant dogs to kids.

—So, keep an eye out, and uh, maybe don't let Sophie outside today.

—Ha. Yeah. Tell me about it. Okay. Well, take care, Jeff. Yup. You, too. Okay now. Take care.

—Okay, bud. I'm sorry, but we gotta take this guy to a shelter. And they can figure out how to get him back to his old—

—Sshhhhh. Hey. I know. But we can't adopt a dog right now. It's a huge decision, and a huge responsibility—

—His name is what? "Dad Junior"?

—Okay. That's very sweet. But we still, uh . . . Okay. Don't make this hard.

—It literally looks insane.

—You know what it looks like? It looks like one of those old illustrations of the dogs of hell. A dog that lives in a fiery pit, snarling and chewing people's souls.

—That *is* what it looks like, sweetie. I'm sorry. It's true.

[*Mom lowers her voice and points at the dog's face*]

—*YOU* ARE NOT WANTED HERE. WE FEAR AND DESPISE YOU.

—YOU ARE AN UGLY FEARSOME BEAST AND QUITE OUT OF PLACE IN THIS HAPPY HOME.

—Um . . . hello?

—"Mom Junior" was taken, I guess?

They let me keep him. I'm still not totally sure why. I guess it was the first time I ever really took a stand against what they wanted to do. I had always been a super docile kid, parenting-wise. I ate the vegetarian food they gave me. I went to bed when they told me to go to bed. I threw zero fits about our family's complete lack of December gift-giving. I went willingly to the Dorje Ling Home of Tibetan Buddhism in Pittsburgh every couple of weeks to sit in a weird-smelling room and do two hours of chants. At no point was I like, guys, I'm really not into this childhood, it seems less fun than other childhoods, and it's making it sort of hard to relate to every other kid at my school.

(By now you're probably also like, Wes, in addition to dogs, what's up with the Buddhism thing. The Buddhism thing is, my mom got super into Buddhism when she did the Peace Corps in Nepal for three years, which is also where she met my dad. He wasn't doing the Peace Corps there. He was just randomly backpacking through Asia, which is maybe why he is not quite as much into Buddhism, less and less so over the years, to the point where last year without any kind of warning he reintroduced Christmas into our family and we had a tree and stockings and stuff, and Mom pretended to hate it but also spent an entire weekend meticulously decorating the tree and then got furious at Dad when he threw it out the day after New Year's.)

My point is, up until Dad Junior, I had been a faithful company man. So they let me keep him.

He was bigger than me and clearly pretty dumb. He didn't understand any of the basic dog commands, and his primary objective seemed to be to eat whatever was on the ground. Also, he was one of those dogs with permanent crazy eyes. His facial expression was Total Disbelief and Alarm, a hundred percent of the time. So any major hang with this dog sooner or later was you sitting there and him chewing something he found on the ground and making a face like, "Hey! Wait a second here!! *How did this get in my mouth?!*"

But I was completely sold on this dog.

For the next two months, he was basically my only friend. I mean, there hadn't exactly been a waiting list on my social calendar, but once I got a dog, the human species really lost all importance for me. It just became all about Dad Junior. He slept on my bed and ate at my feet. I woke up hours before school so I could walk him and play with him, and I ran home from school as fast as I could to play with him again. I literally sprinted home from school. I drew maybe a thousand pictures of him. I wrestled him in the backyard and chased him around the park. I tried to learn his language and communicate in barks and growls. I let him lick my face, and then I would lick his face. You probably think that's an exaggeration. Nope. I licked a dog's face every day, multiple times. The same face he used to clean his own butt. I licked that face without batting an eye.

He couldn't learn tricks or basic obedient-dog behaviors, and in general he had way less personality than most dogs of his size. Mostly he just wanted to eat and sleep. He was in terrible shape and he got tired out way before I did. It was like being best friends with an overweight, senile person.

But I didn't care. I loved Dad Junior so much that I couldn't sleep at night.

• • •

About two months after we got Dad Junior, Mom and Dad took me out to a special dinner. It was at a Himalayan restaurant in Squirrel Hill. There were prayer flags and pictures of mountains everywhere.

"Wessie," said Mom, her eyes kind of teary, "we have some incredible news."

Mom was pregnant. She was pregnant for the first time in her life. It was completely unexpected, for reasons they didn't and probably couldn't explain to me. There were all kinds of medical reasons why it shouldn't have happened. But it did, and Mom and Dad were really, really happy.

I was, too. I mean, of course, deep down I had some vague worry that it would be weird. There would be me and then there would be this other kid who was Mom and Dad's *birth kid*. And I knew that the birth kid would on some level be more their kid than I was. Even if they were insisting that wasn't true. You're as much our kid as you could possibly be, they used to tell me, not realizing it probably should have been, you're as much our kid as *anyone* could possibly be.

But despite all that I was still happy. Because I knew it was making *them* really happy, and even at that age, that's what I was all about. I was a company man.

"And so, uh," said Dad. And he buried his mouth in his beard and turned to Mom, and I knew something bad was coming.

"Wessie, my family had a big dog when I was growing up," said Mom. "And one day he just kind of went crazy. And he attacked me and bit me on the arm."

"Oh no," I think I said, stupidly.

"At your mom's age, bud," said Dad, "and just for a number of reasons, this pregnancy is going to be a very delicate thing, and then after that a *baby* is an even more delicate thing, and we know you love that dog, bud, we really do." And he kept looking at me, and his beard kind of crumpled, and he said, "But we just don't know if we can keep him around."

"Dad Junior is never going to bite anyone," I promised them, shaking my head, desperately trying to keep my eight-year-old shit together.

"You can just never *know* that, Wessie," said Mom kind of quietly.

"I do," I told them. "I do. I really do. He'll never attack you. I promise. He'll never attack anyone. I know him. I really, really know him."

I remember just losing it. I remember the smell of the food and the weird sitarry music and the red fake-leather seat cushions that I was pushing my face into and just completely losing it with sadness and powerlessness while my dad tried to explain that when a dog attacks you as a kid, you can never relax around dogs ever again, and so this has been bad for your mom's health, Wes, and that means bad for the baby's health, too, all this stress and anxiety. Meanwhile, I was crying so hard that I got to the point of getting outside my own body and looking at myself and thinking, *It is somewhat fucked up that you need to cry this much.*

Eventually, my mom said, "Could he become an outside dog?"

I knew deep down that he couldn't. But he did, for a little

while. We put his bed outside on the back porch and put all his toys out there, and I spent as much time out there as I could. But he was bummed out. He just wanted to be inside. It wasn't even that he wanted to be with us. He just liked it better inside where it was cooler and cozier and there was more stuff to sleep on.

And so, after a few days, he ran away.

One morning when I raced out of bed to go play with him, he just wasn't there. The side gate had claw marks on it, so we guessed he had probably jumped over it.

I ran out into the street yelling for him like a maniac. He did not appear. I spent the morning sprinting around the neighborhood, frantically looking for him, and then the afternoon, and then the evening, and part of the night.

For weeks I put up signs everywhere, went knocking on people's doors, called all animal rescue shelters, wandered the streets and parks for hours saying his name, learned how to post to Craigslist and flooded it with MISING DOG POSIBLY STOLEN posts to the point where I got flagged for spam and none of it worked. He was gone. Every night I dreamed I had found him, and waking up from those dreams was the worst thing in the world.

Mom did not help look for him. Dad did, a little. But you could tell his heart was not in it. And he was sad for me, but he was a little relieved at the end of every trip that we hadn't found Dad Junior, and I knew he was relieved, and I hated him for it.

And obviously I hated both of them for making Dad Junior an outside dog. Because that was why he ran away. Or at least that was part of it. He was never going to run away if he could sleep on my bed.

But I think I hated them most of all when they asked me if I wanted to talk about the baby that was coming, and if maybe that was *really* what was making me so upset, because how could they possibly have gotten me so wrong.

Mom lost the baby not long after Dad Junior ran away. She was about five months pregnant. It was because of whatever medical condition made it so hard for her to get pregnant in the first place, which is what made them decide to adopt. I still don't know what that condition is. They never described it to me and I've never asked.

As a family we then went through a pretty terrible period, where Mom was home sick the whole time and Dad would whip back and forth between these two moods:

a) Overly Polite and Formal with Me Considering I Am His Son

b) Way Out-of-Proportion Angry and Impatient about Some Small Thing

It was especially the second mood a few days after the miscarriage when I asked Dad to drive me around again looking for Dad Junior. That was really the first time I can remember him raising his voice at me. But actually it worked, because afterward he apologized in that same overly polite and formal way and promised to make more of an effort to look for Dad Junior, especially on the Internet.

And sure enough, a day or two later, we found him.

Dad Junior had trekked back to his old family way out in the suburbs. He missed them so much that he jumped out of our backyard and ran all the way home. We went out to visit him, and this time the bald, stressed-out, middle-aged guy told me they were going to keep their dog, whose name was actually Henry. They'd made a huge mistake that first time, and they were never going to do that again. He and his wife seemed to think it was all pretty hilarious what had happened. Their two sons understood a little bit better that it was not hilarious and instead incredibly fucked up.

I was watching this dog named Henry gaze with intense loyalty at the older son, and I was realizing I couldn't blame Mom and Dad for what had happened. My dog hadn't left because we made him an outside dog. It was because he was never my dog in the first place. He didn't want to be adopted by me or given a name that wasn't his. He just wanted his old family, because that was where he belonged.

I was watching Henry as we drove away and he was looking at us the way he looked at every car. He was sizing us up like, if he was in better shape, he might chase us, but he wasn't and we all knew it.

I could have asked for another dog after that. But I didn't. In part because I knew I just couldn't handle it if my second dog didn't want to be adopted by me, either. But mostly it was for Mom and Dad's sake.

They were sad in a way that felt like they might never be happy again, and the entire house just seemed to be full of dark heavy air that wouldn't leave.

Of course, I was sad about not having a brother or a sister, too. But I wasn't nearly as sad as Mom and Dad. But actually, that was something to be sad about, too. It was some connection with Mom and Dad that I was failing to have, because I wasn't them, or maybe because I wasn't theirs, in some way that couldn't be fixed. So maybe I did almost get to where they were in terms of sadness.

I mean, I know I didn't. But I wasn't as far away as you might think.

But the sadness did start to fade bit by bit. And after a month or so everyone was doing a little better, and we went out for another dinner at that same restaurant, and they told me they loved me and I was all the son they ever needed, and they told me this was a very sad and difficult episode but it made them realize they had exactly the family that they wanted, and they weren't interested in expanding the family anymore. And we did a thing where each of us went around the table and told the other two about our love for them, and Dad told me that I brought him immeasurable pride and happiness every minute of every day, and Mom told me I was her beating heart, walking around outside her body. And I don't remember what I told them but I don't think it was as good as that. But it still made everyone get teary-eyed and close and happy, at least in the moment.

And that was the only time Mom ever got pregnant, and the only time we ever had a dog or any kind of pet, and that was the point when they really started letting me do what I wanted. That was the moment where ever since, they've given me a ton of trust and independence and let me for the most part take care of my own shit. And in retrospect that seems crazy, because I was eight and a half, but at the time I felt like I deserved it, and I guess they just knew they had a kid on their hands whose biggest motivation was to do the company proud.

ASH: it's a little fucked up that you think of your family as a company
WES: it's just a turn of phrase
ASH: no i get it
WES: i mean you're not wrong, it is fucked up
[*it is four in the morning and ash is looking at wes in a way that he can't figure out*]
ASH: can i sleep here?
WES: yeah
ASH: i just want to sleep here. no sex or anything
WES: yeah no of course not
ASH: not "of course not" but just not tonight
WES: okay

She smiled and very quickly took off everything except her underwear and got under the sheet, and I stripped down to my boxers and got under the sheet, too, and I lay kind of rigidly on my side of the bed but she scooched over and kind of nestled into me from the side, and we lay like that the whole night.

She was asleep pretty quickly but I got no sleep at all, and forget what I said about the happiness of the sushi dinner back in Shippensburg, those three or four hours were definitely the happiest I will ever be.

# THE HATERS
## SUMMER OF HATE
## WORLD TOUR 2016

JUNE 16th • 8:00 P.M. • FURIO, MISSISSIPPI

ELLIE'S

## 20.

# HOW TO ESCAPE FROM A FAMILY THAT YOU THOUGHT WAS COOL WITH YOUR FREE-SPIRITED ADVENTUROUS LACK OF PARENTAL CONSENT BUT IS ACTUALLY CONTACTING THE POLICE IN FIVE EASY-TO-FOLLOW STEPS

**Step One. Be awake when the woman who invited you to stay at this house in the first place contacts the police**

This is going to be around seven in the morning. You're going to be lying in bed with your guitarist/lead singer, and you're going to be awake because of the boner that you've had for the last three hours. At this point the boner has nothing to do with being sexually aroused. It's more of an athletic boner, if that makes any sense. It's more like your dick is seeing how many sit-ups it can do. Okay. You're lying there in the childhood bed of a dude named Quincy and your guitarist/lead singer is quietly snoring into your face, and from downstairs you're going to hear this woman, whom you thought you could trust, shamelessly betray you to the police over the phone. "Could I please speak to Officer Whaley," you will hear her say. "John? Is that you? John, I have three children staying over at my house that I believe ran away from home," you will hear, and it will be like a punch to the gut. "Well, don't come *too* much later because they might be up soon. All right. Thank you, John. All righty then." *Oh shit,* you will think. *Charlize, what are you doing. We trusted you. Shit. Okay. What do we do now.*

**Step Two. Wake up your bandmates**

Okay. Pull on clothes, accidentally smash your toe on something, try not to hop around, and wake up your guitarist and tell her you guys need to get out of there immediately. Then tiptoe out into the hall and wake up your drummer. He has barfed a little bit again in the night, or maybe you just didn't do as good a job cleaning him up as you thought. Anyway, it's immediately going to be clear that he will not be the most helpful part of your team. Meanwhile, your guitarist is in the bathroom and won't get out. So everything is already all going straight to hell.

**Step Three. Take matters into your own hands**

What you need to do is get the instruments packed into the car and ready to go before the police get there, but once you go downstairs and start packing up the car Charlize is probably going to call the police back and tell them to hurry up, so maybe your first task is making it harder for her to call the police. Okay. You're going to take an upstairs phone off the hook and put it under a pillow, and then you're going to very slowly and carefully tiptoe downstairs, where fortunately no one is in the living room, and you're going to spend a few minutes creeping around the first floor like a cartoon burglar, and eventually you're going to spot Charlize through the window, working in the garden. Her cell phone is on the kitchen counter. Awesome. Put it in the fridge. And then just to be super sure she can't call the police you're going to go down into the basement and find the fusebox and flip the Main switch and shut off all the power to the entire house.

Although, this actually is sort of a tactical error, because from outside you hear Charlize go, "Oh, *now* what," because she has noticed that her radio plus all the lights in the house have suddenly shut off, and you hear her come inside and yell, "Ed! Wake up and check the power." So it is safe to say that you've lost the element of stealth, and your only remaining asset is, probably, speed. So run back up out of the basement past Charlize, who upon glimpsing you immediately assumes the worst and screams, "ED! HELP!! ED." Christ. Okay. Run outside to where the drums aren't packed or anything and just pick up a chunk of the drum set and carry it to the car, except the car is locked, so bellow the names of both of your bandmates and run back inside and up the stairs. Corey is just sitting on his bed squinting at nothing. Oh my God. Corey, get your shit into the car, we need to leave right now, the police are coming. Ash, let's go. The bathroom door opens and Ash sullenly exits a bathroom that definitely still has unflushed poop in the toilet. Wow. All right. Just grab the car keys from Corey and hustle back down the stairs with as much of everyone's stuff as you can get, and open the car, and just start cramming shit in there. Amps, drums, the guitars that the church dudes very thoughtfully put back in their cases. Patch cables. Ash is helping you. Eventually, Corey shows up. Meanwhile, Charlize is glaring at you guys from a safe distance and scribbling your license plate onto an envelope. "I'm really, really sorry," you tell Charlize. "We just can't go back home yet." "ED," she just keeps yelling. "ED. EEEEEDDDDDD." Neighbors are excitedly filtering out of their homes to watch what is happening. Okay. You're all packed up. There's no room in the backseat but you'll make it work. "Charlize, your phone is in the fridge," you say. "Thank you so much for hosting us and also saving my life, and please don't call the cops again," and you're about to all squeeze into the car when there suddenly is Ed, on the front porch, in a white shirt and tight white underwear, holding a shotgun, blinking away the sleep from his eyes.

**Step Four. Attempt to reason with a guy with, I'm not shitting you, an honest-to-God shotgun**

Ed. I'm really sorry about this. We just want to hit the road. That's all we want to do. We're super grateful to you guys, and we're sorry about the toilet, which we clogged. Which I clogged. I was the one who, in particular, clogged it. But my understanding is, that toilet was fucked up before we even—what? Wait. What. No. No no no. Ed. We didn't take anything, I promise. That's not what we do. Our point was to play music for you guys, and we got to do that, it was great, thank you, and now we're going to hit the road. The fuse thing was just, I freaked out and made a stupid decision, and if you just go down and flip the switch back, it should be fine. Okay. Ed. That's it. That's all I'm gonna say, and I know you're not gonna like this, but we're just going to get in the car and drive down the road. And I know you're not gonna shoot. So my bandmates are getting in the car, and I'm getting in the car now, and that's what we're doing. I know you're not going to shoot, because you're a good dude. And Charlize, you're a good woman, and I hope you get better. You're really good people. You have a beautiful family. Okay. Bye.

**Step Five. Casually yet swiftly drive the hell out of there**

Drive. Ed doesn't shoot. No one follows you. After five blocks of zigzagging, you are suddenly right in front of the police station. Jesus Jesus Jesus, everyone in the car says, and then pretends that everything's cool. The police pay your car zero attention and in fact may not even be home. And after another fifteen minutes you're on some kind of little local highway. Corey needs to repack his drums so they're in their cases and not banging around and getting all fucked up and also so there's room for someone to sit in the back. So you pull over at a gas station. You get out of the car and stare at your reflection in the window.

ASH: thanks for saying it was you who clogged the toilet

WES: that's what bandmates do

COREY: why don't you guys just fuck already and get it over with

# 21.

## WE MAKE A RUN FOR THE BORDER

Once again, we found ourselves driving a car whose plates were being looked for by the police. But this time it seemed a little more urgent. So stopping to find another used car to buy was out of the question. Instead we figured our biggest priority was to get across state lines ASAP. We actually had no idea if that made any difference, but it seemed like the thing that was most likely to.

Somehow there was no consensus about which way we *shouldn't* go. Like which direction was not a state border but instead the ocean. Ash said east, I said south, and Corey incredibly thought there would be ocean to the north. His position was, we were probably in the sticking-out part of the South where if you go north, you hit the ocean. Ash and I both resisted the temptation to dick on him for this completely insane belief. But our embarrassed silence just made him angrier.

Anyway, we headed west. No one knew what state was in that direction. Texas? Louisiana? Florida? The ocean maybe if all three of us were wrong? It was incredible not to know. It was so stupid that it was actually kind of glorious.

We also figured we had to stay off the big highways. So instead we mostly just took weird little back roads. Ash drove, Corey rode shotgun, and I was in the backseat. Our predominant theme of discussion was what do we do if the police show up and start chasing us.

### What Do We Do If the Police Show Up
### and Start Chasing Us
#### A Decision Tree

**1. Are they in a car or on horseback?**

*in a car:* Then we're not outrunning them, that's for sure.

*on horseback:* We're probably still not outrunning them. Unless the horse's Check Engine light is also on and it has smoke coming out of its butt.

**2. What kind of road are we on? A highway or an obscure little back road? Or some railroad tracks?**

*on a highway:* Get off the highway ASAP and try to find an obscure little back road.

*on an obscure little back road:* Great. Actually, maybe we should find some railroad tracks.

*why would we be on some railroad tracks:* Because *no* highway cop gets paid enough to follow three teenage psychos up some railroad tracks!! Wes hand me a Mike and Ikes.

**3. Railroad tracks are impossible to drive on. Also if a train shows up, it is going to destroy the car and all of our instruments.**

*also the train might get fucked up and this is starting to sound like something we will definitely go to jail for:* Okay. Well, maybe the tracks have like a shoulder or something where you can drive *next* to them.

*but then wouldn't the police just do that, too:* Okay. Well, sorry for trying to come up with a completely fierce plan.
*OW FUCK.* What.
*THIS PIECE OF SHIT SEAT STABBED ME. IT'S FINE.* Okay.


**4. Okay. So we're being pursued by the police. Maybe we can lose them by driving into the forest or whipping around the corner into a conveniently abandoned barn or aircraft hangar and then immediately turning off the car and sitting in the darkness while they roll past all confused and stuff.**

*no. none of those forest/barn/hangar options are gonna work:* Why the fuck not. Wes hand me some washcloths.

*if we drive right into the forest, it's not gonna lead to anything good:* What because of all the trees and roots and stuff?

*it's just not paved, which you kind of need if you're driving, especially fast, especially a shitty car:* Okay. Yeah. I get it. Fine. But if there's a barn, we should get in there.

*okay but how many abandoned barns or aircraft hangars have we passed so far? have we even passed one?:* You know what? I'm gonna stop trying to come up with shit. Because what's the point.

*sorry but we just need to think everything through:* No, it's fine. Sorry. It's fine. I guess we're not losing the police or outrunning them, so we'd have to pull over.

**5. Are the police going to shoot us if we run out of the car once we pull over?**

*probably:* Well, then I guess we kind of have no options at all.

*probably not:* Then let's all run in opposite directions, lose them in the forest or wherever we are, and rendezvous in New Orleans in three days. My old guitar teacher Onnie has a restaurant there. It's called Lime Tree.

**6. So the plan is, everybody scatter and just leave the car and the instruments and stuff.**

*yup:* I'll pay for all your shit. Don't worry. That's always the agreement. Never worry about money on this tour. I've got that covered.

**7. Is this even technically a decision tree?**

*i don't know:* I guess now that I think about it I'm not super clear on what a decision tree is.

At some point in the conversation, I fell asleep and stayed asleep for a super long time. When I woke up, it was past noon, and the police had not yet put our decision tree to the test. Instead, we were in the parking lot of a Buffalo Wild Wings.

WES: are we across state lines yet?

COREY: don't be a dick

WES: how is that question being a dick

ASH: corey was supposed to keep an eye out for a Welcome to Whatever State This Is sign, but he hasn't been

COREY: it probably says on the menu or whatever

It did. We were in Furio, Mississippi. No one knew how it had happened. But it had, and we were all filled with relief, even if that made no sense.

We did not even try to ask if we could play a show at the Buffalo Wild Wings. It was clearly not the kind of bar where bands were supposed to play. It was the kind of bar where you were supposed to watch sports on enormous TVs while experiencing the maximum amount of air-conditioning that the human body could withstand, and also eat meals of only breaded fried meats and dipping sauces. This air-conditioning was incredible, and we briefly discussed eating a breaded fried meat meal, but decided not to, to conserve the cash that we had gotten from Ash's now-probably-frozen bank account. And anyway we had more urgent matters to attend to. Also it was so cold that we were all already getting ice-cream headaches just from the air.

Instead we made another kind of horrifying food purchase at a gas station and set off on a great quest.

ASH: we gotta find a place to play that makes sense for us to play and doesn't suck

WES: yeah

COREY: nnhh

ASH: that's been our problem this whole tour so far

WES: yup

ASH: and we have to accept that it's going to take some time to find a place like that, so let's invest some time in searching for a great place to play, like in one area

WES: yeah

COREY: wes can you stop saying "yeah" to everything because it's fucking annoying

WES: *hell yeah*

ASH: haha

COREY: jesus christ

WES: you know how there's bobby, the guy who hangs out near james brown affirming everything james brown says? i think our band needs a bobby

COREY: i think our band needs a me slapping you around

WES: *yeah*

## 22.

## THE BAND CHANGES ITS NAME TO "CAMPIG" AND THEN LOCATES THE MOST HURTING BAR IN A HUNDRED-MILE RADIUS

Our first task, however, was to identify a place where we could spend the night without arousing local interest. We settled on a campground that was advertised from the road by a banner strung between two trees. The banner was 70 percent white space, 30 percent pictures of bottles of Miller Lite. In the white space someone had scrawled:

CAMPIG

12,—$

It's hard to say what intrigued us more: the idea of staying at a place for twelve dollars a night, or the word "campig." Even Corey perked up briefly.

COREY: what if our band name was "campig"?

[*a contemplative silence*]

ASH: it's a little close to danzig, so i'm wondering does it make me think of loud angry hairy jock metal

COREY: no. no one will think that

WES: what if people think it's a kind of pig

COREY: jesus wes. listen to yourself

WES: i was just doing your thing that you were doing earlier

COREY: what thing

WES: the thing that you were like with the name air horse where you were like what if people think we're a horse, ugh, i hate that

COREY: air horse sucks as a name but i don't remember making that specific point

WES: you were like air horse makes me think of a horse singing with a human voice and then you melted down existentially

COREY: yeah because that's a nightmare hellscape thing to think about but this is completely different because it's not a horse and it's not even a pig. it's campig

WES: i see

COREY: even if it was a pig, a pig singing is awesome

ASH: we can try campig if both of you promise to stop talking about it

It turned out that in order to pay twelve dollars you had to be willing to sleep in your car, which generally people only do when their car is an RV. So we debated whether that made sense for us. But it turned out not to be a debate at all when no one was willing to argue the position of Yes, Let's Sleep in This Atrocious-Smelling Car Tonight. So instead we just paid eighty dollars for a cabin. It smelled rotty and mushroomy but also like incredibly powerful lemons that were made in a factory.

We spent the whole afternoon and most of the evening ricocheting around the entire county, looking for bars or other performance spaces, trying to keep track of the CAMPIG campground so we could find our way back to it, and lying to people about our dads.

That was the strategy Ash came up with. It was, one of us would walk into a store or gas station and tell whoever was running it, Excuse me, Mister, uh, I'm looking for my daddy and I don't know this area too good, so uh, can you tell me where the closest bar is, because [*breaking down to a whisper*] that's probably where I'm gonna find him.

Look. I know it was super wrong of us to do this. But it did help us find a bar a pretty high percentage of the time.

It also turned out to be a fascinating social experiment that exposed us to a whole diversity of Mississippi dude humanity. Some dudes got big-eyed and husky-throated and gave us free food. A bunch of others got stiff and weird. And two dudes actually laughed in my face. One of them said, "Well, young man, the bad news is, you're not much of a liar. The good news is, you're probably not cut out for politics." And the other just yelled, "My daddy was the same way! We should start a club!" and then continued watching local news and ignoring me.

But for the most part we got a bunch of directions to bars, which was good. The problem was none of those bars wanted us.

It was clear that this was going to be a problem for the entire tour. If a place was an established music venue, it already had an act booked that night. And if a place wasn't, it didn't want to just randomly become one, especially not for our sake. We were clearly underage and not from around there. We looked like trouble. Or at least serious inconvenience. We were clearly something that was not going to improve anyone's life in any way.

What we needed was a place that was as weird and prone to bad decisions as we were. But the hours piled up and we didn't find that place. We didn't even seem to be close. Also, I don't want to go into the details, but when three people eat nothing but Twizzlers, Combos, and warm Dr. Pepper all day, it gives the car a new and terrible smell that should only exist in an alien penal colony.

Then a little after sunset we found Ellie's.

Ellie's was sort of the bar equivalent of our Honda Accord. It was un-air-conditioned and older than all of us combined. There were about twenty people in there, and at any given moment at least four of them were barfing out clouds of Marlboro Red smoke. People's faces tended to have this kind of faded, sour look. Everyone was white except for two ancient-looking black dudes with cigars and a backgammon board at a table near the door. It was mostly, but not all, dudes. Two different clusters of men had a woman in them, and each woman looked like the kind of thirty-something who actually looks like fifty-something.

The closest person to us in age was probably the bartender. His hair was a big fat slicked-up dollop of wet blackness, and his stubble was intimidatingly rich and even. It made his face skin look like cheap, sturdy corkboard.

"Y'all looking for somebody," he asked us.

His voice was higher than any of ours. It was also uncomfortably beautiful. Like Prince's but with more friction, or Robert Plant's with less. His eyes were wide and a little sad and the kind of very light brown that made you nervous. His faded pink T-shirt had entire distinct families of armpit holes.

Ash just studied him with what I thought at the time was dislike.

"Actually we're looking for somewhere to play tonight," I said.

"We're a band," Corey said. "We're called, uh, Campig."

The bartender blinked.

"Y'all called what," he said.

"Campig," said Ash, pushing her chin out at him.

"Canned Pig?"

"Camp—*Cam*."

"*Cayun*."

"*Cam. Cam*pig."

"It's like the word 'camping' but without the *n*," I said.

"Oh," said the bartender, frowning suddenly. "I get it. Cam, pig." He said it with the tone of a person who had just been told where veal comes from.

"It's a terrible fucking name," Corey realized.

But the bartender stopped frowning as abruptly as he started and said, "No, it ain't. I like it."

"Can we play here," Ash asked him.

He looked us all over.

"I don't see why not," he said, smiling like he knew a secret.


We loaded in. None of the bar patrons spoke to us. Many of them seemed determined to pretend that whatever we were doing wasn't happening. But it was.

Our setup was not optimal, but not horrible. We had enough room over in one corner to space ourselves out, and we weren't obstructing anyone's path to a tray of egg rolls or anything. So that was good. But we had no microphones or PA system to plug into, so vocals and levels were clearly going to be a problem. Also, my part of the floor was sticky.

"Y'all don't sing," wondered the bartender, who turned out to be named Cookie.

"We sing," retorted Ash. "We just don't mic ourselves."

Out in the parking lot, though, Ash was sort of freaking out about it.

ASH: what the fuck are we doing. we need mics and mic stands

COREY: we need tops one mic and one mic stand

ASH: no. you guys need to sing too

WES:

COREY:

ASH: especially tonight if we don't have any mics

COREY: i'm not singing

ASH: just double me on the choruses

COREY: no one's gonna hear me

ASH: they will if we have mics

COREY: no i mean no one's going to hear my voice over the sound of the meat grinder

ASH:

COREY: the meat grinder that i will be feeding my dick into

ASH: don't be a fucking asshole right now

COREY: i'm just saying that meat grinder is super loud

ASH: wes will you sing

WES: yeah sure

COREY: you're also not gonna hear wes's voice

WES: yeah? because of the meat grinder?

COREY: no because your mouth is full of ash's sloppy cooz

ASH: hey corey?

COREY: yeah

ASH: what the *fuck* is your problem

She kind of said it with her entire body. Like it was one of those sentences you had to step into, like a punch. It raised the overall Parking Lot Tension Level by about a thousand percent. My hand started throbbing. It might have been bleeding again. But at the time I was thinking, *my hand is bleeding because it senses that I might have to punch someone, and it's probably Corey but I'm not sure.*

I was thinking, *we are about to have an epic brawl, right here in the dirt parking lot behind Ellie's.* But because I am a hopeful idiot, I was thinking, *maybe this will be the kind of brawl that actually leads to some beautiful psychological turning point for everyone involved.* Like the fight that allows everyone to see one another for who they truly are or whatever.

Anyway, that didn't happen and instead Corey backed down. He might have been a crazy social-cues-ignoring confrontation-seeking hothead. But in that moment, Ash completely outcrazied him. She had that look in her eye that I remembered from out on the highway shoulder, when she was twirling the lug wrench and getting ready to lay waste to a Jeep full of cult members. Corey was not even a little bit up to it.

COREY, *unintelligibly*: sahh uhh

ASH: what?

COREY: i said it's all good. sorry.

ASH: good.

So we went back in there to play a show. I figured Corey had been defused. At least for the time being.

But that turned out not to be true.

## 23.

## COREY ELEVATES HIS BEING-
## AN-UNSTABLE-MESS GAME TO
## A WHOLE OTHER LEVEL

We got about a minute into the first song. And then suddenly Corey started soloing.

The song didn't call for a drum solo. But he started soloing anyway.

He just took a massive loud awkward solo over everything. He bashed his toms and smashed his cymbals in an apelike frenzy, and it was clear that he was intent on doing this for a while, so Ash and I stopped what we were doing and let him do his thing.

I say "frenzy," but the thing was, he had no facial expression at all. His body was creating total mayhem, but his face was completely still. So that was about as creepy and messed up as it could have been.

After a while he stopped. Then he counted us back in as though nothing fucked up had happened. So we started playing.

Then another minute into the song, he did it again. He started soloing insanely, and Ash and I stopped and waited it out.

This happened four or five more times, and each time, Ash and I just silently waited it out. I'm not sure why. I guess it was a battle of wills. No one wanted to give the other side what they wanted. And he clearly wanted a reaction. So Ash and I just patiently kept trying to play songs and waiting out these drum tantrums that kept happening.

We were up there for about ten minutes. Obviously, it felt a lot longer than that. Most of the audience just grimly endured what we were doing. One or two people left. The guys playing backgammon kept playing backgammon. Cookie kept serving people drinks.

Then, ten minutes in, a dude from one of the clusters of dudes walked up and positioned himself right in front of us.

At first he just stood there, swaying a little bit and staring us down. His buddies watched him and giggled.

He was short and ridiculously jacked. Somehow he had muscles in the area between his shoulder and his neck. Those were probably his biggest muscles. Also he had a Macklemore haircut and a number of smeary, murky tattoos.

"Come on now," he started shouting. Corey was the one he was addressing. "Play a song or don't. But don't play that shit."

Corey, soloing violently, refused to look at him.

Uh-oh, I thought.

"People don't want to listen to that bullshit," the guy yelled.

"Give him hell, Rudd," one of his friends hollered.

Meanwhile, Corey stopped soloing. But he didn't look at Rudd or at us. He found a random point in space to frown at thoughtfully instead.

"This ain't your basement," Rudd told him. "This ain't your bedroom where you can just fuck around. People didn't come here to have to listen to that shit. Now come on."

There was kind of a gentle quality to the way he was saying it.

But the fact that he was essentially one enormous bicep made his gentleness more terrifying than rage.

Fuck, I thought.

Corey, still staring at nothing, erupted into another solo. It went on for about ten seconds. Then he stopped and carefully examined his snare drum like it had instructions for what to do next.

Rudd kept gazing at him, his mouth sort of twisting downward.

Then he said, slowly and calmly, "Am I gonna have to kick your ass."

Oh holy shit, I thought.

Ash was just kind of watching it unfold. She actually seemed to be smiling a little bit.

Corey rhythmically bashed and muted his crash cymbal five times: PSHT, PSHT, PSHT, PSHT, PSHT.

Rudd's eyes widened.

"I ain't gonna ask you again," he said.

Corey rumbled something on his toms.

"All righty then," said Rudd, and that was the moment I decided to help, so I said, "Hey, man, look," trying to sound calm, and as the words were leaving my mouth, Rudd turned to me and clamped his hand onto my chest, and I shut up, and we looked at each other, and one of his eyelids was pink and inflamed and rubbery looking, and I have no idea what would have happened next if Cookie hadn't called us back to the bar.

"Band," he yelled. "Campig. Come on back here take a break and I'll get you some waters, and Rudd, I got a cold one with your name on it, so why don't all y'all come on back here."

Rudd looked at me for a beat or two longer. Then he coughed, or burped. It was some complicated alcoholic bodily reflex. He went *hurmp*, and something gross happened in his mouth.

Then he shrugged, took his hand off my chest, and headed over to the bar.

I immediately unplugged my bass and got the fuck out of there and was sitting at the extreme other end of the bar before I really knew what was happening, and after a moment or two Ash was there, too, and Corey.

Cookie set down three waters in front of us, and then he brought three whiskeys, too, and winked. Ash sipped hers. I picked up mine but couldn't get myself to drink any of it. Actually, I didn't want to use my hands for anything because they wouldn't stop trembling. Corey picked up his whiskey and drank it like he was washing down an Advil.

Cookie grinned and brought Corey another, and he slammed that one, too, and we just kind of sat there.

Was it lost on me that the reason for all of this—the Corey-Ash hookup that made everything weird—was the exact thing that, way back when, I had pretended to be upset about? Back when Corey had told me they had hooked up, and I was like, I'm upset, because now it's gonna get weird, because what if you stop hooking up and start hating each other, or something? But in fact the unspoken but obvious reason that I was upset was actually just simple jealousy? But then it did get weird in exactly the way that

I predicted? So I was right after all when I said that thing that I didn't even mean?

I don't have an answer for you. Because at this point I sort of forget why all those sentences are questions in the first place. And I'm not gonna reread them to try to figure it out. Because that seems exhausting, but the main thing is, just writing about this is making me kind of light-headed. So, my bad.

Anyway, sitting there at the bar, we were all totally silent. None of us knew what to say to one another.

But pretty soon we didn't have to say anything because Cookie came back over and wanted to talk.

I was only then just noticing he was super tall and also kind of jacked. He was probably six foot three, and he had giant hands. Each hand was the kind that looked like it could grip your entire head and lift you off the ground.

"You kids," he said, grinning. "Shoot. Where y'all from?"

"Pennsylvania," I said.

"Well, I dug it," he said. "Dug all y'all."

We probably looked at him like he was being a dick.

"No, I mean it," he said. "I ain't just being nice. Y'all was up there, taking chances, and it was real cool. Real cool, y'all. Just a little experimental for this crowd, I guess."

Somehow no one told him that the drum solos were not part of our artistic vision as a band.

"Are y'all just going around looking for places to play," Cookie asked.

"Yyyyyyyyyyyyyyyyy," said Corey.

We gazed at him. But he didn't finish the word. He just looked down at his hands and started doing flams on the bar with his thumbs. Flams are when you do a soft hit and a loud hit as close together as you can.

"Yes," said Ash.

Corey continued flamming.

"Well then can I ask y'all something?" asked Cookie, refilling our waters. "Do y'all want to play a real blues bar?"

He had that smile again of knowing a secret, or at least thinking that he did.

"Yeah," said Ash.

"Course y'all do," Cookie told us. "Listen. I'ma tell you what y'all need to do. Listen. Y'all need to head down to Clarksdale and play the Crossroad. I'm serious. That's where kids like y'all, a band like y'all, needs to be playing. Crossroad Bar and Grill's a legendary blues venue and that's the kind of show y'all need."

"Yeah?" said Ash.

"*Oh* yeah," said Cookie in his weird sweet high voice. "All of them big names come through there and play when they just wanna play for ordinary people. Not for big crowds or no rich folk. You just wanna play a room of some real people who like real music, you come to the Crossroad and play, and ain't nothing about it in the paper, on the Internet, on the radio, because people just know. All of them big names. Bobby Bellflower, Sonny Wallis Jr., Cricket Petway, man, you name it."

"How would they ever possibly let us play there," said Corey.

Cookie smiled and said, "Well. If y'all interested, I could get you a slot."

"Yeah?" said Ash again.

"They know me," he said. "They know my daddy, my whole family. I could get you a slot tomorrow night if y'all want it. And I'm telling y'all, it's what y'all need."

We processed this.

"Y'all want it?" he asked.

Corey was the one who said, "Yeah."

Cookie grinned and went into the back room.

Corey didn't say anything else. But he nodded to himself, and frowned, and reached out, and clapped me on the back two or three times, like he didn't want to but he believed it was the right thing to do.

And look. We had just played yet another horrible show, and our drummer had made it clear that he could become a self-destructive idiot at a moment's notice. So there was no real reason to think that this next show would be any different.

But at that moment I was awash just in the warm thought of, *Holy shit. This is the one.*

Cookie came back out and told us he booked it, tomorrow night at ten, a one-hour slot, and we could spend the night at his daddy's house after the show.

*This is the one*, I couldn't stop thinking. *This is the show that fixes everything.* Because all we needed was an actual stage and an actual crowd. We just needed some real place to take a chance on us. Our problem wasn't that we sucked. Our problem was that we had been playing literally impossible gigs.

Cookie was telling us about his dad's house in the valley.

Apparently, it had a lot of rooms, so we didn't even need to worry about it.

I was no longer afraid of him. I no longer worried that he was going to envelop my face with one of his big hands and lift me off the ground. Instead, I wanted to high-five that hand a million times. Because he was going to take us to the promised land. He was our big doofy angel of God.

Basically, I felt like suddenly we had God's attention, and He was like, GUYS, MY BAD ABOUT ALL THAT STUFF BEFORE.

WES. YOU SPECIFICALLY. I'M SORRY ABOUT THE ASH-COREY HOOKUP SITUATION. I WAS REALLY ASLEEP AT THE WHEEL WITH THAT ONE.

FROM NOW ON, I GOT YOU GUYS. AND TOMORROW YOU SHALL PLAY THE SHOW YOU'VE ALWAYS DREAMED OF.

YOU SHALL PLAY AT A REAL VENUE WITH A REAL SOUND SYSTEM AND A VENERABLE LORD-OF-THE-RINGS-LOOKING SOUND GUY AND EVERYTHING.

YOU SHALL PLAY FOR A VAST, APPRECIATIVE AUDIENCE, AND YOU SHALL ROCK THEM MERCI-LESSLY, BUT ALSO WITH GREAT SOPHISTICATION AND RANGE. AND THEY SHALL BE FREAKING OUT IN AN UNCONTROLLABLE ECSTASY THE ENTIRE TIME.

AND ONSTAGE YOU SHALL FEEL A CLOSENESS TO ONE ANOTHER THAT I RESERVE ONLY FOR THE MEMBERS OF THE SICKEST BANDS. YOU SHALL

PERIODICALLY MAKE EYE CONTACT, AND YOU SHALL
NOT EVEN HAVE TO SAY ANYTHING. YOU SHALL JUST
NOD, AND GRIN, OR LIKE SNEER OR SOMETHING, OR
YELL SOMETHING SORT OF NONVERBAL LIKE, "YAH,"
LIKE THE GUY FROM CAKE, AND IT SHALL MAKE ALL
THE CRAZINESS AND STRESS AND HEARTACHE THAT
HAS HAPPENED SO FAR COMPLETELY WORTH IT. AND
THEN SOME. BECAUSE I AM GOD.

Holy fuck. God. Thank you. I am truly grateful. I can't even
start to thank you enough.

DON'T EVEN WORRY ABOUT IT.

Also sorry I said "fuck" just now. And I guess in general sorry
for swearing basically all the time.

WES. COME ON. THAT SHIT IS TRULY THE LEAST
OF MY WORRIES. BECAUSE THINK ABOUT ALL THE
OTHER TERRIBLE SHIT THAT IS HAPPENING ALL THE
TIME EVERYWHERE. LIKE POVERTY AND TERRORISM.
IN FACT I SHOULD PROBABLY GET BACK TO DEALING
WITH ALL OF THAT. IT'S JUST NONSTOP SOMETIMES.

Well, anyway, thanks.

NO. THANK YOU. FOR THE FOUR OF YOU ARE MY
CHOSEN BAND.

Wait. What.

## 24.

## YEAH BECAUSE MEANWHILE BACK
## AT ELLIE'S COOKIE HAS SOMEHOW
## JOINED OUR BAND

At some point a tall and kind of downtrodden-looking woman walked in.

"Brought your stuff," she kind of whispered to Cookie, stepping behind the bar.

"Thanks, baby," he said, and he kissed her on the mouth and left.

She remained behind the bar, puffing a cigarette and resentfully surveying the landscape of equally resentful-looking drunk people.

Pretty soon Cookie was back. He had a guitar, a mic bag, and a couple of mic stands. He grinned at us like, *It's Christmas in June, and your gift is me.*

"Well, don't just sit there," he said to us. "Get back onstage with me."

Suddenly, we were his band. It happened before any of us could figure out what was going on. He was up there calling the songs, and we were playing with him, and we were unmistakably his band.

And I'd like to think that we would have left or mutinied or something if he had sucked. But that's hypothetical. Because he didn't suck.

He was really, really good.

He played guitar like someone who has been playing for hundreds of years. At no point did he play anything that sounded like a mistake, or that seemed to be in any way difficult for him to play. And then, on top of that, he had a singing voice that was even more beautiful than his speaking voice. He had a very straightforward vocal style, super unembellished, no vibrato or melisma or anything. But every note was beautiful. It had all this brightness and sweetness in it, and it made your heart beat a little faster. It was like if Coke could sing. Not Coke Zero, obviously. I'm talking red-label, bunch-of-calories, immediately-gives-you-diabetes original delicious Coke.

So he was fierce at guitar and fierce at singing. But he might have been the fiercest at being a bandmate. We were up there mostly playing rootsy blues covers, like "Preachin' Blues," and "Catfish Blues," and "Tupelo Blues," and "Boom! Boom!," and "Way Down in the Hole," and Cookie was keying in on every single thing that each one of us was doing. He was effortlessly harmonizing with Ash, and playing parts that matched right up with mine, and glancing over at Corey to stay on top of the beat, and just in general supporting all of us and keeping track of us like one of those dogs who's been bred for thousands of generations to herd sheep, and now has no sheep, so he's doing it to humans instead.

It was of course different music from what we'd been doing. But I was on board with it. We all were.

Ash was singing lead about a third of the time and letting Cookie sing lead the other two-thirds, and sometimes even trying to harmonize, and she wasn't doing any of the growly fuck-you vocal stuff that we were used to hearing from her. She was singing everything pretty straight, and her guitar parts were much more evened out and easy to follow. She was kind of completely transformed.

I was fully occupied with getting through each song without fucking it up. The songs weren't super familiar to me. But, as a musician, if I'm good at anything, it's using my ear and having a sense of the form and being able to hear my way through stuff. So I was able to play competent bass, and that felt good.

Corey was drunk. But, unexpectedly, this just made him docile and submissive. I guess it was because it was taking every ounce of his concentration to try to keep time and play like a person who wasn't drunk. So he just kind of locked it down and frowned with concentration and made a very simple pocket.

And people really seemed to like it.

Our first song was "Mother-in-Law Blues," and eight bars in, we had everyone's attention. The backgammon guys stopped playing, the clusters of drunk swaying people stopped joking and arguing, and everyone just looked up at us and started nodding to what we were doing.

It was the complete opposite reaction from before, when everyone's top priority was to ignore what was happening. Not this time. People were getting into it.

When Cookie pushed his mouth into the mic and started singing, a couple of guys mouthed along. When Ash pushed her volume knob up and started soloing, people cheered. And when we finished, people applauded. Kind of a lot. There was whistling and whooping and everything. Even Cookie's downtrodden-looking apparent girlfriend looked mildly psyched. And Rudd, who had been watching Corey like a hawk, visibly relaxed the muscles between his neck and shoulders.

So we kept playing, and people kept liking it, and it was sort of exactly the feeling I had been seeking all along.

But it sort of wasn't, either.

It felt like cheating, that we were making everyone happy with songs we hadn't written, and a guy we hadn't escaped jazz camp with. I mean, it *was* cheating. Because he was the best member of our band. And we were letting him call the shots. So why did it even need to be us up there? It could have been anyone. And that didn't feel great.

But I decided to just go with it. Because clearly we were doing something right.

So we played for a couple of hours, until about eleven, and people got really into it, and more people came in off the street, and it wasn't necessarily that I felt like I was the Wes that I had always wanted to be, or that we were the band that we wanted to be. But I was a Wes and we were a band that *other people* wanted us to be. And that was better and worse at the same time. And part of me was like, this is probably what it's like to be an adult, and that a little bit sucks, but it sort of doesn't matter if it sucks or not, because it's reality and you just have to deal with it.

I mean, that makes it sound like I was pissed. I wasn't. People were dancing and clapping. We had a nice little thing going on. Corey wasn't being a dick. I was doing my job. Ash sounded good and Cookie sounded great. It was far and away our most successful gig, and it's shitty to want anything more than that.

Cookie was acting like our best friend afterward, and maybe he was.

"I guess Pennsylvania boys know how to *play*," he kept telling people, reaching over the bar and clapping me or Corey on the shoulder. Now it was him and his girlfriend tending bar, because it had gotten so crowded. Basically, Ellie's contained the entire adult population of Furio, Mississippi, or at least the part that wasn't watching air-conditioned sports and eating fried breaded meats.

At some point Rudd came over to hang out. He mostly wanted to talk to me. This was probably because I was the most polite and responsive.

"Now *that's* music," he told us, a bunch of times in a row. "That there is *music*. Hell yeah. Promise me that's the kind of music y'all are gonna play from now on."

I found out a lot about Rudd. He was a former Boeing engineer, now trying to start his own business making jetpacks and hovercraft, and his oldest son was probably gay, and he wanted me to be super clear on how he did not have any kind of problem with that.

He even apologized for trying to pick a fight. "Look," he said. "I wasn't gonna sock you or nothing. I knew you weren't a bad kid. I *was* gonna sock your friend. I was gonna toss him out the fucking window. Your friend was being an ass. But I wasn't gonna fight you, man. *Ermp.* Put you in a hold, maybe. You ever learn any holds?"

It did not take long to reach a point where Rudd felt comfortable demonstrating some martial-arts-type holds on me. They were pretty painful but I tried not to be a puss about it.

"Here's what you gotta do in a fight," he told me. "You're a skinny little shrimp. Now, I don't intend that as a criticism. I just mean, you're a tiny little kid. So your prerogative has got to be end the fight, ASAP. Get a mouthful of water if you can, or any type of liquid, and spray it in the guy's face. You gotta put your lips together and spray it. Pffffft. Right in the eyes. That's a big advantage because the reflex is, I'm gettin' sprayed in the eyes, close my eyes, turn my head away. *Harmp.* All right. No liquid, then you need to headbutt him right in the nose. Pop him with this part of your head right here. It's way stronger'n his nose. Stronger'n a fist, too. Plus a fist obviously you gotta wind up so he sees that coming. Headbutt's far and away your best bet. Far and away. Headbutt him like, POP, and you'll break that dude's nose nine times outta ten. You hear me? Pop. Fight's over. Hit him too hard, you might even kill him. Bottom line, ain't no dude gonna keep fighting with a broken nose. But you gotta hit him *hard.* All right? POP."

"Or kick him in the nuts," I asked.

Rudd was disgusted. "I guess," he said. "If you want to be a dick."

• • •

Corey was slamming whiskeys pretty hard. I wasn't drinking anything. Ash was sipping again, and just shook her head when anyone tried to talk to her, which happened a lot, because she was a girl in a bar.

"Think we can play Garfunkel somewhere," Corey yelled a couple of times, but we couldn't figure out where.

Eventually, I realized Corey had become completely catatonic, and I had to pack up his stuff because there was no way he was capable of doing it. So I did. I packed us all up while Corey and Ash sat at the bar being two different levels of drunk. It was crowded and kind of deafening by then. Multiple different beers got spilled on me while I was crouched on the ground putting drums in cases and stuff.

I went back to the bar and Ash and Corey stood up.

"We'll drive over to Clarksdale together tomorrow morning," Cookie yelled at us over the noise. "Y'all got a number I could reach?"

We all just shook our heads.

"Meet me back here around eleven," he told us, and we nodded, and we walked out of there.

A policeman was just hanging out front, smoking a cigarette and talking to a guy in a trucker hat.

We stopped in our tracks. All of us. I had a bass drum in my arms. Ash had her guitar amp. Corey had nothing in his arms and was too drunk to stand in one place. He had to plant and replant his feet every three seconds or so.

The policeman squinted at us. He was bald except for a tiny soul patch. It was one of those way-too-small soul patches that on first glance just looks like the chin has a belly button that is a little bit overflowing with lint.

We looked back at him. No one said anything.

Then he smiled and said, "You three sounded good."

"Thank you," I said.

"You practice a lot?" he asked.

"Yes, sir," I said.

"Not going to let him drive, are you," the policeman asked, tilting his head at Corey.

"No, sir," I said. "I'm driving."

He nodded but didn't say anything for a few moments.

Then he kind of snickered.

"Well, go ahead, load up," he told us, and we did, and got the hell out of there.

Back at the campground, people were setting fires and smoking cigarettes around them. We parked in front of our cabin. I was irrationally worried there would be a person in there, but of course there wasn't.

Corey had completely passed out. I tried to wake him while Ash watched me.

WES: corey
COREY: hhhhhhhhhhhhrrrhrnnhgggngnnhh
WES: come on man
COREY: ffffff
WES:
COREY:

WES: corey?

COREY:

WES: you want to come insid

COREY: nnnNNNNNOOO

WES:

ASH:

WES: should we just leave him in the car?

ASH: big time

We left him in the car. The bed would have been a little small for three people anyway.

Ash took off her shoes but nothing else and just lay on top of the covers and aimed herself at the wall.

I took off my shoes and got on top of the covers, too.

After a few minutes I kind of scooched over toward her, like an inch.

I would not be able to tell you what my plan was. I guess my plan was just, move toward Ash until something good happens. So that's what I did. Every few minutes I kind of scooched toward her.

After maybe twenty minutes, my hand was sort of grazing her butt.

She didn't make any kind of response.

I very slowly put my hand on her butt.

She made a kind of sighing noise.

I was trying to figure out what to do next when she said, "Wes."

"Oh hey," I said, pretending to be surprised or something. I guess I was hoping I could convey the idea of, *I was asleep, too, so*

*who knows how this happened. Perhaps my hand found your butt,
and perhaps your butt found my hand. It is impossible to know.*

"Don't do that," she said, and I felt awful and kind of shrank
away.

"Sorry," I said.

"It's fine," she said. "Just go to sleep."

"Yeah."

I lay there in misery. In my head, I headbutted myself in the
nose as many times as possible.

But after a few minutes she flopped over and asked, "How
come you don't drink?"

I just shrugged.

"It's okay that you don't," she said. "I was just wondering."

"Someone's got to drive," I said.

"It doesn't always have to be you," she said. Then she reached
over and grabbed my dick.

I mean, she couldn't really get a handle on it, because it was
in my pants and stuff. She more or less just grabbed a random
handful of my crotch, and gave it a little squeeze, and let go, and
the world as I knew it basically exploded.

"Good night," she said kind of loudly, and flopped back over
and fell asleep pretty quickly, but for the second night in a row, I
mean, let's just say that I didn't.

# THE HATERS
## SUMMER OF HATE
## WORLD TOUR 2016

JUNE 17th • 3:00 P.M. • CLARKSDALE, MISSISSIPPI

PINEFIELD

## 25.

## ALTHOUGH I WAS ABLE TO GET SOME SLEEP AFTER MASTURBATING INTO THE SINK AGAIN

Let's not even talk about that part.

Let's also not talk about the part where Ash and I opened the car and discovered that Corey, in his sleep, had allowed himself to do some serious peeing. Because we definitely did not talk about it at the time. We just stood around stoically saying nothing while he stumbled out of the car and tried to change his clothes with his eyes shut. His eyes were shut because of his industrial-grade hangover.

"Corey?" I did ask at one point. "You need anything?" But his only response was a demon noise that he made with his throat. It sounded like *khoooomm*. So that made it feel like me helping him was probably not on the table.

While we're not talking about stuff, let's not talk about the weird silence in the car the entire time we drove back to Ellie's, where Ash was being super blank and wordless for God knows what reason but probably among other things her continued terrible relations with Corey, and Corey was pretending to be in a coma, and I was trying to think of something to say the entire time but couldn't, and it was one of those silences that keeps getting more and more acute and unbearable, like a kettle on the stove freaking out more and more, and the only thing that reset it was Corey making that demon noise again every five minutes or so.

I wouldn't even say the car smelled worse after Corey peed in it. Just more complicated. It was a more complex bouquet of aromas in there that you almost didn't want to categorize as "good" or "bad." It was way too complex for that. It probably smelled like the swamp that Yoda lives in.

Anyway, we got to Ellie's, and it was 11:18 because we got lost for a while, but Cookie wasn't there. So we just sat around in the parking lot and ate the rest of the Twizzlers, which the heat of the car had microwaved into a new yet still somehow Twizzlerish rubbery substance. Also we drank Dr. Pepper that was so hot that every few sips one of us would have to spit it back out.

"Hey, Ash," said Corey all of a sudden.

"Yeah," she said.

"Do you think growing up so rich has given you a fucked-up view of the world," he said.

I found myself too exhausted and stressed out to intervene. *Fuck it,* I told myself. *This probably needs to happen.*

"What do you mean," she said, in this almost bored-sounding voice.

His eyes were still squinted almost all the way closed.

"I mean, if you grow up super rich, like you can buy anything you want, does it fuck up how you see the world and like other people and stuff."

"Still don't know what you mean."

"Yeah, you do."

"No, I don't."

It felt a little bit like I was on the set of the world's worst morning TV show. A show called *Morons in the Morning, with Your Exhausted Stressed-Out Host, Wes Doolittle.*

"Like you can just buy your way out of any situation," said Corey. "And you probably think it's pathetic when other people can't."

Ash frowned very sadly, mostly with her forehead, and nodded to herself.

"And like you get bored with people really easily, because you're used to people like serving you and giving you whatever you want, and in general everyone wants to be nice to you and be your friend because you're rich, so you feel like you never have to try because everyone automatically loves you no matter what you do."

"You think I feel like I never have to try?"

"I was just wondering."

"That's what you think I'm like?"

"I don't know. Maybe. You tell me."

"No, you tell me, Corey."

When she said his name out loud it sounded for a moment like it was becoming the part of *Morons in the Morning, with Your Exhausted Stressed-Out Host, Wes Doolittle* where one of the guests gets up from the couch and the other guest immediately jumps up, too, and then huge security dudes with headsets come sprinting in. But we didn't quite get there.

"I'm just saying," said Corey, "how could it not give you a fucked-up view of the world."

Ash paused. Then she initiated perhaps the most epic sarcasm battle I have ever witnessed in my life.

"Yeah," she said.

"Yeah?"

"Yeah. No, you're right."

"Well, I probably *am* right."

"No, it's a great point. Thanks."

"Sure, no problem."

"I really appreciate how honest you are."

"Don't worry about it."

"I just really appreciate when people are honest with me, instead of fawning all over me like a bunch of assholes, which is what normally happens, obviously, because I'm so rich."

"Sure thing."

"I've actually literally never had a genuine conversation with anyone before right now. So, seriously, thank you."

"You're welcome."

"No. Hey. *Thank you.*"

"You're super welcome."

"I mean, it's *never* happened. Not even once."

"Yeah, probably not."

"I think maybe it's also because I'm a girl? And girls my age are the single most powerful people in the world? Everyone constantly listens to them and respects them and gives them everything they want? You know how it's like that for girls? That's probably part of what we're talking about."

"Well, it actually probably is because everyone wants to sleep with you."

"Oh yeah. That's definitely the best kind of power to have. There's no way *that* shit ever fucks up your life."

"Not as bad as it fucks with other people."

"Sure. Tell me about it."

"You want me to tell you about it?"

"*Please* tell me all about it, Corey."

"You really want me to?"

"Yeah."

"Everyone thinks you're super hot and wants to fuck you, and it clearly *has* fucked up how you see people, because you think you can just hook up with people, and then just freeze them out, just be super cold and shitty, and it probably doesn't even register with you how bad that fucks with their heads, because there's no reason for you to give a shit."

"I *don't* give a shit," agreed Ash. But the fire had kind of gone out of her voice a little bit.

"You don't give a shit, and why should you," Corey told her. "You're just, uh."

We waited for him to finish his sentence.

He burped in what looked like a painful way.

"I'm just what," said Ash.

"Hang on," he said, and he got up and walked slowly and carefully around the side of Ellie's, and then for a while we listened to him barf violently.

While this was happening, Cookie's pickup truck pulled into the lot.

"I'm gonna ride with Cookie," Ash told me.

"Yeah," I said. "Okay."

"Too much drama," she said, holding up her hands like I had a gun.

Cookie, even more stubbly and grinny and Coke-voiced than last night, scribbled me some directions to his house, in case we lost track of him on the highway. But they were completely illegible. They looked like this:

HIWY 30 2 "QTB"

THAN KEEP AN EYE UT "4" BIB RED BARM (LM MIM)

R L R R @ MCGONADS

"I'm sure you'll make it just fine," he told me, and winked, and off we went.

It was only until after I started driving that I realized we didn't even have an address.

Fuck, I thought.

We didn't have an address, and we had no phones. So if I lost them, then basically, the entire tour was over. Because how the hell would we ever find them again.

So either Cookie was disorganized to the point of being an idiot or he sneakily didn't want us making it to his place. And I didn't want to get super darked out with those types of shitty thoughts, but I did kind of feel like it was probably the second one.

And Ash sure wasn't making any special effort to make sure we got to Cookie's dad's house okay. So maybe she wanted us gone, too.

Maybe she was done with us. Because we were too much

drama. Not exciting drama. The annoying kind. We were boys and she belonged with a man.

One of us had given her half an hour of substandard oral sex and now was on an existential meltdown of binge-drinking and then producing bodily fluids. The other was a pathetic virgin who masturbated in sinks and was afraid to drink alcohol in the first place. So why would a girl who was nineteen, and had illegally dated a member of Animal Collective, ever want to put up with that.

I knew these were shitty dark thoughts that I shouldn't be dwelling on but I couldn't help it.

Even if she wasn't done with us as a band, I was starting to think, maybe she should be. Maybe we didn't deserve to be in a band with her. She belonged to a different world than we did. We belonged at jazz camp. We belonged with the Adams and Tims of the world. If everything was in its right place, we'd be calling each other "cat" and "froond" and wearing filigreed vests made out of alligator skin. And Ash would be onstage at clubs and concert halls. She'd be in front of a real band playing huge music for real people. And the longer we tried to stay with her, the more we were holding her back and dragging her down, and it was shitty of us to do that.

It was shitty of us, I couldn't help thinking, it was just super selfish and shitty, and a couple of times on the highway I found myself relaxing my foot on the gas pedal, and letting Cookie and Ash start disappearing past the cars in front of me.

I was just thinking, I could make this easy for everyone right now, and let their pickup truck escape into the distance, and we could turn around and start the long drive back to Pennsylvania, or turn ourselves in to the police, or whatever.

But each time I did that, I thought, *Wes, that would be a mistake.*

*Because yeah. Maybe Ash doesn't want you tagging along.*

*But what if Cookie actually turns out to be a psychopath rapist murderer.*

I couldn't dismiss this thought. I was thinking, *Wes, you can't ignore that there is something kind of off about this dude. He might try to pull some shit. And if he does, you need to be there to stop it. You* and *Corey.*

*Although who knows how much help Corey is going to be.*

*Look at him trying to be passed out on that seat. He's snoring but he still seems to be awake somehow. His eyes are a little bit open and he keeps flopping around in an irritable panic.*

*How long has it been since he last brushed his teeth? Remember that time he once tried to argue that you don't need to brush as long as you floss? Man.*

*Poor Corey.*

I was sitting there in the driver's seat not quite letting the pickup truck get away and looking over at Corey sometimes to make sure he wasn't dead or peeing again, and in addition to the stuff about Cookie, I was wondering whether Ash would be a little more understanding if she knew Corey's family actually was kind of poor.

I mean, "poor" can mean a lot of things. Corey's family was

the kind of poor where you'd forget they were poor until something would happen to remind you of it, like they wouldn't replace a broken pane of glass for a while if it was the summer or a part of the house that didn't face the street. Or all of a sudden they just wouldn't be able to use their car, because they didn't have two thousand dollars to spend on a new transmission to get the Check Engine light to turn off to get the car to pass inspection. Or they'd invite your parents over for dinner, and you'd watch the way your mom ate the cheese from the predinner cheese plate. The same bright-orange mostly salt-flavored cheese that you and Corey would eat a bunch of in the basement. You'd watch your mom pick at it, and you would just know from her eyes that she was thinking, *wow, this is the most budget cheese there is*, this pity that she was trying to hide and that you really hoped you were the only one who could see.

Here's the kind of poor they are. Both of his parents are musicians. His dad is a pianist who wanted to be Elvis Costello *and* Stephen Sondheim simultaneously and wrote a few unproduced musicals and led a couple of super hurting piano-driven bands and just in general never made it. And at the same time he doesn't like teaching piano and has had a huge amount of trouble holding down a job outside of music, because everywhere he goes he feels like his bosses are evil or stupid. This is a recurring thing that you pick up on if you're Corey's friend and you're paying attention. And Corey's mom is a jazz singer who got certified as an accountant when Corey was ten, but she also has trouble finding work, partly because she got started so late and partly because she just really hates being an accountant. She'll even complain about it to you,

Corey's random teenage friend, when she's picking you guys up from band practice. So you know she just hates the hell out of it. And then Corey's older sister, Becca, was born seven weeks premature and didn't get great treatment right away and probably as a result but also maybe just genetically she's got cerebral palsy. I mean, she's really smart and with it and everything, but she has a huge hitch in her walk and balance problems and her speech is kind of smashed together and hard to understand, and she's needed a lot of special medical attention and physical therapy her whole life.

So, bottom line, it's a family with a super unstable income, frequent periods of no health insurance, and crazy medical bills, and so they're definitely poor, like they definitely get food stamps, and bill collectors are constantly calling their house, and Corey's drums are all hand-me-downs from his uncle, and the only vacations they take are just to Corey's mom's parents' house in Delaware where they sleep on cots in the living room and basement, and maybe if Ash knew all that, she'd be a little more understanding about why Corey lit into her for being rich and, I don't know, hopefully you are, too.

That's the only reason I'm bringing it up. I sort of wish you didn't know any of it. It's the same with telling people I'm adopted. It's just, now you're thinking about *poor,* and that's different from thinking about *Corey.*

I liked it better when you knew Corey's parents only as these oppressively caring doglike people who love their son so much that they have to constantly thwart his efforts to leave his own house. Because now instead you're thinking of them as these semi-deadbeat failed musicians whose debt is probably going to ruin Corey's life.

Which might be true. But not as important. I think, anyway.

Anyway, I trailed that stupid pickup truck for three stupid hours, with no stops or human companionship because Corey was pretending to be dead the entire time, and I managed not to lose them, and eventually we took an access road and came to a rest on a little unpaved meadow in front of a giant house, near a handpainted sign that said PINEFIELD.

WES: corey

COREY:

WES: we're here man

COREY:

WES: hey corey

COREY:

WES: corey

COREY: WUNGH

WES: we're here

COREY: fuu uu u ung

WES: we're at the place

COREY: fuuucckkh h

# 26.

## MEET THE PRITCHARDS

The house was huge and weird. It was clearly meant to look venerable and ancient, with slabby chunky stone and elaborate roof tile, but there was just something off about its shape and proportions. The windows were cartoonishly big, and the various pieces of roof were at unnecessarily crazy angles to one another. Also it was too new looking somehow. It looked like an old Scottish castle got married to a reality-TV mansion who was just way too young for it, like as a third or fourth marriage, and this was their awkward kid.

Anyway, we all got out of the cars and stood in that field and looked at one another. I could hear some muffled thumping coming from inside the house.

"Great driving, man," Cookie told me. Something about him was still off. More off than before, even. "I mean we was up there just talking songs and music and *life* and the rest of it and getting lost in conversation, and I'd just completely forget you was back there, and then I'd think, ho, damn, I'm supposed to be guiding those two little Pennsylvania dudes, oh no, did I lose 'em, but each time I look in my little mirror there you was, and I'd go, ha ha, well *damn,* the boys are still hot on my tail, God bless 'em, so great little piece a driving."

I looked at Ash. Something about her was off, too. Her eyes were cloudy, and she couldn't get her mouth all the way closed.

"Thanks," I said.

"Don't even worry about it, little buddy," said Cookie, "don't you even worry, and *you* need some Gatorade, Corey my man, that'll fix you right up, let's get you in the house get some Gatorade into you, and ohhhhh NO. Ha HA. Look out."

Corey and I turned.

A bunch of people were slowly marching out of the house with musical instruments.

Wordlessly, we stood there and watched them approach us.

We would later learn that this was not any kind of organized band. It was just a group of random inhabitants of the house who were having a spontaneous living-room jam session and then saw us and decided to get up and walk out of the house to greet us in the form of continuing to jam.

The group included a guy who was probably Cookie's dad and the owner of the house. So that made this greeting feel a little more ceremonial and legit.

Nonetheless, this was not a band band. Like it wasn't the kind of band you would be able to look up on Wikipedia. Although who knows. People put all kinds of obscure stuff on Wikipedia.

# List of the Band of People Slowly Marching Out of Cookie's Dad's House to Greet Us band members

From Wikipedia, the free encyclopedia

The Band of People Slowly Marching Out of Cookie's Dad's House to Greet Us is a more-or-less-completely-for-shit American acoustic jam band that formed spontaneously in a house outside Clarksdale, Mississippi, in 2016 and immediately disbanded afterward because it wasn't actually a band at all. It was just a random jam session that Wes mistook for a band. But we still put it on Wikipedia because Wikipedia is an attempt to centralize all human knowledge, and that is incredibly badass and we take that shit for granted a lot of the time.[?]

## Current members [edit]

### Probably Cookie's dad [edit]

Instruments: lead guitar, chanting

The guy that Wes assumed was probably Cookie's dad was a member of the original TBOPSMOOCDHTGU. He wore loose-fitting clothing, his body was the perfectly round shape of a giant egg, and his beard was like a bristly steel-wool lifeboat that his head was sitting in. His guitar playing consisted of nonstop technically proficient soloing, which he doubled by chanting gibberish in a gentle, reasonable tone of voice. It was his gentle but undeniable charisma that made Wes assume that he was Cookie's dad, which indeed it turned out he was. His favorite gibberish syllables were "wuzza" and "fuh-gee." [1]

## A tall spindly man of roughly the same age [edit]

Instruments: rhythm guitar

The other guitarist was a tall spindly man who was way less good at guitar. He was kind of frantically strumming the only chords he seemed to know, which were A major and E minor. He was just toggling back and forth between them endlessly. It was like watching a guy playing unwinnable ping-pong against himself.[2]

## A curly-headed shirtless guy in his twenties or so [edit]

Instruments: recorder

There was one chubby curly-headed dude playing a recorder, wearing no shirt at all, and skipping and galloping playfully from side to side like a hooved figure from Greek mythology, e.g., Zacchus, the Greek God of Being a Shameless Jackass.[3]

## An all-female percussion section [edit]

Instruments: tambourine, maracas, Uruguayan candombe drum, gong

The percussion section was four women who varied in both age and musical skill. The youngest, about fifteen, holding a tambourine, seemed to be trying to deconstruct the very notion of rhythm itself. The oldest, maybe thirty or forty, was also not really on top of things rhythmically, in that she could not get all the way through rippling her gong without collapsing in laughter like a maniac. But the college-age girl on the candombe drum was keeping that shit together. And then the other who-knows-how-old woman was contributing quietly on the maracas, but for her it was mostly about shuffling around with her elbows above her head and her arms flailing hither and thither like tree branches in the wind. Sources[7] have estimated the per-capita number of flowers in this rhythm section's hair at, conservatively, a billion. [4]

## Former members [edit]

### A 100% naked guy who was passed out near the front entrance on a couch under some tablas [edit]

Instruments: tablas

This guy was a member of the original TBOPSMOOCDHTGU. He left the band in 2016 due to being completely passed out naked on a couch under some tablas.[5]

## References [edit]

1, 2, 3, 4, 5. ^ your memory, from which you will never be able to erase any of this, especially the sight of a naked passed-out dude just chilling under some tablas and no one is freaking out or even acting like this is a big deal

As far as I could tell, it wasn't anyone's birthday, or the Super Bowl, or any other reason to have thirty people at one house. But as Cookie led us on a little tour, we could not help but notice that there were, minimum, thirty people in there. Maybe closer to fifty. I had a lot of questions that I didn't ask. Were all of them related to Cookie? How many of them lived there permanently? And where did they all sleep? Normally, the answer to this question would be in the rooms that are designated for sleeping. But that was not an option in this house. Because it was a house of zero bedrooms, and in fact, very few rooms at all.

You're probably thinking, Wes. That's impossible. A house is nothing *but* rooms. Yeah. I know. But basically every roomlike space in this house flowed into the next, through eight-foot-wide doorless entrances. Even the closets had no doors at all. So it was sort of all one big aboveground rabbit warren.

Actually, it sort of had the vibe of an Ikea, because the design was so open. But then, decor-wise, it was pretty heavy on tapestries and cushions and incense and people just dreamily lounging around, so it also was a little bit the vibe of the home of a pampered Turkish sultan. And then also it was like a Dave's Used Instruments in the sense of, there were guitars everywhere, and egg shakers, and djembes, and didgeridoos, and güiros, and vibraslaps, and basically every acoustic instrument known to man.

At the way end of one wing on the first floor, we did finally find a few doored-off rooms. These were heavily insulated little studios with speakers and drum kits and pianos and stuff. One was connected to a sound booth.

On the walls were a couple of rows of framed gold and platinum records, all "Presented to Jarold Pritchard," and I stood there examining them, and that was when the house started to make sense a little bit.

"Yes, sir," said Cookie, coming up behind me. "Big Pritch produced all of those."

They were records by Bobby Womack and Wilson Pickett and Lou Rawls and Etta James. A lot of them were autographed.

Wilson Pickett's said, "THANKS 4 NOTHIN' PRITCH!!! HA HA HA HA HA —W. Pickett."

"So your dad's more of a producer than a musician," I said.

"Oh, I wouldn't say that," said Cookie. "No. You can't say that about Big Pritch. He's a *guitar player's* guitar player. But listen. You want your own big old house in the country, you want to take care of your people, listen up. You gotta put that guitar down and get back behind the glass. That's just how the industry goes. Now let me tell you about it."

Fortunately, at that point his phone rang and he had to take it.

The three of us were left kind of halfheartedly inspecting the instruments in the biggest studio.

"This is pretty cool," I said.

Neither of the other two responded.

"Great rehearsal spot, for sure," I suggested.

Corey played a middle C on a piano that probably cost more than his parents' house.

"So uh," I said.

They looked at me.

"You guys want to rehearse?" I said.

"Sure," said Corey.

But Ash said, "Not right now."

Corey nodded angrily to himself.

"I mean, if we're playing tonight, I guess, I think it'd be a good idea," I said.

"Not right now," she said again.

"Ash, what's going on," I heard myself say.

"Look," she said. "Cookie and I smoked up on the way over here, and so I'm just pretty high right now."

"Oh," I said.

She was glaring at me as though I was being a dick.

"Yeah," she said. "So I don't want to play our stuff. That's just not what I need to be doing."

"Are you going to be sober by the time we play?" I asked.

"Yeah," she said. "Probably. It's not gonna matter, so just be chill."

"Sorry," I said, feeling my throat get hard.

"In general, I really need you guys to be chill. Just chill the fuck out. Okay?"

"Okay," I said. "Are we not being chill?"

"You're not," she said. "Neither of you is. Like, if you have to ask that, then clearly you're not."

"Okay," I said.

"Especially you," she told me. "You're so fucking worried about everyone. You're like trying to be everyone's dad. You're what. Sixteen? Just chill the fuck out."

"Okay."

"I don't get why you can't relax and just try to enjoy shit," she said, revving up. "I'm sorry, but it's so fucking stressful to be around you. You're just always staring at everyone. You're like staring at everyone, all the time, and analyzing everything and trying to figure out how you should react to everyone, and it stresses me the fuck out, and you need to turn it off. I need you to fucking turn it off, just for like an hour."

"Ok *ay* ."

"Can you do that? Can you turn it off? Just for one hour?"

"Y , yyeah."

She stared at me. "Fuck."

I didn't reply.

"Are you crying right now?" she said.

"N , *no.*"

She watched me stare at the floor with my chin all stupid and wobbly.

"*Fuck,*" she said quietly, and then Cookie came back and told us our gig got bumped because it's a Friday night and they needed the slot, but if we just show up tomorrow night around seven, we'd probably get to open for Deebo Harrison, and in the meantime we could definitely chill here tonight, so it's all good, just enjoy yourselves on the property and relax, oh and Ash, Big Pritch wants to meet you.

Ash said great.

They left.

Me and Corey stayed.

Corey sat at the piano and played a little bit of the Brad Mehldau arrangement of "Exit Music (For a Film)."

That took me out of it just a little bit. Because it's always kind of a shock when a drummer plays a nondrum instrument. It's like a dog speaking English.

WES, *eventually, calming down*: jesus
COREY: well what the fuck did you expect, wes.

He said that and it put me right back in it.

"What should I have expected," I asked him.

"You should expect to get bitched out. Because Ash is a bitch. She's been bitching me out since Knoxville. So she finally just bitched you out, too. Oh well. Get over it."

"Corey, what's your deal."

"My deal is you're a hypocrite."

"The fuck are you talking about?"

"You're a huge fucking hypocrite. That's what I'm talking about. You told me to go fuck myself because Ash and I hooked up, you got all self-righteous and pompous about it, you said you'd never do that and tried to make me feel like a dick, but now you guys are hooking up, so, you know, what the fuck."

"We didn't hook up."

"Oh. So you guys just sleep together now, every night, without hooking up. Sure."

"For two nights, and yeah. That is what happens."

Corey was staring at me like he found out that all this time I actually *had* been doing grievous harm to my dick.

"Well, that's fucking weird," he said finally. "And pathetic."

"It's not as pathetic as being so bad at going down on someone that you can't even get a hard-on afterward."

In retrospect, I would say that Corey absorbed this blow with a lot of poise.

"Fuuuuck you," he said, with that same "Anybody home?" melody, and then he walked out of there, and I was alone.

There was an iPad lying around, so just to do something I used it to check my messages, and this time I did have email from my parents. There were seven or eight or so.

Apparently, right after dropping me off at camp, they had gone to a yoga-and-meditation retreat without telling me. It was the kind of super intensive retreat where you give up all contact with the outside world. So even before Ash and Corey and I left our phones in practice space G, my parents had left their phones with a yoga retreat receptionist.

I looked at the timing and figured out that it wasn't until we were at Charlize and Ed's that my parents found out I was gone.

"We're not going to punish you," went the first few messages. "We're not mad, Wes. We're just worried. PLEASE tell us where you are and whether you're okay."

I didn't read more than three. I mean, it wasn't really that surprising that they had gone to the retreat. They had done stuff like that before. But for some reason I was imagining what would happen if I had died. Like if Ash's aggressive borderline-lunatic driving had put us under the wheels of a semi or something. My parents wouldn't even have known about it for a day and a half.

I wrote back as long and detailed an email as I could muster.

dear mom and dad,

i'm fine. we're somewhere in mississippi or maybe louisiana. i don't really know where because we don't have phones but we're all fine. we have plenty of money and food and a car and we'll be back by the end of camp. don't worry about me. you guys have always taught me to be independent and rely on myself and it's coming in handy now.

i am very sorry that this is inconveniencing you guys and making you worry. but it's important and i have to do it.

love,

wes

p.s. how was the retreat?

p.p.s. tell corey's parents that he's fine too.

There was all kinds of other stuff I should have wanted to do on the iPad. Snapchat, Instagram, Facebook. Figuring out on a map where we'd been and where we could go. Seeing if there had been anything about us in the news. Even just getting to put on any song I wanted for the first time in three days.

But I didn't. What I did was, I logged out of email and sat there with the iPad on my lap and stared at the wall. I couldn't even tell you what I was thinking. I had a thought bubble above my head with the ". . ." of someone typing but not hitting SEND.

That's the state I was in when a bunch of Pritchards wandered into the room.

Some of them I recognized from the jam session that had slowly marched out of the house to greet us. Others I did not recognize at all.

"I heard y'all are opening for Deebo Harrison tomorrow night," said one.

"Yup," I said.

"Y'all must be real talented," said another.

"We're okay," I said.

"What are y'all called," said a third.

"We're called the Magical Singing Boner," I said.

"Ha ha ha ha ha," said a fourth without actually laughing.

"Want to jam with us?" asked a fifth.

I didn't. But I did. Because I thought maybe it would help if I shut off every other part of my brain for a while and just played music.

So we jammed. It kind of worked. I mean, it didn't. But at least it was an opportunity for me to practice being more chill around people.

It was just another spontaneous jam session, and I was realizing that jam sessions just broke out in the house all the time among random groups of instrument-playing Pritchards, and there was no goal that they were ever trying to accomplish. They weren't out to write a song or make a recording or start a band. It was just about jamming, and it seemed like that was both a good thing and a bad thing.

No one seemed to be trying terribly hard. A high enough percentage of Pritchards were good enough on their instruments that they didn't make you want to stop playing music forever. There were two different saxophonists, but miraculously for saxophonists, neither one was trying to solo over everything, and instead they were content to brainstorm little riffs and stabs and other rhythm parts. And the pianist, a tiny shaggy guy who couldn't seem to get his eyes all the way open, played an interesting kind of funk stride piano that got everyone else in line, and he and I traded bass lines for a while as the various percussionists did their best to keep up.

One nice thing that was happening was, every time I

brought out some new bass line or other idea, this pianist was demonstratively psyched. His head would whip over in my direction, and he would make a point of writhing around and doing that one specific happy-musician face where you pretend that you've just smelled something completely horrible.

So that was pretty nice, and it did take my mind off of things a little bit, and we continued that way for a while until eventually the pianist dug into his hoodie and pulled out an enormous bag of marijuana and a pipe and a lighter, and he handed it to the tambourine girl, and she put the tambourine down and casually packed a bowl while he locked eyes with me.

I tried to make a face of dignified concentration.

He grinned and nodded maniacally.

Look. I'd smoked pot a few times at parties. But I'd never really felt anything. Not hungry, or giggly, or paranoid, or whatever you're supposed to feel. Mostly I just felt kind of out of touch with everyone else. Like suddenly everyone around me was way more impressed by basic camera-trick Vines, like ones where a guy pretends to jump through a window of a moving car, and I would sit around pretending to have my mind blown by it but secretly thinking, *guys, what are we all doing with our lives right now,* but then mainly just thinking, *if I open my mouth, I will definitely reveal myself to be a huge terrible hater, so I should probably figure out how to escape before that happens,* so I guess yeah a little bit paranoid.

But anyway that was the inferior-quality, probably-just-dirt-and-moss-from-a-parking-lot weed that was available to the trombone section of the Benson High School Jazz Band. This Pritchard weed was a different thing entirely. And I feared it with all of my heart.

One reason for that fear was the look on this pianist's face. It was the face of uncontrollable psychosis. He was nodding and winking and baring his teeth maniacally. I mean, he was probably just trying to convey his enthusiasm for drugs. But in fact it looked like he was possessed by a demon. Specifically, a sheep demon. Because of his general shagginess and the sheepy way he was bucking his head around insanely.

The tambourine girl offered me the bowl.

I shook my head and tried to smile in a polite but nonchalant manner. I was trying to nonverbally communicate the idea of, "Thanks for offering me drugs. By the way, I have been around drugs a bunch of times in my life and am completely cool about them. Anyway, I'm good for right now. But I'm definitely not being uptight or weird. So, thanks, and, hopefully now we are done having an exchange about this."

This nonverbal communication was a complete failure. The tambourine girl frowned and pushed the pipe closer to my face.

I looked into her eyes. They were kind of a green-flecked seawatery blue.

She put the pipe to my lips and lit it.

I didn't want to be a dick. So I inhaled a little bit.

She motioned for me to keep going. I did.

She smiled.

I decided, fuck it, and breathed in as deep as I could. She smiled a little deeper and puffed out her cheeks. I puffed out my cheeks. She had freckles and bright red hair and a long, narrow face. I held it for a while.

Five minutes later I was done coughing violently, and trying to play bass again, except the world was chaos and existence was a nightmare.

## 27.

# I GUESS YOU WOULD CALL IT A DRUG EXPERIENCE GONE WRONG, EXCEPT WHAT WOULD IT MEAN FOR A DRUG EXPERIENCE TO GO RIGHT, LIKE WOULD THAT JUST MEAN SITTING AROUND KIND OF INERTLY BLISSING OUT TO THINGS, LIKE A HAPPY VEGETABLE, BECAUSE I DON'T KNOW, THAT SOUNDS EVEN WORSE, LIKE IT'S SORT OF LIKE PREPARING TO DIE AS HAPPILY AS POSSIBLE

So I was still trying to concentrate on playing bass. But that had become increasingly difficult, due to the variety of terrible things happening in my head.

These things were mostly each taking the form of a different terrible Wes.

TRYING TO CONCENTRATE ON PLAYING BASS
WES: ba-dup boobidy bump, ba dup bup

PERMANENT VIRGIN WES: hey

TTCOPB WES: ba-dup boobidy bump

PERMANENT VIRGIN WES: hey wes

TTCOPB WES: uh, hey

PERMANENT VIRGIN WES: hey i was just checking to see if we were still a virgin

TTCOPB WES: umm

PERMANENT VIRGIN WES: i mean i know we are so i guess i'm just checking to make sure you still know that

TTCOPB WES: yeah i know that

PERMANENT VIRGIN WES: okay good

BAD FRIEND WES: yo guys what's up

PERMANENT VIRGIN WES: that's probably never gonna change just so you know

BAD FRIEND WES: what's never gonna change? wes being a bad friend?

PERMANENT VIRGIN WES: no we're talking about wes being a virgin

BAD FRIEND WES: oh yeah

PERMANENT VIRGIN WES: and how wes is going to live his entire life without ever having sex with a woman because why would any woman ever want that

BAD FRIEND WES: right right because of his looks for example

PERMANENT VIRGIN WES: yeah he's always going to look like a little kid with his floppy hair and no muscles and women are going to look at him and think why would i want to have sex with a little kid

BAD FRIEND WES: yup

TTCOPB WES: um

PERMANENT VIRGIN WES: a little kid who probably has a little kid dick

WON'T EVEN HAVE A GIRLFRIEND EVER PROBABLY WES: and cries like a little kid too a lot of the time

PERMANENT VIRGIN WES: oh wow you're even more pathetic than me

WON'T EVEN HAVE A GIRLFRIEND EVER PROBABLY WES: hahahahahahahahahahaahha yup

PERMANENT VIRGIN WES: who even gives a shit about having a girlfriend

WON'T EVEN HAVE A GIRLFRIEND EVER PROBABLY WES: wes apparently

PERMANENT VIRGIN WES: maybe just start with hooking up with a girl first, except he can't even manage that

BAD FRIEND WES: yup yup yup to all of that hey have you ever noticed how wes thinks he's a great friend despite being the kind of best friend who feels and acts superior to you

TTCOPB WES: trying to concentrate here

BAD FRIEND WES: in his head he's constantly dicking on his best friend for having no sense of social cues or whatever which is ironic because he also has zero ability with social cues and at least corey is always honest about who he is and not pretending to be a fake better version of himself

WON'T EVEN HAVE A GIRLFRIEND EVER PROBABLY WES: yeah girls can smell the creepy dishonesty coming off of wes from a mile away

POOR ORAL HYGIENE WES: or maybe they're smelling the rancid dairy product smell that his breath sometimes has

TTCOPB WES: guys maybe we can cover all this later when i'm not trying to play bass

MUSICALLY UNCREATIVE WES: yeah about that

TTCOPB WES: oof

MUSICALLY UNCREATIVE WES: are you eventually

gonna play something interesting or is it just gonna be more of the same

ALSO JUST NOT A GREAT BASSIST WES: at least try to not drag tempo-wise

ALSO JUST NOT A GREAT BASSIST WES: okay now you're rushing

HIS ORIGINAL PARENTS DIDN'T EVEN WANT HIM WES: hey guys what are we talking about

ALSO JUST NOT A GREAT BASSIST WES: dragging again

MUSICALLY UNCREATIVE WES: we're talking about wes being not that great

HIS ORIGINAL PARENTS DIDN'T EVEN WANT HIM WES: yeah no kidding did you guys know that his original parents didn't even want him

PERMANENT VIRGIN WES: yup

BAD FRIEND WES: yup

POOR ORAL HYGIENE WES: yeah i knew that

HIS ORIGINAL PARENTS DIDN'T EVEN WANT HIM WES: okay just checking

HIS ADOPTIVE PARENTS FRANKLY AREN'T THAT INTO HIM EITHER WES: i feel like i should point out that his adoptive parents frankly aren't that into him either

TTCOPB WES: guys i know we're sort of having fun here joking about all of this but actually it's not really that funny

HIS ORIGINAL PARENTS DIDN'T EVEN WANT HIM WES: you're telling me it's not funny

MUSICALLY UNCREATIVE WES: it's brutal

PERMANENT VIRGIN WES: yeah i don't know about you guys but i'm not joking at all

HIS ADOPTIVE PARENTS FRANKLY AREN'T THAT INTO HIM EITHER WES: one thing that is funny though is wes's pathetic sense of wanting to be a dog to people who don't care as much about him as he wants them to

BAD FRIEND WES: oh yeah that is pretty funny

TTCOPB WES: guys it's getting a little hard to play bass right now

HIS ADOPTIVE PARENTS FRANKLY AREN'T THAT INTO HIM EITHER WES: i mean how hard does he have to work to ignore the fact that he's got two parents who in their ideal world wouldn't have him

HIS ORIGINAL PARENTS DIDN'T EVEN WANT HIM WES: *yup*

HIS ADOPTIVE PARENTS FRANKLY AREN'T THAT INTO HIM EITHER WES: yeah i mean he's got parents who if they truly had what they wanted, they'd have some other kid right now, some kid whom they'd be biologically required to love way more than they love him, but that didn't work out so they're stuck with him instead, and they're being pretty nice about it and they mostly always have been because they're good people, but the only reason he's theirs is that they can't do any better, he's the plan b that happened because their plan a fell through

HIS ORIGINAL PARENTS DIDN'T EVEN WANT HIM WES: yeah and i would just add that he'll never be loved as much as he would if his birth mom and dad had kept him from day one and made him a part of their family and their lives, think about the life that he was supposed to have that he's missing out on, he'd be living in caracas and speaking spanish and listening to who knows what kind of music and talking and fighting and laughing with his parents and maybe his brothers or sisters, who knows, and maybe he'd be poorer and maybe his whole situation would be super dysfunctional, but it would be real and you can't replace that

HIS ADOPTIVE PARENTS FRANKLY AREN'T THAT INTO HIM EITHER WES: yeah everyone involved decided that the right life for him was the one where he doesn't have the real thing, the authentic thing, every adult in his life decided that the thing he should get is just the good-enough thing, and

TTCOPB WES: *please quit*


BAD FRIEND WES: oh for fuck's sake

BAD FRIEND WES: are you trying not to cry again

ALSO JUST NOT A GREAT BASSIST WES: jesus christ

PERMANENT VIRGIN WES: wes, we're just trying to help

WON'T EVEN HAVE A GIRLFRIEND EVER PROBABLY WES: yeah we're just trying to help you be honest with yourself for once

HIS ORIGINAL PARENTS DIDN'T EVEN WANT HIM WES: we just see you lying to yourself all the time and trying really hard and we're all standing around going, kid, come on, give up already

HIS ADOPTIVE PARENTS FRANKLY AREN'T THAT INTO HIM EITHER WES: you just don't seem to get that the harder you try, the less things work out for you

TTCOPB WES: please just let me play music and forget about all this shit just for a few minutes

TTCOPB WES: let me just focus on music just for a little while and try to make one good thing

MUSICALLY UNCREATIVE WES: but that's exhibit a, you sad stupid kid, because listen to what you're playing

ALSO JUST NOT A GREAT BASSIST WES: the harder you try to come up with interesting stuff, the less interesting you sound, the worse you play, so just give up

BAD FRIEND WES: exhibit b, think about corey, man, the harder you try to be a good friend, a good dog, the more obvious it is that that's just not what you're wired to do, because you're a fake and a fraud, so can you please give up already

WON'T EVEN HAVE A GIRLFRIEND EVER PROBABLY WES: exhibit c, ash, who clearly does not want some clingy needy sad-sack little kid chasing her around, and the more time you try to chase her down and win her over, the more you are that kid

PERMANENT VIRGIN WES: so give up, let her go, just give up

ALL WESES: give up, man

ALL WESES: give up

TAMBOURINE GIRL: hey are you okay?


What?

I said are you okay. You look a little sick. Let's get you some air.

Where would we get it from, though.

Outside.

Ohh.

Come with me. Take my hand.


Ohhhhhhhhhh.

How do you feel now?

Yes. Good. Yes. Ohhhh wow.

I'm shayin'.

You're shaying.

Shayin'.

Shay—*Saying*.

Ess-aytch-ay-ee, ay-enn-enn-ee.

Sheh—, Shuh-nay-nuh.

Nope. Essaytchayeeayennennee.

Shuhh. Oh my God. I can't spell.

Run your fingers through the grass.

Or, what's the backward of spell? When you take letters and make words out of them? There's a super basic word for that?

Take your fingers and run them through the grass, like *this*.

Oh my God. I've suffered permanent brain damage.

Just temporary brain damage.

Are you sure? How can I know for sure?

You know because you've damaged the part that would know that it's temporary.

I've damaged the part, that would know, that uh. Fuck.

You'll be fine. You're fine right now. You're perfect. You just need to breathe the air, and drink some of this.

Mmmmmmmp. Kay.

How's that.

Hhhhhmmmmhh. It's really good.

You need to be hydrated, because all life came from the sea.

Well, uh. I guess it did. In a sense.

In a sense, innocence.

Whoa. I never thought of that.


Repeat after me. Shae, Anne.

Shae, Anne.

ShaeAnne.

ShaeAnne.

Hello.

Wes. Uh, that's my name.

Hello, Wes-uh-that's-my-name. Do you want to walk with me?

Sure.

Walk next to me. Like this.


So do you live here?

Sometimes. When my mom goes on tour.

She's on tour now?

She's in Japan for another two weeks, then a week in South Korea. She sings with a jazz and world music choir.

Which one?

Do you know a lot of jazz and world music choirs?

Well, not a ton.

Which ones do you know.

Well.

. . .

I guess basically none.

My mom's is called the Cotopaxi Extraterrestrial Chorus.

Okay.

Sometimes they sing with Jon Anderson.

Okay.

He's the lead singer of a band called Yes.

Oh wow!

Wow?

Yeah, I mean, that's a big deal. The lead singer of Yes? That's huge. What's so funny.

Nothing.

What.

You're sweet.


I was wondering what's up with all the Gatorade everywhere.

Gatorade sponsors a lot of alternative religions. Not just ours.

Oh.

Has anyone told you about Jaroldism?

Um, not yet.

We need boys your age, so please just keep an open mind.

Will do, for sure.

. . .

Oh. That's a joke.

I like joking with you.

I was like, I guess now I'm in a cult for the rest of my life.

No, Uncle Jarold went to school with all those guys who started Gatorade, and he invested with them as soon as he could, and it did real well. He had a few investments that did real real well.

Ohhh. So having a house like this, it's not just from producing.

No. Uncle Jarold says, it's not enough just to make money. You have to make your money make *more* money before the government dives in and taxes it to pieces.

Welllllll.

. . .

Well, no. Never mind.

What.

Well, my parents are public school teachers, so you know, taxes, to me, I don't think of them as a bad thing *necessarily*, and

I don't talk politics. Chase me.

What?

Chase me!

Okay, you caught me. Now what are you going to do with me.

Yeah, just, hang on, one sec, because, woooo.

I'm hanging on.

Yeah, I just need to, catch my breath.

You better catch it soon, though.

Yeah, my lungs are just kind of fu

Too late!

I caught up to her at the hot tub. It was a big wide hot tub on the deck. She just slipped right into it. Clothes and all. A bunch of people were already in there. Cookie was in there. Ash was too. Big Pritch was in there with his chest fur trapping hot tub water like dew. A couple others I thought I recognized and three I thought I didn't. It was big enough not to be crowded.

Ash didn't make eye contact with me. I didn't make eye contact with her.

Well get in here, Fast and Furious, said Cookie.

I was still kind of shaky but trying not to show it. I stripped to my boxers. It seemed to take an hour. I got in between ShaeAnne and Big Pritch. The water was incredible. It was like stepping into a cloud of God's breath.

ShaeAnne was ducking underwater and hanging out for what seemed like a suicidally long time. Then the surface of the water would give birth to her panting, gasping, laughing head.

Big Pritch rotated his big round beard-lifeboated head to me like the turret of a tank. He had squid eyes.

The best artist is the best thief, he said.

What?

You're the boy who thinks the best artist is the best thief.

ShaeAnne gasped and ducked back under the water.

Yeah, I said.

Tell me what makes a good thief.

A good thief, uh, doesn't get caught.

And what's a way not to get caught.

Be super sneaky about it I guess.

You'll never get caught if nobody knows you stole.

Ohhh.

He kept staring at me with his squid eyes.

The water clumsily burped up ShaeAnne's sleek, wet, narrow head. Her hair was plastered to her face. You could see it was dull blond at the roots.

Now would you like to know the irreducible fact of the universe, Big Pritch asked me.

Pa, what you telling him, Cookie called over to us.

Sure, I said to Big Pritch.

The irreducible fact of the universe is: *scale.*

Scale.

Yes.

Can you tell me what that means.

No.

Oh.

Heh. Heh.

Ha ha.

ShaeAnne plunged back under.

Can't nobody tell you what it means but here's what it *is.* No matter who you are. What you are. Where when or how you are. There's always something bigger than you and always something smaller than you. Always something faster than you. And always something slower than you. Always something older newer lighter heavier brighter darker. Anything.

You mean not just people but anything.

He leaned in close. His eyes were eight inches from mine and his breath was burnt leaves.

If it all gets too big for you, he told me, if it feels like it's too much. *Zoom out.* And if it all feels too small. Too far away and meaningless.

He pulled back away from me.

Zoom in, I said.

He turreted his head away from me and got his cigarette back.

I looked around the pool. Ash's eyes met mine finally. I looked away from her. I looked up at the house. I tried zooming in. I zoomed in on each window. It was hard to see inside. I went floor by floor. I heard ShaeAnne bubble up again somewhere behind my head. One attic window had the screen pushed up. It opened out onto the roof.

I looked at it for a long time.

## 28.

# THEN I HOISTED MYSELF OUT OF THE HOT TUB AND WALKED INTO THE HOUSE DRIPPING WET IN MY UNDERWEAR AND NO ONE EVEN BATTED AN EYE

By the time I got up to the attic, I had mostly dried off.

I had collected little melodies in my head from passing through all the zones of music in the rest of the house. They were all overlaid in my head echo space like kids talking in the halls between class. The loudest was a recorder melody that was two or three notes away from being the theme song to *Barney & Friends*.

I don't know how I knew it was him who had opened the window, because you couldn't see him from the deck, but I stuck my head out of the screenless attic window and sure enough, there was Corey, sitting over at one end of the roof with his legs dangling over the side. He was scooping his hand into a jar and then messily eating whatever was in there off of his hand like an animal.

"What are you eating," I called.

He wordlessly held up a jar of peanut butter.

"Oh shit," I said.

He put another pawful in his mouth.

"Shit shit shit," I said, and I climbed out of the window and hustled over to him as quickly as I could. The roof was a very smooth expensive-seeming tile. I was sort of crouch-running. He didn't look back at me.

I mean, obviously I was panicking and thinking the whole time, *this is my fault. This is because I said that shit to him in the studio. I was so shitty to him that he is trying to kill himself.* Because that's what this had to be. He didn't have his EpiPen, and he had put himself where no one could find him if he started having an allergic attack. And where he would probably fall off the roof. And the terrible Weses were starting back up in my head, but I was doing my best to drown them out.

When I reached him he wasn't swelling up or seizing up or breaking out in hives. But he wouldn't look at me, either. He was just staring down into the garden at the side of the house.

"Fuck, fuck, fuck," I said.

But he didn't respond.

"Corey, I'm sorry I said that shit in the studio," I said. "Fuck."

But he didn't even seem to hear me.

"Are you not having a reaction," I asked.

"I'm not allergic," he said finally, and his voice was strained and high and thick.

"What?" I said.

"I always thought I wasn't allergic, so I tested it."

"Oh," I said. I didn't know what to say. "Well, thank God."

"Thanks, God," he said.

And still not looking at me, he took another pawful of peanut butter and ate it, kind of trembling.

"I've been out here for a while," he kind of mumbled.

I was trying to figure out what else to say. Because now, actually, I was realizing I was furious at him.

I was completely goddamned ripshit. Because what the fuck

was he doing. I wanted to headbutt him in the face because what the fuck was he trying to do.

"You fucking idiot," I almost said, but then he turned and I saw that his eyes were all screwed up. They were wobbly and bloodshot and big-pupilled and scared.

So instead I just said, "Did you get super high or something."

He nodded.

The way he was looking at me kind of changed everything.

"Well, let's get you inside," I said.

He jumped to his feet. But he did it way too fast, in a way that was clearly not about going back inside. It was instead about being an insane and possibly suicidal maniac. He had to throw his hands out to catch his balance.

"Jesus, Corey," I yelled. I wasn't sure if I should grab him.

"Is it fucked up that I'm out here," he said, breathing hard.

"Yeah," I yelled. "Yeah. It's a little fucked up. Let's get you inside, man."

"I'm doing a fucked-up thing right now," he asked, or announced, and flung the jar of peanut butter down into the garden.

"Yeah," I said, trying not to panic. "But it's all good, man. Let's get you inside."

"No," he said, now kind of bending over and really staring at the garden, like he was trying to read something written in the plants, "no, no no no, because, I mean, I mean does that mean, I mean, because, does that mean, I mean does that mean that *I'm* fucked up?"

"No, man," I said. "No. You're not fucked up."

He shook his head, though.

"You're acting like you know that," he said, trying harder to read the plants. "But you don't."

"Yeah, I do."

"You don't know I'm not fucked up."

"I do. I promise I do."

"How could you know."

I didn't reply right away.

"How could *you* know," he said again, and he looked up and looked at me, and I realized I was smiling at him.

It wasn't because of anything he'd done. He was still a psychotic maniac who I didn't recognize. There was nothing for me to be happy or relieved about.

But something took over my face and my brain and I felt happy and relieved anyway, and I was smiling at him in this small, relaxed, calm way, because my face knew that it would help him, because it was something that I could use to douse his crazy panic.

I mean, in that moment I just kind of became someone different, who could see into the future and who saw myself helping Corey back in through the window, and I knew it was going to happen.

"I know you're not fucked up because I know you," I said. "I know you better than I know anyone. You're my friend. You're not fucked up."

He just stared at me.

"You're like anyone," I said. "You're like me. You do fucked-up things sometimes. But you're not fucked up."

He stared at me a little more, and I saw him just starting to come back to normal, but he was starting to breathe really hard, and shake, and heave, and he was starting to lose his balance, so I did something else. It really seems like it shouldn't have worked. But it did.

"Give me your hand," I said to him. And I reached out to him.

And he put his sweaty sticky peanut buttery hand in my hand, and I squeezed it, and I started walking and leading him back to the window, and he followed me, and we made it all the way across the roof. And I went inside, and he came in after me, and I said, "All right."

And I gave him a hug, and then he started crying and couldn't stop.

It was a truly epic amount of crying. We stood there in the attic and he put me in kind of a headlock and got peanut butter in my hair and just wept uncontrollably. For the first minute or two I was choked up and sort of sniffling along with him.

But his crying went a lot longer than mine.

COREY: HRN     , RN N        RRRNNNN, , NK
WES: it's all good, man
COREY: OORRRRNNN , N , NT    NTK K        , ,    ,
*ohhjjh*
WES: get it all out
COREY: jjjjjh , jjhhh , h         h u u uRRrRRNNN    U
UUuurrnnt

WES: just get it out

COREY: ooOHhhh god , oh, , g god ,       jjjJJJJJHHHH

WES: allllllllll good


I was hoping he was just crying and being sad with as few thoughts as possible. Because the more thoughts he was having about why he was out there, the wronger those thoughts were going to be. I knew that for a fact. I just knew what was going on in his head. I knew that he wasn't going to be able to realize that he was just fucked up on drugs and loneliness and a bad hookup and none of it was permanent.

Finally he calmed down and lay down on his back on the floor, and I got him some Gatorade, and I found an iPad and a Bose speaker, and I asked him if there was anything he wanted to hear, and he said *Chutes Too Narrow*, so I put on the first track, and we sat there and listened to James Mercer strum and casually sing his way into that big second A section.


COREY, *eventually*: damn.

WES: you were just way too high, man

COREY: yeah

[*james mercer hits that high note on "told" that is the one time in his entire singing career that he sounds not completely in control*]

COREY: yeah it's probably it's uh

WES:

COREY: it's uh probably good not to get too deep into uh into coming up with reasons i was out there, right

WES: the reason you were out there is you were on drugs

COREY: yeah.

*[james mercer does that jungle-gym melisma on "behind" that sounds a million times easier than it is]*

COREY: look, i just want you to know, i wasn't out there because of shit with you

WES: thanks man

COREY: you're a good friend and you basically just saved my life and i'm not mad at you for making me a hater

WES: well you're a good fr

COREY:

WES: wait you're not mad at me for what

COREY: for turning me into a hater

WES:

COREY:

WES: what

COREY: you're a hater, you've made me into a hater, but i'm not mad

I was almost too baffled to say anything.

WES: when did i make you a hater

COREY: i mean right from the start. like one of the first times we even talked to each other. i played you this exact album. remember?

*[james mercer gets to that low register part where he sings in his talking voice like he's putting his kids to sleep]*

WES:

COREY: i was super psyched about it, because i was super

psyched about the shins. i thought they were our beatles. so i was like, hey check this band out, and we listened to it and you just had this look on your face of completely refusing to like it

WES:

COREY: and then after a loooong time you were like, this is the band from that movie garden state? and i was like yeah. and you were like, the band where natalie portman says this band will change your life? and i was like yeah. and you didn't say anything more than that. but that was all you needed to say. because we sat there and kept listening to it and it was like, well, yeah. this band isn't changing anyone's life

WES:

COREY: and all i could think was, holy shit i'm glad i didn't tell you the shins were our beatles

WES:

COREY: and that was it. i couldn't love the shins anymore. i couldn't love anything. i had to hate on everything. like you

That did happen. I remembered it. I did say, This is the band from *Garden State*? The band that will change your life? And I did mean it like, this band isn't changing my life.

But I didn't remember it as me hating on Corey's favorite band, the Shins. I remembered it as me and Corey finding a way to hate on the Shins together. Because that was what we did. Because Corey had already made *me* a hater.

Honestly, I really kind of liked the Shins, but I hadn't thought Corey was putting them on for us to like.

WES: yeah but corey that was only after you showed me how to be a hater by hating on kool & the gang

[*two james mercers sing that harmony on "confrontation" where it always sounds to me like the levels are completely fucked and it's sort of hilarious but maybe only i hear it*]

COREY: what? no. the shins was first

WES: no man. kool & the gang was first

COREY: no because you hating on the shins was the whole reason *why* i hated on kool & the gang

WES: no, you hated on kool & the gang, and then together we listened to the shins, and i wanted to show you that i could hate on stuff too, because i thought that was the thing that *you* liked to do, so

COREY: dude. no. come on. shins were first

WES: no. it was definitely kool & the gang

COREY: shins

WES:

COREY:

WES:

COREY: the shins, man

WES:

COREY: i'm 90 percent sure

WES:

COREY:

WES: i mean i really think kool & the gang was first

COREY: maybe like 80 percent

WES: but now i'm thinking about it and i guess i can't be totally sure

COREY: *fuck*

WES: i guess there's a chance because i'm going through my memories and i guess i don't know for sure what the order was, like i can tell you what it feels like but maybe i've always been remembering it wrong, or maybe now i'm remembering it wrong

COREY: *oh my god. why do we have to be stoned right now*

[*james mercer hits that one plaintive note on "heard" the third time through the chorus that is the first moment in the song where he allows himself to feel true painful emotion and it takes the song to a completely different place somehow*]

WES: maybe we need to just drop it for the time being

COREY: yeah. we need to drop this immediately. because trying to remember shit stoned feels like it's destroying my memories forever


Yeah. That was how it felt for me, too. It felt like my memories were old crumbly photographs and the act of pulling them out was smudging and blurring and breaking them, and the closer I tried to examine them, the tighter I gripped them, and the worse it got.


WES: well, hey

COREY:

WES: i'm sorry. i've b

COREY: don't worry about it


And by this point his voice was back to normal. It was back to being Corey's dry cool kind of surprisingly deep voice, and it told me we were exiting the raw hot gooey place we had been in, of crying and being vulnerable and saying unspeakably honest things to each other.

WES: no but just let m

COREY: seriously, don't worry about it, because if you start apologizing, then i'll start, and we've both got like a million things to apologize for, and it's just too much shit for right now, so don't worry about it

WES: all right

[*track three starts with that suspended chord from the guitar that then breaks off into that bouncy little mountain-goat descent with the stamping bass-drum into the cymbals and the big minor strum and james mercer triumphantly yelling*]

Part of me was definitely sad to be leaving the raw hot gooey place. But maybe a bigger part was relieved. And then a third part was thinking, *If you and Corey were girls, you would probably be in that raw hot gooey place all the time. You would constantly be telling each other brutally honest truths about your relationship, and it would cement your bond but also provide you with constant pain. You would probably be a gibbering lunatic by now.*

WES: there's kind of a good hot tub outside if that interests you

COREY: oh yeah?

WES: yeah it's pretty big and people seem to like it

COREY: are some of those people girls

I'm just saying, you can only be in that place for so long.

WES: i don't want to oversell it but it's a hundred percent girls and all of them are softly moaning in ecstasy a hundred percent of the time

COREY: oh *tight*

WES: yeah. it's super tight

COREY: my dick is trying to gnaw itself free from my torso just thinking about this

WES: yeah i wasn't even in that hot tub for ten minutes before i caught my dick drawing elaborate escape plans on a rag

We headed downstairs and left the Shins playing for someone else to find.

COREY: hey is one of those girls the girl you were chasing around the lawn like a lunatic rapist viking

WES: you saw that, huh

COREY: i'll never be able to unsee it

WES: look. she wanted me to chase her

COREY: well all right but now let me ask you something

WES: sure

COREY: do you think that last thing you said made you sound like less of a rapist

## 29.

## MAYBE IT WASN'T A HUNDRED PERCENT BUT THERE
## WAS A GOODLY NUMBER OF GIRLS IN THERE

One of them was ShaeAnne still. It was a younger crowd at this point. Big Pritch had left. So had Ash and Cookie. I tried not to think too hard about where they had gone or what they were doing.

Initially, ShaeAnne seemed to be ignoring me. But soon I realized it was part of an elaborate Courtship Initiation Sequence.

COURTSHIP INITIATION SEQUENCE CHECKLIST

☐ Give long smoky look to Object of Courtship (OoC) as he approaches hot tub and slowly raise leg out of water until big toe is pointing more or less at him

☐ Abruptly drop leg back into water and ignore OoC for about ten minutes

☐ Glance sort of half-eyeliddedly back at OoC, and if he is not looking, which he's probably not, then I guess just keep making identical half-lidded glances over there every few seconds until he happens to be looking back

- ☐ Once brief eye contact has been made, giggle mysteriously
- ☐ Immediately submerge head and entire body underwater
- ☐ Drift slowly over to OoC's foot area
- ☐ Give his shin a brief but painful bite with a lot of your teeth
- ☐ Drift back across the hot tub and emerge nonchalantly from surface of water as though nothing fucked up has happened
- ☐ Continue to ignore OoC and instead strike up conversation with Friend of Object of Courtship (FoOoC) despite the fact that FoOoC is clearly in the middle of flinging some big-league woo at a different girl, the girl being that candombe-drum-playing girl from earlier and the woo being it's hard to tell but based on the angles probably fondling her butt
- ☐ Respond to OoC saying, "Hey, ShaeAnne, come over here" by craning neck and giggling more mysteriously than before
- ☐ Turn away from OoC completely
- ☐ Then, from across the hot tub, drift slowly backward onto OoC's lap like a car backing into a garage
- ☐ Refuse to speak not in Spanish

I need to note in passing that Corey was pitching an unprecedented game at the candombe girl. It was like suddenly he had switched brains with Drake. He just walked up to this girl who was at least a few years older than him and eased himself right in next to her, and almost immediately they were having an intimate murmury conversation with their heads like six inches apart, and before long, his hand was almost definitely on her butt. So he had clearly made a full recovery and I was relieved and impressed. Even kind of intimidated.

I mean, I was doing okay with ShaeAnne. Actually I guess I was doing great. She was calling me *azucar papi* and *amor latino*, and she was literally smushing my dick under her thigh.

I sort of wanted to correct her Spanish, because it was nonsense garbage Spanish and those phrases didn't really mean anything. But even if they did, whatever they meant, they didn't apply to me. I wanted to tell her, I don't speak native Spanish, either. I'm a nonpracticing Buddhist. My mom's ancestors are from Poland. My dad's are from Wales and Sweden.

But the main thing was, I didn't want to get into it. You bring up race stuff with white people and either they get awkward and defensive and want to tell you why you've misunderstood them, or else they want you to drop everything and teach a college seminar for them, and either way it's just exhausting.

Also I was trying not to think about Ash, which meant that I was.

But part of me was like, *Wes. There's a nice girl here who is into you and who also saved you from a possibly life-threatening panic attack. And she just wants to have fun.*

So after a while I relaxed and let myself have fun.

I started giving her a shoulder rub. Then a neck rub and then a back rub. To mix it up a little I added quiet sci-fi sounds to the rubs like *bwoyp* and *bbyyyyyyyeeewwwwwwwWWHIT* and *ernt ernt ernt ernt*. She laughed less mysteriously than before. After a while she turned and sized up my face and kissed me, and we made out for a while, and Corey and the candombe girl were also making out, and everyone who wasn't me or ShaeAnne or Corey or the candombe girl kind of conspicuously got out of the hot tub and went somewhere else. ShaeAnne's breath smelled and tasted sort of bad but a comfortable earthy kind of bad like farm animals, and her various areas of skin kept catching on my areas of skin like rubber on rubber. We kept making out and did other dumb stuff like tap each other on the face and make more sound effects and breathe weird on parts of each other's skin to create weird new sensations. And the sun started to go down and the mosquitoes got worse and we decided to go into the house and we ate some vegan fritters and yogurt and we smoked some more pot for some reason and we played some more music with a bunch of other people except I wasn't playing bass and instead I was playing these percussion instruments that I didn't know how to play and so was she and both of our playing was pretty much for shit but it didn't really matter and every now and then we would stop playing to make out some more and my lips were kind of dry and raw but I didn't really care and then at some point she got up and took my hand and brought me to my feet, and we started walking, and I knew we were looking for a place to have sex, and that's when my heart started racing, because I was thinking, this is how it happens.

We walked through the house looking for a secluded spot but everywhere we went there were Pritchards lying around and eating and drinking and smoking and playing and ignoring us or giving us these sly little grins that I really wanted them not to make, I didn't want them to be part of it, and I asked ShaeAnne once if we were going to the studios because maybe that would be private but she said people are always going in there to record, at all hours of the day, and we kept walking and I couldn't stop thinking, this right here is how it happens, this is where and when it happens, and this is who it happens with, and I was trying to stay calm but my heart was bounding around insanely.

And then we turned a corner and there was Ash, patiently sitting cross-legged on a little cushion bent over her unplugged Les Paul, practicing, and looking at her I just knew immediately that she and Cookie hadn't hooked up and weren't ever going to and that I was an idiot for thinking they would and she glanced up at us and I wanted her to be upset and jealous and pissed off but I knew for a fact that she wouldn't be, and she wasn't, she just gave us this funny lopsided grin for a couple of moments and then went back to playing guitar and we kept walking past her.

We walked and walked and walked and didn't pass anyone else and finally we were somewhere pretty dark and abandoned and ShaeAnne put her hands on my shoulders and pushed me down onto the floor and I thought *this is it* and it was it. She guided me onto my back and pulled on the bottoms of my briefs and I pushed them over my knees and feet and I was completely naked and not hard at all. She straddled me and pulled her top off and her breasts flopped out and I heard them more than saw them. She reached behind herself and kind of carefully took my not hard dick into one hand and pretty soon I couldn't really think about anything else and pretty soon after that I was hard and she took her hand away and I heard her opening some little crinkly package and I felt her put the cool plasticky middle of the condom snugly on the front of my dick like she was shrinkwrapping it and I felt her fingernails through the plastic like the legs of a crab fingernailing their way down my dick and she rose up a little and adjusted her panties and breathed harder and opened her mouth and her breath was like vegan fritters and farm animals and her eyes were dark and I saw them very clearly somehow and her hair was stiff with chlorine and itched like straw on my face. The moment she put me inside her I came. I mean the exact moment.

FUCK, I said, and I curled up around her like a snail, and kept coming about a hundred times, and I said fuckfuckfuckfuck, until she said sssshhhhhh, and pushed me back down onto my back and just lay on top of me, and that was how it happened.

Shit.

What.

Just, shit.

Shhhh.

I mean, I feel bad for coming, you know, instantaneously.

Don't feel bad.

Why not.

Because you won't next time.

And twenty minutes later, she was right, I didn't, and then an hour later after we smoked even more pot like idiots, I *really* didn't, I mean to the point where I kept getting a stomach cramp and needed to take a break, and eventually during one break we just agreed to call it quits, and I think I was asleep before I had even climbed all the way off.

# THE HATERS
## SUMMER OF HATE
## WORLD TOUR 2016

JUNE 18th • 8:00 P.M. • CLARKSDALE, MISSISSIPPI

CROSSROAD BAR & GRILL

# 30.

## OBLIVION

I awoke to the sound of the Sailor's Hornpipe.

The music was coming from behind a door. It was being played on a recorder.

It took me a full minute or so of all-hands-on-deck thinking to figure just those two things out. Because I was in a deep brain fog.

The light of day revealed that ShaeAnne and I had chosen to have sex and sleep right smack in the middle of the floor. She had put her clothes back on in the night. But I had not. I was completely naked.

There was the muffled sound of a flushing toilet.

Then a nearby door opened. And out stepped the recorder-playing curly-haired guy.

I skittered into a corner like an insect and covered my dick with my hands. The guy winked mischievously and continued to play. ShaeAnne flopped over and mumbled something irritable. I crouched and grabbed my boxers and tried to put them on without exposing myself. At some point the guy realized that he was not a bringer of whimsy but instead a bringer of terrible mortifying embarrassment and he left. ShaeAnne continued to try to be asleep.

I was alone. I was at a brain speed of about two thoughts per minute, and one of those thoughts was just Corey's demon noise.

It took about an hour to find the rest of my clothes. This turned out to be more than enough time to fully realize the shame of sleeping the entire night totally naked right in front of the door to what turned out to have been a pretty popular bathroom.

COREY: basically everyone saw your taint

WES: oh god

COREY: i was headed to the bathroom myself but i spotted you guys from a safe enough distance that i had time to turn and run away without seeing your taint or anything else that would force me to move to the Yukon forever

WES: great

COREY: i ended up peeing out the window

WES: is there only one bathroom in this entire house

COREY: basically yeah

WES: fuck

COREY: around sunrise you guys really became kind of a tourist attraction

Breakfast was slices of toast. Except the toast was made out of bread that wasn't bread at all. It was just a bunch of nuts and seeds glued together.

WES: what about you? did you hook up with that girl

COREY: there was nowhere private so no

WES: right

COREY: the thing about me is i'm not a crazy taint exhibitionist who wants everyone to see his taint

WES: yup

I found Ash having breakfast alone in an abandoned corner of the house, between an elephant sculpture and an unused hookah. She, too, had seen me naked. But that was not all.

"You guys had sex like twenty feet away from me," she said, munching the weird toast.

My heart basically stopped.

"There's no way," I said.

"Yup," she said, munching.

"We walked all the way to the other end of the second floor."

"I can tell you for a fact that is not what you did."

"No. Come on. You're fucking with me."

"I wish I was. You got maybe ten steps out of my room, and then you stopped, and got down right in the middle of the floor, and immediately started fucking."

"Oh my God. I'm sorry."

"It's okay. It was clear you had no idea what was going on. Plus it was pretty dark in there."

"Oof."

"You were just pale shapes from where I was. But I could hear everything."

"Yeah."

"The first time there was about thirty seconds of foreplay, she put a condom on you, and it was pretty much over before it started."

"Pretty much."

"I have to say, it was impressive how long you came. You came nonstop for a really long time."

"Yup."

"A *really* long time. Your balls must have been like little deflated balloons after that."

"Yyyyup."

"Look. Don't feel bad. The first time for a guy is never good. You got it out of the way and you went right back at it. And that time it sounded like things went pretty well."

"We didn't go right back at it."

"Oh yes you did. You guys went *right* back at it. You weren't even done coming. You were like, fuck, sorry, I came instantaneously, and she was like, well, you won't this time, and you guys just started making out and going at it again. You didn't even change condoms, which I have to tell you is gross. And defeats the purpose."

"That's really not how I remember it."

"Well, your memory is fucked up, because that's what happened. I was there. In the future you need to change condoms if you're going to have gross porny multiple-male-orgasm sex."

"Thanks."

"Honestly, my recommendation would be, don't have that kind of sex in the first place."

"Thank you."

"Maximum, keep it to two orgasms. Or at least give yourself more time before the third one."

"You mean more than an hour."

"I mean, more than the ninety seconds you gave yourself to smoke a bowl before a third round of pain-fucking."

"Ninety seconds?"

"Yeah."

"There's no way. It was at least . . . *half* an hour."

"No. You waited for exactly as long as it took you to speed-smoke a bowl and then she basically tortured your dick. For a really long time. She was flipping you around and putting you in all these positions and you were like, ow, wait wait wait, time out. And she was like, *no* timeout, *no* stopping, just shut up and don't even think about stopping because I am a psycho."

"It wasn't that bad."

"It sounded horrible. And it took forever. That's when I should've broken it up."

"Well, thanks for not breaking it up, because that would have been weird."

"Um, I did break it up the fourth time, and that's what you should be thanking me for."

"There was no fourth time!"

"Ohhhh yes there was. You were half-asleep. You were just lying there murmuring, Please, no, and she was ordering you around in broken Spanish."

"No. Come on."

"Yeah. Finally I yelled, 'He wants you to stop,' and she was like, 'Are you sure,' and I was like, 'Um, yeah.' And then I think you both fell asleep because I didn't hear anything."

"Oh," I said.

She munched the weird bread and studied me.

"Well, thanks for listening to me have sex four times," I said. I was a little mad and she could tell.

"Hey," she said in a different tone of voice. And she made that weird lopsided grin again and gave me a light punch in the arm that I think she hoped would be playful. But instead it was just awkward and dumb.

It was the first truly awkward thing I had seen her do and it took me out of being mad somehow.

"Why did you stay and listen," I said.

"Yeah," she said. "I should have left. But, I don't know. I guess I wanted to make sure your first experience was okay."

"You did?"

"I guess, yeah, I did. And the main thing is, look. You just don't get that many opportunities to listen to someone you know fucking."

"Huh."

"It's just really interesting. I recommend it."

At that point Corey walked in, so we stopped talking about it.

"This bread looks like a bear took a shit," he told us, like he was a reporter for local news.

I was still in a total mental fog. But I could at least pick up that things were a little better among the three of us. We were all capable of sitting around talking and joking and stuff. It was like things had been reset a little bit.

Also, Ash made it clear that it was just gonna be the three of us opening for Deebo.

"Cookie knows I want to play my songs," she said. "And he knows that's just you guys and not him."

We rehearsed all afternoon. We were all pretty cracked out and achey and terrible-smelling. But the music clicked in a way that it hadn't before.

It didn't sound the way it had in the jazz camp practice room. That was electric and insane and kind of out of control. At the Pritchard studio, it had a completely different feel. We played our set and it felt like wearing a really old good T-shirt. The songs didn't cut anymore. They just *sat* in this cool, soft, comfortable way.

Ash sang quieter, Corey and I locked in about 3–5 bpm slower than usual, the amps buzzed less, and the guitar and the bass had a cleaner Meters-y vibe. It felt good and we didn't talk about it. We played all afternoon and none of us tried to overanalyze it or be some rah-rah unnecessary cheerleader. Specifically, I didn't do those things. Those were normally my specialty. But I managed to just chill out and be a third of the band, no more, no less.

I remember thinking it was working because we just didn't have any shit anymore that we were keeping from one another. It was all out there. We had all seen me naked. We had all seen Corey go insane from drugs and alcohol. And as for Ash, maybe we hadn't seen her at her worst. But we had seen her stoned, and mean, and even awkward. And both Corey and I had definitely done all the hooking up with her that we were going to do, and it was all past us somehow. All that was left was music.

Cookie didn't even show up to listen to us. I guess Ash had

told him not to. That was the vibe I got, but I didn't ask her about it. We didn't see him until he came to tell us that dinner was ready and that after we should get going to the Crossroad.

"Y'all feelin good," he asked us.

"Feeling great," Ash told him.


Dinner was the same situation as before of mysteriously someone had made some food and everyone got to just walk into the kitchen and randomly take some. It was an enormous bowl of some kind of weird lemony bean salad. It was huge and vegetarian and it made me kind of sad. It felt like something my mom would have figured out how to make one weekend and then we would have to eat it for three or four days.

I knew I had to write or call my parents again. But I also knew that I could go another day and it wouldn't be that big of a deal. And that made me sad for whatever stupid reason.

I saw ShaeAnne through a window eating outside by herself, and I went and joined her.

"Yo," I said.

"Where were you all day," she asked me.

"Playing music," I said.

"You left me all alone," she said, pulling up grass in little handfuls. I felt shame. But also panic.

"Oh," I said. "I'm sorry. I didn't know you wanted me to stick around."

I knew as soon as I said it that it was idiotic.

She said nothing and just rolled her eyes.

"Are you gonna come see us play," I asked.

"I don't think so," she said.

I was relieved. But then I felt even worse.

"Well," I said. "Hey. I had an amazing time last night."

She ripped out some more grass and rolled her eyes even harder.

"All of yesterday," I said, panicking. Everything I said was a mistake. "You're really cool to talk to. And funny. And obviously really pretty and sexy. So it was just a great day."

She just hiked her eyebrows up and nodded miserably to the grass.

"It was my first time," I said. "So."

She looked at me.

"Sorry I'm being weird," I said.

"Me, too," she said, smiling finally. And she threw grass in my face.

# 31.

# DEEBO

The Crossroad was a little like Ellie's. Except bigger and not depressing. It was set back in the woods off the two-lane highway, and it had no parking lot so there were crooked lines of parked cars on either side of the access road. The XROAD sign looked like it had done all the fading it was ever going to do and was now an ageless unchangeable artifact from another dimension. Inside there were enough tables for about a hundred people but almost everyone was standing around the bar. It was an even mix of black and white, and in general people were less downtrodden and more cheerful and it was kind of impossible to tell anyone's age.

The sound system was intense, and the sound guy weighed at least three hundred pounds and had a lot of questions about my mic levels that I couldn't answer. We were too late to do a sound check. We didn't even have time for Corey to set up his drums. "Just use the house set," the sound guy told him. "House *set*," agreed Corey in a fake-deep voice that made it clear that he was super intimidated.

All we had time to do was meet Deebo Harrison.

He was sitting with his band at a table off to one side. They were all wearing loose-fitting shirts, and their vibe was one of, they weren't having a very important conversation, but they still didn't feel like we should be interrupting it.

Deebo didn't get up when we walked over to him. He was pretty short. The top of his head looked like no hairs had ever grown on it at any point in time. His eyes were small and it hurt to look at them. His hand when I shook it was dry and tough and briefly popped my knuckles out of place.

Cookie introduced Ash, but not us. "This is the legendary Ash Ramos," Cookie purred. "She and her band come down all the way from Pennsylvania."

"New York," said Ash.

Deebo sized each of us up.

First Ash. Then Corey.

Then me. No one said anything.

Finally, he turned back to Ash.

"Go on when you're ready, then," was all he said.

Honestly, I wasn't ready. But I told Cookie I was. And so did Corey, again in his fake-deep voice that indicated that he was fending off a crippling panic attack.

But Ash was the most freaked out of all.

I'd never seen her afraid before. Not when Rudd was getting ready to throw Corey through a window, and not when Ed stomped out of his house with a shotgun. But she was afraid now. She was twitchy and spacey. She kept sneaking glances back to Deebo's table and swallowing. All of a sudden she seemed about five years younger.

"He's the real fucking thing," she told us.

"Yeah, but so are you, honey," Cookie said to her.

"So are *we*," I said.

"We are going to rock everyone to within an inch of their lives and then kill them," said Corey.

But she just kept shaking her head and glancing over at Deebo's table.

"I don't belong here," she said, and her voice sounded five years younger, too.

We told her she did belong here. We told her we all did. I don't know if we believed ourselves as we said it, though. I kind of tricked myself into thinking, yes, I did. Because anyone can belong anywhere. I think you have to believe that or else eventually you become a Nazi or something.

But Ash wasn't buying it.

"What the fuck are we doing," she kept whispering.

"Boys," said Cookie eventually. "Can I talk to Ash alone for a quick minute."

Outside Corey and I kicked stones into the woods and had a disagreement about whether Cookie was going to screw it up for us.

COREY: looks like we're cookie's cover band again

WES: no way. ash won't let that happen

COREY: ash *will* let that happen because she is pissing her pants right now because we have to open for a dude who probably fashioned his guitar with his bare hands from a tree

WES: she just needs to remember to be the crazy highway ash with the lug wrench

COREY: cookie's not gonna let her

WES: no. i think she's over him

COREY: look, man. it's cover time. just embrace it. i'm gonna get hammered

WES: why would they ever serve alcohol to an underage dude with zero dollars

COREY: to get him to stop randomly stealing other people's drinks

WES: i see

COREY: yeah

WES: actually that's not the worst plan ever


Then Ash came outside.

The look on her face was something I hadn't seen before.

"Are we playing with that creepy fuck," asked Corey.

Ash just shook her head.

I knew it wasn't a good head shake.

"What's gonna happen," I said.

"I just want to do this one with Cookie," she said.

Corey and I were both quiet.


It was like Corey and I were each waiting for the other to blow up. But neither of us did.

That probably made it harder for her and that was probably why we were doing it.

Finally, I just said, "Well, have a good show."

"Yup," said Corey.

She nodded. She looked like she wanted to say something else. But she didn't.

Instead, she just walked back into the Crossroad, and we were left alone outside.

Neither of us said anything or looked at each other. I mostly just stared into the woods and tried to wait out the need to cry. My eyes were burning again and my throat was hard and I knew it was the dumbest shit ever.

When Corey spoke, his voice was high and clear. He wasn't going to cry but he also wasn't himself.

COREY: well. i think it's time to go

WES: mm m

COREY: yeah

WES: back to cooki e's dad's   h   ouse?

COREY: well, no

WES: oh

COREY: i think i wanna call my parents, and drive home

WES:     yeah

COREY: you can call yours and we'll figure it out

WES:         yeah

COREY: they'll pick us up somewhere or wire us some money for gas and we'll just drive back

WES:       mm

COREY: you wanna get your bass case and patch cable and stuff?

I don't know what to tell you. I didn't. I guess I didn't think Corey would actually leave without me.

And I wasn't ready to go back to my parents. There was no reason. They weren't even mad at me.

WES: you know,  i don't
COREY: oh
WES: i    want to stick it  o ut
COREY: you sure?
WES: y   eah

And I was mad at Ash. I was sort of furious at her. But I just didn't want to leave her yet. It just wasn't time. And again, I was thinking, if I leave Ash alone with Cookie, there's a chance something horrible could happen. It was the pickup on the highway all over again.

COREY: well, good luck, man
WES: yeah
COREY: i understand. i hope it works out
WES: be s afe,     okay?
COREY: yeah you too

We both stood there for a little while longer.

COREY: well, see you in pittsburgh, and, uh, don't let em cut off your dick.

And he turned and walked down the access road until he got to our Honda Accord with his drums in the back, and I watched him get in and kind of slam the door after himself, and the brake lights turned on, and the headlights, too, and the car lurched back into the road and pulled out to the end and waited for a few cars to pass and then eased onto the highway and out of sight around the time I heard clapping from inside the Crossroad, and Cookie kind of muffledly saying, "Ladies and gentlemen, Ash Ramos." I heard her start with a simple little blues tag, and Cookie joined her at the turnaround, and she started singing about how it was early in the morning and she heard the rooster crow for day.

They sounded good together. I had to admit it to myself. I wanted them to sound bad, and I knew that was petty and stupid. But anyway, they didn't. They sounded good and legit and I knew that it wasn't the pickup truck all over again after all. Ash had found the right band for her, and it was a duo. It was her and Cookie. And Corey knew that it was time for us to leave and I should have known it, too.

And probably I was just staying because I was in love with someone who didn't love me back. And because I thought I belonged in a good band that could go on tour and play great shows, even though I didn't.

So I was standing around thinking, *Ash doesn't love you, and music isn't right for you, and you just let your best friend drive away, and your parents might try to pretend otherwise but they don't need you back anytime soon.* I was thinking, *Wes, all you really have is yourself.*

I guess that probably sounds super lonely and terrible. But actually I wasn't sad about it. As soon as I saw Corey drive away, I stopped being sad, or angry at Ash, or anything. I stopped feeling feelings at all.

Because it was just me at that point. I was all that I had to worry about. So I wasn't worried. I just didn't really have feelings anymore. I wasn't anxious or hopeful about what would happen next. What I would do or what would happen to me. I wasn't even that curious about it.

I just stood there thinking, *At some point, something else is going to happen, and then I'll know what it is, but until then, I don't mind not knowing, and maybe even more than that, I just don't care.*

I don't know how long I stood there. It felt like a really long time.

Eventually, a car pulled onto the access road and took the Accord's old spot, and a man and a woman got out. Each was tall. The woman had the same kind of wrung-out trampled-by-life look of Cookie's girlfriend back in Furio. The man had sleepy eyes and tattoo sleeves and a long stemmy neck. He wasn't fat but his belly was all settled downward like a sock half-full of something.

I watched them come down the access road. They were taking long slow steps. Her shoulders were hunched, and she looked like she was trying not to look furious. He looked kind of calm and almost bored, but maybe that was just his sleepy eyes.

When they were close the man asked me, "That's Cookie Pritchard up on stage right now?"

It was clear that he already knew. But I nodded anyway.

As they passed me, I saw a gun tucked into the man's belt, and in my new feelings-less state, I just stared at it and didn't really feel anything.

They went in and the door closed after them and nothing seemed to happen. Cookie and Ash continued playing the song they were playing. It was just me alone outside again. I still had that feeling of *something is going to happen,* except it had sort of evolved into *something is waiting for you to do it.*

For some reason I found myself walking around the outside of the Crossroad. I walked around the side past the kitchen entrance and the exhaust vents and out back where the dumpsters were and around the other side where the power and telephone lines were attached to the building. I got to the side door that led directly to the stage and watched Cookie and Ash through the smudgy little window. They were all I could really see. Ash was deep into the music. But Cookie was gazing out into the audience with this weird intense pout that looked ridiculous on his face.

They finished, and there was some applause, and Cookie got up kind of quickly and muttered, "Well, that's all for Ash and me, let's bring Deebo up here," and there was more applause, and then I could hear the other guy in the crowd yell something, but I couldn't quite hear what it was over the noise.

Then everyone got quiet and I could hear him a little better.

"Haven't seen you round here in a while," I could hear the man say, or something like that.

Cookie just stared out at what was probably the man, blinking and swallowing.

"Hey," I heard the man say. "What are you getting for this gig? You two gonna split it fifty-fifty or what?"

Ash's eyes were huge and round and darting back and forth between Cookie and whatever was out in the audience.

"You know my little sister's working double shifts," I heard the man say. "Six, seven nights a week. Because if she doesn't, your daughter doesn't eat."

"My daughter isn't really any of your business, O," said Cookie finally, and that immediately set off a bunch of noise, with the man named O and the woman who I guess was O's sister both yelling, and the audience getting loud again, and I stood there not making out what anyone was saying. And then a few people grunted or shrieked and around the corner of the building I could hear the front doors of the Crossroad fly open and people running outside to their cars and starting them up, and I didn't know for certain but I was pretty sure O had pulled out his gun, and I could kind of hear him yell about this deadbeat son of a bitch bringing his new skank around here and how O wasn't sitting around on his dick any longer waiting for a family fucking court judge to get his shit together, and I knew I needed to think of a plan but the plan-making part of my brain wasn't really responding and so just to do something I deployed my patented Wes Doolittle Go-To Panic Move and went over to the circuit breaker on the side of the house and flipped the Main switch, and all the lights went out, not just inside but out where I was, too. All of a sudden I was in the darkness. Inside I could hear a huge amount of shrieking and shouting and some stuff crashing to the floor but no gunshots as far as I could tell, and I opened the stage door and yelled, ASH, into the darkness, and then WHAM something smashed into my chest and face and knocked me to the ground.

It was Cookie. He kept running. The door slammed shut. I lay there on the ground trying to get my breath. The door opened again and this time it was two people. It was Ash and the guy named O.

I could hear Ash breathing kind of raggedly. It looked like O was holding her arm. "Cookie," yelled O a few times. "Cookie, be a man for once in your damn life." There was no response from Cookie, wherever he was. "You call him," O told Ash. "Cookie," she tried to yell. Cookie was gone. "Louder," he said. "Cookie," she tried again. I kept lying there. "You even know he had a kid," he asked her. "Yeah," she said. "But all we do is play music together." I got my feet under me, and no one seemed to hear it. "I don't care what you do together," O told her, and I knew it was the wrong choice but I very quietly crept close to him and he was peering past me into the woods and his head was about a foot and a half above mine but I could see it pretty well in the moonlight and I could see his big nose and before I could talk myself out of it I gathered myself and right as I heard him whisper "shit" I jumped up and dolphin-bounced my forehead right into his nose, hard, I jumped and I nodded the place above my eyes right into his nose as hard as I could, and a huge burst of light went off in my head,

## 32.

## AND I HEARD HIM MAKE
## A NOISE LIKE HAAARRRM,

and he fell to one knee and I heard no gunshots and felt nothing and then Ash had me by the hand and we were running into the woods and we were pretty deep in there before we stopped and looked back through the trees at the police lights flashing.

## 33.

## DEER IN THE HEADLIGHTS

We sat there under a bush and watched the police talk to O and take him into custody and help him with his bloody or broken nose. We couldn't really hear what they were saying. A few times they sent flashlight beams flickering into the woods, and we crouched down to duck them but they wouldn't have reached us anyway.

Ash still kind of had that high nervous tween voice when she spoke.

ASH: are you okay?

WES: yeah

ASH: you're sure?

WES: pretty sure

ASH: ohhhhhhhh god

I had a feeling she was going to tell me how stupid I was, and I was right.

ASH: ohhhhhhh my god that was fucking dumb, wes

WES: i know

ASH: no, you don't know. that guy had a gun. that was *so* fucking dumb

WES: no, i know he had a gun

ASH: then why the fuck did you do that?

WES: yeah, it was probably a mistake

ASH, *starting to freak out*: how are you so calm?

WES: i don't know

I really didn't know. But I was pretty calm. My head was starting to pound, but that was it.

ASH: where's corey? is he okay?

WES: he left a while ago, so i think he's fine

[*ash nods. her chin is trembling*]

WES: he's driving back to pittsburgh right now

I was calm because it was still just me. All I had was me and it was still just me trying to be ready for the next thing.

But then the next thing that happened was that Ash pushed her face into my chest and cried, shaking and sniffling, and I put my arm around her and hugged her closer, and she burrowed in there sort of mouth and nose first like a dog, and at that point it was kind of impossible to still have no feelings.

She didn't cry for very long. Afterward she mostly had her voice back.

ASH: wes i'm sorry

WES: no it's okay

ASH: no. i made a huge fucking mistake

WES: i mean

ASH: it should have been you and corey up there with me

WES: well, but i get it

ASH: no. please don't say that. it should have been *you fucking guys* and i knew that and cookie fucking knew it too

WES: it's fine, though

ASH: *it's not fine.* it's not fucking fine, because he's a shitty person

WES: cookie?

ASH: yeah. he's a shitty dad

WES:

ASH: he told me about his daughter, and he was like, i never see her, because i hate her mom, but it's okay, because her mom's family is taking care of her, and if i wasn't free to do what i want i wouldn't be happy, and then i wouldn't be a good dad to her, so it's for the best for both of us

ASH: he said all that shit to me on the drive yesterday and i didn't say anything because i was stoned but i was also too chickenshit

ASH: and then later i was practicing guitar alone and he sat next to me and put his gross hand on my leg and tried to make a move and all i said was, i'm not into men, and what i should have said was, do you know how bad you're fucking up your daughter's life? do you have even a little idea of how shitty and selfish you are?

ASH: i let him break up our band and he's a shithole and i hope that other dude finds him and beats the shit out of him

WES: maybe *we* can find him and i can headbutt his face

ASH: no. i don't want to see his face. i just don't want him to exist in my life for another fucking second

We sat there in the damp forest and kept watching the police. I could hear O's sister's voice angrily trying to tell them something about the big picture. Cookie was nowhere to be found.

Ash and I were leaning against each other and her arm was around my waist and her hair was tickling my neck and I didn't need it to be anything more than that.

ASH, *eventually*: so. you want to get back on the road

I didn't know what that meant. Like if it meant, let's keep being on tour, or just, let's get out of this forest where there's deer and Lyme disease and stuff.

WES: what about our guitars

ASH: we'll figure it out tomorrow

WES: okay

ASH: we'll find somewhere to stay tonight, and come back tomorrow for our stuff, and then we'll figure it out

WES: okay

ASH: i emailed onnie today. he's expecting us. so maybe we can just go straight to new orleans tomorrow. we'll figure out how

WES: okay yeah

So we made our way out of the forest and to the two-lane highway, and started walking in the direction that Corey had gone.

We walked single-file at the extreme edge of the shoulder, which was pretty narrow, and cars passed us and some of them slowed down, but we didn't want a ride with any of them. We just walked and talked and Ash told me more about what it was like to have a dad who didn't really care about you, or care about anyone, and I'd tell you about it but you don't need to know it and I don't want you to.

And she told me if it turned out that I got that girl pregnant, then I better be ready to move down to Mississippi and become a full-time dad. And there was undoubtedly a non-zero chance I did get that girl pregnant, because we had definitely botched our whole condom procedure.

WES: shit

ASH: you'd be a good dad though

WES: i don't want to think about it

ASH: you'd be a great dad because all you do is sacrifice yourself for other people and for some reason it doesn't make you miserable

WES: that's not *all* i do

ASH: well most guys don't *ever* want to do it, so you're a great guy

WES: i dunno. i was shitty to shaeanne today

ASH: she committed many sex crimes against you last night, so it's fine

WES: i guess, yeah


My head was throbbing kind of violently and I was pretty sure my hand was bleeding again under the wrapping. But for some reason I was amped about it.

ASH: hey

WES: what

ASH: i never ever ever want to have a kid, i mean *never*, but if i ever changed my mind, i would want you to be its dad

WES:

ASH: i don't ever want to get married. that's never gonna change. but if my hormones get all fucked up and i decide i need to have a kid, you're the only guy i know who would make an even half-decent dad, so i'd probably ask you to be the dad of that kid

WES: well

ASH:

WES:

[*ash reaches out and takes wes's hand*]

ASH: hey. i'm not fucking with you here

WES: no. i know

ASH: no but i've been thinking about how it probably seems to you and it probably seems like i've been fucking with you, but wes, i know you like me

WES:

ASH: i mean i know you want us to have a thing and i've kind of wanted that too

WES:

ASH: i mean i was mad when you were hooking up with shaeanne, and then afterward, the next morning when i was giving you shit, i mean i was jealous

[*ash squeezes wes's hand and then lets go*]

ASH: but we're not gonna have a thing. not now. it's not the right time. what it's time for is, it's time for us to have a band together. that's what i need and that's what we need. but i just want you to know, i know you like me. and i like you too. i like you in all kinds of ways.

WES:

ASH, *a little huskily*: i just don't want you to think i've been fucking with you.

WES: i'll be your kid's dad

ASH: you will?

WES: i will. i'm in

ASH: you have to do all of its diapers though

WES: eighty percent

ASH: one hundred percent because it's still a way better deal than being pregnant

A car flashed its beams at us. We ignored it. It veered onto the shoulder. We yelled and jumped out of the way. It groaned to a stop.

Then we recognized it.

COREY: GET IN GET IN

WES: OH HELL YES

ASH: FUCK YEAH

COREY: SHUT UP AND GET IN THE CAR

We got in the car and hugged the shit out of him like he was our long-lost brother presumed dead in the war or something.

Corey had gotten about fifteen minutes away from the Crossroad before turning back. The reason he turned back was me.

He just figured I couldn't really have wanted to stay behind. I was just being an idiot in the moment. Also, he knew his parents were probably going to end his life when they finally got him back. But they were *definitely* going to end his life if they found out that he had abandoned me with insane people in the middle of Mississippi.

By the time he returned to the Crossroad, the police had blocked it off and shut it down. But somehow he sweet-talked his way into

1) befriending a cop

2) figuring out what had happened

3) *getting into the Crossroad* and looking for us in there

4) walking out of the Crossroad with both our guitars and Ash's pedals and everything

WES: holy fucking shit

ASH: corey how the fuck did you do all of that

COREY: the usual dickload of lying

WES: wow

ASH: what did you say

COREY: i said i was deebo harrison's drummer and he sent me back to make sure he didn't forget anything and he was probably gonna fire me if i didn't get in there, so please, officer, my job's on the line

WES: oh wow

ASH: that's fucking awesome

WES: you probably could have just told the truth but i am still so proud of you right now

COREY: i gave myself a fake name

WES: no you didn't

COREY: "bone wilson"

ASH: NO

COREY: i swear to god i was like, excuse me, officer, i'm bone wilson, deebo's drummer, and he was like, well hello there, bone, what can i do for you

Like I said, the vibe was incredible.

Then it kind of changed in a hurry.

COREY: so ash where can we drop you off

ASH:

WES: no no no ash is still touring with us. we're gonna go play a show tomorrow

COREY:

WES:

COREY: nnnnnnope

WES: come on, man. we can still play a great show

COREY: i'm not playing with her. sorry

ASH: corey, *i'm* sorry

COREY: oh yeah?

ASH: yes. i'm really sorry. i panicked, and i did the wrong

thing, and i hurt you guys and sold myself out, and i have to live with that, and it feels shitty

COREY:

ASH: so i'm sorry

COREY: apology accepted, but i'm not gonna play with you anymore

WES: corey, come on, man

COREY: it's not happening

WES: she said she was sorry

COREY: i heard. great. still not happening. i'm not playing with her

ASH: corey, what do you need me to say

COREY: ash, there isn't anything you can say, because bottom line you don't think i'm good enough to play with you. there's no way around it. and i don't feel like trying to change your mind anymore. so i'm dropping you off and wes and i are driving home

ASH: in what car.

The way she said this roughly doubled the Vibe Terribleness Quotient.

COREY: clearly, this car

ASH: you mean *my* car?

WES: guys

COREY: i mean the band car, the car of the band, a band which you are no longer in because you left the band tonight

ASH: uh *you* left the fucking band, including your best friend who had to stay behind and deal with a guy with a fucking gun

WES: guys can we jus

COREY: sure, yeah, because *you* became best friends with a super-herb who goes around herbaceously making enemies with dudes who have guns

ASH: oh that's a great fucking point, i wonder if i did that because my drummer sabotaged my last show by pretending to be a fucking ape

COREY: well maybe *that's* bec

WES: I WILL HEADBUTT BOTH OF YOU IN THE FACE IF YOU DON'T SHUT UP

At that point mostly I just felt incredulous that I was still dealing with this shit.

WES: here's the deal. tonight i headbutted a guy in the face. yesterday i got out on a roof and had to deal with corey going insane from drugs. i've also talked down a guy with a shotgun and cut open my hand on diseased highway glass. we've all made some sacrifices on this trip. but i probably have a concussion and the wound on my hand is definitely infected. so i'm gonna need you guys to *drop it*

COREY AND ASH:

WES: corey, we're not driving back to pittsburgh. we're driving to new orleans. if you still don't want to play with ash once we get there, that's fine. but you have to drive us there. or shut up while someone else drives. and ash, you have to be cool with whatever corey decides once we do get there. and that's what's gonna happen

COREY AND ASH:

WES: that's what's gonna happen or i'm gonna headbutt you both in the face. i don't give a fuck anymore. i've been through too much shit. all right?

COREY:

ASH:

COREY: oh SHIT

ASH: FUCK

WES: NO. NO NO NO

COREY: FUUUUUUUUUUUUU

There was a deer in the headlights.

I had always thought that deer-in-the-headlights thing was a myth. But this deer was in our headlights, and he was definitely just standing there staring at us, and it seemed like it did not even occur to him that he could get out of the way.

We were all screaming at him. He did not hear us or care. For some reason Corey was not braking. We got close enough that we could see the deer's entire facial expression. It was the panicky bug-eyed expression of someone who is watching a movie that he doesn't even a little bit understand. It was basically the face of my mom after she made me explain Snapchat to her. Actually, it was an expression I recognized from Dad Junior.

We did not end up hitting the deer. Not because he moved. We missed the deer because Corey steered us off the road.

We rattled into the shoulder. The car juddered and heaved and bounced up and down. The right wheels dipped into a ditch. There was a horrible RRRRRRRTTTCCCHH scraping noise on the underside of the car. Everyone was screaming. Corey pulled us out of the ditch and BOCK something smacked the side of the car right next to me. It was a fencepost hitting the right side mirror and KKSSHH I heard it explode and shatter into a million pieces. Everyone continued to scream. We lurched away from the fence. We lurched right back toward it and BEERRKK a different fencepost punched a huge gash into the side panels including the door that I was gripping and I felt it groaning like a living thing.

We lurched all the way back onto the road. It took a few minutes to realize we were driving again. The car was making a few more noises than before. But it was still a functional car, and we kept driving it.

Ash was the first to start laughing and then Corey started in and pretty soon we were all laughing like maniacs, and after that things were fine.

# THE HATERS
## SUMMER OF HATE
## WORLD TOUR 2016

JUNE 19th • 9:00 P.M. • NEW ORLEANS, LOUISIANA

LIME TREE

## 34.

## SOMEHOW WE NO LONGER EVEN WORRIED ABOUT GETTING PULLED OVER EVEN THOUGH WE HAD VISIBLY BEEN IN AN ACCIDENT AND HAD NO RIGHT SIDE MIRROR

Suddenly anyone could just say anything and it was not a problem.

ASH: you know i did think i was better on my instrument than you guys

COREY: *knew it*

ASH: i didn't even realize that i was thinking it though. i just assumed it

WES: huh

ASH: honestly, i'm probably the worst one in this car

COREY: you definitely are at jazz

WES: you're worse in the sense of more limited

ASH: mmm

COREY: yeah wes and i can do a bunch of things pretty well and you can only do like four things

WES: four to six things

COREY: but you're fierce at those things, so don't worry about it

ASH: i'm not fierce at anything

COREY: look, you'd have to be, because otherwise we and our dicks would have fled from you many days ago

ASH: thanks dickhead

I mean, anyone could really say anything.

ASH: corey, can we talk oral sex technique a little

COREY: i'm never gonna improve without feedback so please give it to me straight

ASH: you gotta slow it down and i mean *way* down

COREY: ok

ASH: just really simplify what you're doing. in general try to make circles with your tongue

COREY: got it, got it

ASH: and no matter what happens, you need to be out of there after five minutes, good or bad

WES: huh that's interesting

ASH: there's nothing worse than knowing a guy is *trying* to get you to come, like he thinks your cooz is candy crush and he's trying to get three stars or some shit

COREY: it would have been great to know this approximately four days ago

ASH: you're telling *me*

Even when they turned on me, I was fine with it.

ASH: wes you didn't go down on me but i think you'd be even worse at it

WES: please explain

ASH: you'd just sit there completely still with your mouth

open and hope that i would start fucking your face and you wouldn't have to do anything

WES: actually yeah that sounds ideal

COREY: no no no that's not wes. here's wes

ASH: i listened to him have sex for more than an hour. he basically just lets himself be a sex prop

COREY: no no no here's wes going down on you: lick lick lick . . . "all right all right all right"

ASH: oh yeah because he wants to achieve consensus!

COREY: his finishing move is making a spaceship noise into your cooz and then asking you if he's getting an A

ASH: hahahaha

WES: i will headbutt every face in this car

I gave Ash more band names to consider. And pretty soon Corey couldn't help himself and started going along with it, too.

**All of Them Knew They Were Robots:** "Okay. It sucks because this is the first good name either of you has ever come up with, but there's just no way this isn't a Mr. Bungle tribute band. Everyone in this band has given up on writing their own music and instead they just play note-for-note-faithful Mr. Bungle covers once a month at the same bar in Houston because they all work at NASA, and this is how they blow off steam on the weekends, and their spouses are all pretty sick of it, except for the lesbian girlfriend of the glockenspiel player, because she's the only cool one."

**Meow Meow Kitty:** "Pros: Regardless of how good this band actually is, it automatically gets everyone's attention. Everyone instinctively YouTubes the shit out of them. Because everyone is obsessed with cats. Cons: This band is three lip-syncing Japanese girls in miniskirts, and literally nothing would be worse than having their fans."

**Jennifer Lawrence's Armpit:** "Here's a thought experiment. What happens if this band becomes successful to the point where someday you *meet* Jennifer Lawrence? Is there even a 10 percent chance you would manage to be cool about it? No. There is a zero percent chance that neither of you would go insane and do something antisocial. Pick someone you'd be cool around and maybe I'll consider this."

**Padma Lakshmi from Top Chef's Armpit:** "That's sort of better, except, okay, then, who is this band. Answer: This band is four super pimply fifteen-year-old part-time stoners who are either trying to rip off Phish and like String Cheese Incident or instead Slayer and Gojira and like Hatebeak, and either way it's just sloppy chaos. You guys don't know Hatebeak? Hatebeak is a hardcore band whose lead singer is a parrot. Look. Wes. Corey. None of these names have anything to do with *us*. Come up with some names that are about *us*."

**Cookie's Gruesome Death:** "Okay. That's two good names you guys have come up with. But way too close to Death Cab for Cutie. But you guys are starting to get okay at this."

**Perfect Taste:** "Jesus. No. That name literally means nothing. That band plays acoustic college rock and their lyrics are the worst thing you can possibly imagine. They're what happens when three fratty hetero dudes sit in a room and try to imagine what it would be like to be a sensitive poet. Just thinking about this makes me never want to play music again."

**Charlize and the Eds:** "I do like the idea of calling myself Charlize, but I'm not gonna tell you again about Name and the Somethings."

**The Haters:** "It's too, uh."

" . . . "

"It makes me think of, um . . ."

" . . . "

"Well, let me sit with that one."

We weren't even halfway to New Orleans when Corey let us know that he was deciding not to leave after all.

COREY: so can we talk about our set tonight
[*ash just grins at him*]
WES: yeah what are you thinking
COREY: i dunno i had a few ideas

And after Ash putting him in a hug stranglehold from the backseat that almost made him drive off the road again, he told us his ideas, which were mostly just the idea to maybe throw in a few covers of bands we liked. We could punk them up and dumb them down and make them our own. Because it's not the end of the world if people know what bands we listen to. Actually it's kind of good.

ASH: what bands were you thinking
COREY: well
WES:
ASH:
COREY: i was thinking the shins
ASH: why the shins
COREY: because they're what i listen to when i just don't give a fuck anymore
ASH:
COREY:
ASH: well that's a great reason to listen to shit
WES: corey knows *i'm* into it
COREY: yeah wes and i can't get enough of that delicate sensitive ass shit
ASH: then let's do the fucking shins. i think a shins cover could be really good
COREY: YEAH BITCH
WES: ash who are *you* into when you've run out of fucks to give
ASH:
COREY:

ASH: ok. you guys want to know? for real?

WES: yes

COREY: YES

ASH: when i no longer give a fuck, sometimes i listen to . . . the sad ass stylings of . . .

WES AND COREY:

ASH: mariah carey

COREY: OH MY GOD

WES: MIMI

ASH: shut up shut up shut up

WES: i think what you're *trying* to say is shoo doo doop

COREY: WE BELONG TOGETHERRRRR

WES: you'll always be my ba-a-a-abyyyy

ASH: SHUT UP WES'S TURN

WES: oh that's easy. my go-to is the original triple threat: singer, bandleader, *and* one hell of a bassist

COREY: oh no

WES: a living legend out of jersey city named robert bell . . . but you might know him better as . . . *kool*

ASH: oof

COREY: *no*

WES: I'M TALKING ABOUT KOOL AND ALLLLLL HIS FRIENDS A.K.A.

ASH: stop with this shit

COREY: *wes what are you doing*

WES: "THE GANG" LET ME HEAR YOU SAY KOOL & THE GANG

COREY: i will never say it

Just in case you are thinking everyone was pissed: No one was pissed. Everyone was amped. The sun was about to come up. We were three hours outside of New Orleans, we smelled like a horror movie, and we were a band. We were the Haters.

WES: ash it's pretty cool that this whole time you were secretly the girliest girl in america

ASH: you're a dork and corey's a pussy

COREY: each time you say the word "pussy" i know it should give me a boner but somehow it doesn't

ASH: pussy

COREY: yeah all that's happening is my dick is achieving inhuman levels of floppiness

WES: i'm rock hard but it's for kool & the gang

## 35.

# WE AWOKE TO A MONKLIKE, SHAVEN-HEADED MAN TAPPING THE DRIVER'S-SIDE WINDOW

We got to Lime Tree a little before nine, and no one was there, so we parked in a shady corner of the employee parking lot and opened the windows halfway and we all fell asleep in the car, and the guy who woke us up was Onnie himself.

It was around noon. He was a small older dude in a tight-fitting black T-shirt that said GEAUX SHORTY on it. His eyes were black and crinkly and he carried himself kind of like a ballet dancer and kind of like a pigeon.

"Oh my God," said Ash, "ONNIE," and she jumped out of the car and wrapped him in a hug, and Corey and I stumbled out of the car and blinked and squinted and tried to be respectful of what was clearly a high-level sacred teacher-student bond.

"It gives me a lot of joy to see you," Onnie told her, gripping her shoulders. His voice was round and precise.

She kind of hung her head bashfully.

"You've come a long way and you've followed your heart and it gives me tremendous joy."

"Well, don't say that until you hear me play something."

"You'll always be my favorite student and I'm prouder of you than you can know."

"Well, I just hope we don't suck tonight."

"You won't," he said. "You won't suck." He looked at us. "Nice band," he said. "Golly. Look at the three of you."

"Were you for real in Slayer," Corey asked him.

"Ah," he said. "For the briefest of moments. Just filling in as a favor to Tom."

"Oh damn," said Corey. "That must have been, uh."

We waited for Corey to find an adjective.

"I just hope one day I'm in a band even half as sick as that," said Corey finally.

Onnie did the slowest blink I have ever seen, and smiled.

"Do me a kindness," he said. "Cherish this part. Before the triumph and the failure. Now, when you're too young to win or lose. Before you know what winning or losing would even mean. Try to be here, now, and cherish it. All right?"

He took us across town to a narrow airy little house with flood damage still visible on the outside, and he gave us some towels and robes, and we each put our clothes in the washing machine and showered up. The shower felt unbelievable. It felt like I was molting my skin like a snake.

Onnie made super basic sandwiches for us on incredible bread, and he told us we could practice in the basement if we needed, or go out into the city, just be sure to lock up behind ourselves, and come to the restaurant for dinner at six, and then we'd play afterward. We nodded and said goodbye, and he left. We sat there with clean skin and hair in his coarse plaid robes eating the sandwiches, and it was hard not to feel like in some way the tour was already over.

We spent about an hour running through covers. We did "Gone for Good" (the Shins) and we did "Vision of Love" (Mariah), and we did "Funky Stuff" (Kool & the Gang). We pared them down and roughed them up and flattened them out and slowed them down and sped them up, and each one was definitely a Haters song by the end.

Then we spent another hour writing a little song of our own called "Love Is a Hate Crime" that began just like the first thing we played together, back in practice space G, with Corey thumping slow quarter notes and me ringing out half-note E's. We all sang on the chorus. In my case and Corey's maybe you wouldn't call it singing so much as yelling. But it felt pretty cool to use your voice and your instrument at the same time. It felt like the next step for us, and we were just starting to take it.

It was still a few hours to go until dinner, and even though the sky was dark and violent looking, we went out into Onnie's neighborhood with a couple of acoustic guitars and a cajon for Corey, and we just walked the streets playing and singing, and a bunch of kids started following us around and laughing and yelling, and we ended up at some basketball courts and set up shop there and ran through all our songs under the intense cloudy sky that was refusing to rain.

We got a few dozen fans that way. I mean, some kids hated it. But some kids loved it. And those were the only kids we gave a shit about.

I felt a stupid combination of feelings. Like my heart was hot with happiness, but I was mad at myself for being so happy, because I knew it was just going to hurt that much worse when it was all taken away. So I couldn't really enjoy it, except I was almost shaking from enjoying it so much. I almost couldn't walk home.

Someone offered us weed, and for a moment it seemed like one of us might have broken down and said yes. But we all ended up saying no.

"We're just too mentally unstable for that shit," apologized Corey.

"Good to know," said the dude, nodding slowly. "Good to know about yourself."

Driving back to Lime Tree, it felt like the part of waking up from a dream where you're pretending you don't know yet that it was a dream. Even though you do. Like you know you're not really flying, but you're pretending you don't know, just to have a few more moments of it. And you're pretending the world around you is that same beautiful insane shifting dream place you would never get tired or bored of, and you still have that stupid perfect dream understanding of yourself and everyone and everything. You still have that feeling of you'll never feel confused or disappointed again.

We parked in the employee lot. There was a police cruiser out front but we didn't make anything of it. The whites of the leaves on the trees were showing in the hot heavy wind. We each grabbed a couple of things from the car and walked into the restaurant, and standing there waiting for us were a couple of police officers, and Corey's parents, and mine.

# 36.
## THE HATERS

Corey panicked and ran. He didn't even put down his cymbals. He just hugged them to his chest and whirled and ran out the door, and his parents ran after him, and so did the cops, and the cops ran him down in less than a block, because these were highly athletic, professional cops, and Corey is not an athlete in any way. So he got handcuffed facedown on the sidewalk and then screamed at by his mom while his dad paced around irritably waiting for his turn, and in other circumstances it would have been hilarious.

Ash asked Onnie if we were going to get to play, and he shook his head sadly, and she got angrier than I had seen her get, and she said some things to him that definitely she felt shitty about later. But he probably didn't mind because he is a monk from another untouchable dimension of human experience.

My parents were the angriest ones there. My mom kept starting to say something and then just pursing her lips and shaking her head. And all my dad could say was, "God*damn* it, Wesley. God *fucking* damn it."

Onnie was the one who had told them. You couldn't really blame him for that. Ash's mom was on his case nonstop as soon as the jazz camp called her. She felt like the entire thing was Onnie's fault somehow.

So he told everyone's parents when Ash emailed him, and right away my parents flew down to New Orleans. Corey's parents drove. Ash's dad stayed in the Netherlands to watch Ash's half sister Jessica lose at tennis to a Polish woman in the second round of something called the Topshelf Open. Ash's mom stayed in New York for kind of no reason.

Ash burned out kind of quickly on yelling at Onnie and telling him he was a fucking pussy who'd do anything any rich fuck told him to, and she went over to a table and slumped into a chair and watched me get chewed out by my parents, who by then had figured out some of the things they wanted to say:

—I didn't know how much danger I had put myself in

—I didn't know how much danger I had put my friends in

—No, just listen

—There was no *way* I had any *idea*

—I hadn't stopped to think about the terrible worry this had caused so many people, not just my parents, although, God, the last four-plus days had been a total hell

—Or the hundreds of hours the police had spent looking for me when God knows what else they could have been doing with that time

—Not to mention the *tens* of thousands of dollars this was probably going to cost

—The fallout from this, the damage you've done to your future, is just, we're speechless, Wesley

—Oh don't you say a *word* right now, don't say a *single word*, because this is just incredible, this irresponsibility, *incredible*

—*Zip it*

—*Don't say a single goddamn thing* because neither one of us is anywhere *near* in the mood

—I don't even know who I'm talking to right now, Wes

—It is so unlike you to be this thoughtless and irresponsible that I feel like I'm not even talking to you

—It's so not you that we are *at a complete and total loss for words*

I could've been a dick and pointed out that they clearly were not at any kind of loss for words. Or I could've gotten angry back at them and asked them what about that retreat they went on that they didn't tell me about. How what if I died that first night and they wouldn't even have known right away. Or I could've just reasoned with them. I could've said, you know what, guys, I've been so good for so long, you had to know something like this was coming. You can give me a freebie just this one time.

But I didn't do any of that. It was such an insane unfamiliar feeling being the object of their anger. I sort of just sat in it and let it wash over me. It was like being in a cold ocean. At first it's a shock to the system. But after a while you're used to it and you can just be in the cold water for a while.

Ash sat motionlessly, alone, watching me and my parents. And I was looking back at her from time to time, and there was this quiet little misery in her eyes, and I knew what it was from, and the only thing I wanted was for her not to have to feel it.

Meanwhile, outside, Corey was being yelled at so hard that he was just lying there straight-up pretending to be dead.

I sort of don't want to weigh you down with everything that happened after that. Because my parents were right about the fallout and the damage. There was a crazy amount of shit to deal with afterward, and it took forever. To the point where you had to ask yourself if it was even worth it.

First, there was the legal stuff. Ash got nailed by highway police radar drones in Maryland, Virginia, and Tennessee for so many speeding violations in her mom's car that her license got suspended, and then the way bigger thing was, I got charged in Mississippi with a count of reckless endangerment for cutting the power to the Crossroad, plus a count of aggravated assault on Orryn Simmonds Sr., plus a few other random counts just to be a dick, and all the charges eventually got dropped but I still had to go down there a bunch of times and talk to lawyers and a judge, and my parents had to accompany me to every single thing, and it cost a crazy amount of money and time and just in general made me feel horrible, because it was my mess but other people had to help clean it up.

Plus the judge dropped the charges only on the condition that I do three hundred hours of community service back in Pittsburgh, and so since then I've had to spend every Saturday working at the Food Bank with other court-ordered community-service kids whose shit tends to be just way more serious and fucked up than mine, and most of those kids are actually pretty okay to hang out with but one of them is a sociopath named Marcel who showed me a pigeon that he killed in the parking lot, and every time I have a shift with him I am legitimately afraid for my life.

Meanwhile, Ash's parents laid down the law and threatened to cut her off completely unless she moved in with her mom's parents back in rural France. So that's where she is now. Actually, her photos of it look kind of beautiful. But Ash says every day she contemplates becoming an arsonist. That's when I hear from her, which is less and less, because she's just not great about being in touch, online or otherwise. Which is not surprising. But it's still kind of tough.

Part of it might be that when she got her phone back, we all got to hear the recording of that first practice-room session we had, and it's definitely not that good. I mean, it's not horrible. But it's sloppy and sort of monotonous and just not the thing we thought it was. And so you can't blame her for wanting to get some distance from it.

Corey's parents went even more crazy than Ash's. They told Corey I wasn't allowed over at his house anymore, and he wasn't allowed to go over to mine. And they confiscated his drums and told Benson's music director that he wasn't allowed to do music this year, either. It wasn't just because of the tour. Corey said his dad sat him down and said, Corey, I'm going to be very honest with you, because it's what you need to hear. I don't want you to pursue music for a living. Because it's just not a good life.

Corey fought back for a few days and then gave up. Because against his parents, there's only so much you can do. So now he's the kid at Benson High School who used to play drums until his parents took them away from him, and instead he's just a dude taking classes who doesn't have a thing and basically at all times is planning to fake his own death and escape to the Yukon or something.

As for me, I kind of dropped out of music at school, too. Because Benson got a sophomore transfer named Omar Brighton who happened to be the number two–ranked bassist at Bill Garabedian's Jazz Giants of Tomorrow Intensive Summer Workshops. He's a really good dude, but it's impossible for me to be in school jazz band with him. He's just too ferocious at jazz bass. He actually is a jazz giant of tomorrow. And I basically just feel like it's unfair for me to be taking half the songs when they could be going to someone who loves them and doesn't just like them. So after about a month, I dropped out as politely as I could. I didn't have a ton of time for it anyway, what with all the legal stuff and the trips back to Mississippi and the Food Bank hours with Marcel the pigeon murderer.

Basically, it all got pretty heavy and sad.

But it wasn't all sad. I did at least get back in touch with some people to apologize. And ShaeAnne and Charlize and I have stayed in touch. ShaeAnne and I text each other little emoji nonsense stories every few days. And Charlize and I remind each other to stay healthy, go to checkups, and avoid broken highway glass. Her text personality is way more excitable than her in-person personality. On Sundays she sends me super Christian messages, and I send her super Buddhist ones, and then she says "WES U CRACK ME UP!!!!"

My parents and I went through a whole thing. But they calmed down after a month or two. They told me that they realized that the last five years or so, they had let themselves just kind of stop worrying about me, because I was such a good kid. But now that's all changed, and they'll never not worry about me again. And I know that sounds terrible, but it makes me happier than before.

We've at least gotten to the point where now it's kind of a family joke that I'm this depraved criminal mastermind. Every time I come home from anything, my dad asks if I've finally managed to put an end to that Batman character once and for all.

And I guess the best part of it is that they got me a dog in September for my birthday. It's a brilliant diabolical move, because now I can't leave Pittsburgh for basically as long as he's alive. He's this weird awesome poodle corgi mutt, and definitely not as big as Dad Junior but much smarter and more personable and not the kind of dog who will terrorize my mom. I named him Air Horse. Even Corey admits that's a great name for a dog.

• • •

And even though Corey has no drums and we aren't allowed to go to each other's houses, we've still been spending a bunch of time listening to tunes and messaging each other back and forth.

I've kind of listened to music differently since the tour. Everything I used to hate about a band, I don't hate anymore. It just feels like a way to know them a little better.

Recently, kind of all of a sudden, we started writing our own songs.

I do mine on bass and Corey does his on his dad's MIDI keyboard late at night. They're not very good but that's actually why they might be really good. We send each other skeleton tracks and add stuff and change stuff and I don't know. It's starting to sound interesting.

Obviously, making these tracks doesn't give you the same feeling as being onstage playing a show. But in some ways it's kind of better. If you work on a track long enough and get comfortable with leaving mistakes in there, it starts to have the same sound of playing live where you can hear that everyone is breathing the same air. Plus Corey is surprisingly sick on a keyboard. He rips in a completely unapologetic fashion. He has one eight-second riff on "Dogs Ate Cookie" that sounds like he has been training for decades in a remote mountaintop sanctuary just for this very moment.

At some point we're going to show these tracks to our parents, and maybe they'll let us hang out again, and maybe

Corey can get his drums back. But the tracks aren't ready yet.

What they need is Ash. And we've been sending files to her basically every single day.

But like I said, she's just pretty bad at keeping in touch. So every single day for weeks we've been hoping to get something back from her, and we never do.

At least not until last night. We got an email around 10 P.M. Later we calculated that it was 4 A.M. in France. There wasn't anything in the subject or body. But attached was one of our tracks with guitar added in. Plus she added a track of her own, just acoustic guitar and voice. It was this simple folky Hank Williams kind of song like nothing we had heard from her before.

In both of those tracks she sounds fucking great. Like she always does. And so it's hard not to be fired up right now. Maybe this is just the beginning. Maybe she's going to start sending us stuff every day, and maybe soon we'll put all these tracks up where you'll be able to hear them. And maybe one day she'll move back to the States and we can get serious about this shit.

But I don't know. I know I shouldn't get ahead of myself. There are plenty of reasons why it probably won't work out. It's hard not to be obsessed with what could happen, but I should really just have the attitude of, what already has happened, if that's all I get, that's enough and I'm grateful.

I mean, it's not. But I am.

I want to end this the way the tour ended.

My parents eventually said, well, say goodbye to your friend, because the police are saying it's time to go. So I walked over to where Ash was sitting.

She was still slumped over with an elbow on the table and one hand buried in her hair, and her eyes were still traveling back and forth between my parents and me.

The rain was finally starting to hammer down outside, and you could feel the shift in the air right away, from one kind of heavy to another.

She was actually smiling a little bit, and I realized I was smiling, too.

"Shredfest," she said, and it took me until the flight home to remember what that meant.

## ACKNOWLEDGMENTS

**first acknowledgment:** the inadequacy of these acknowledgments

**second acknowledgment:** my loyal, brilliant, and patient editor, Maggie, who got me into the YA game in the first place, and is also why Ash, Corey, and Wes escape jazz camp before page, I don't know, 250

**third acknowledgment:** my equally loyal/brilliant/ patient agent, Claudia, at WME, who is not just good at her job to the point of being some kind of warrior princess or something but also a superb read and drinking buddy; ditto Laura, Anna, and Sarah

**fourth acknowledgment:** Susan, Leily, Michael, Chad, Jeff, and the rest of the heroically supportive Abrams team, who are responsible for this book's readability and visual and tactile beauty, and who frequently tolerate me being on the premises loudly writing emails without shoes or socks

**fifth acknowledgment:** Angela Abadilla, Calvin Stemley, and the incomparable Dwayne Dolphin, who are the musicians and music teachers who shaped me as a musician but even more as a person, which is good because in the end I never became all that much of a musician

**sixth acknowledgment:** Mom, Dad, Lena, Eve, and Grandma, who are the family that is the reason everything I write is about families

**last acknowledgment:** Tamara, who is my first read and my last love.

## ABOUT THE AUTHOR

Jesse Andrews's debut novel, *Me and Earl and the Dying Girl*, a *New York Times* and *USA Today* bestseller, was published to critical acclaim and starred reviews. His adaptation of the book for the big screen won both the Grand Jury Prize and the Audience Award at the 2015 Sundance Film Festival. Jesse is also a musician and screenwriter. He lives in Boston, Massachusetts. Visit Jesse at www.jesseandrews.com.